CW01559003

MURDER IN OXFORD

By Christina Koning

THE BLIND DETECTIVE SERIES
The Blind Detective
Murder in Regent's Park
Murder at Hendon Aerodrome
Murder in Berlin
Murder in Cambridge
Murder in Barcelona
Murder in Dublin
Murder at Bletchley Park
Murder in Oxford
Murder in Paris

MURDER IN OXFORD

CHRISTINA KONING

Allison & Busby Limited
11 Wardour Mews
London W1F 8AN
allisonandbusby.com

First published in Great Britain by Allison & Busby in 2025.

First Edition

ISBN 978-0-7490-3231-9

Typeset in 11/16 pt Sabon LT Pro by Allison & Busby

By choosing this product, you help take care of the world's forests.
Learn more: www.fsc.org

Printed and bound in the UK using 100% Renewable Electricity at
CPI Group (UK) Ltd, Croydon, CR0 4YY

EU GPSR Authorised Representative
LOGOS EUROPE, 9 rue Nicolas Poussin, 17000, LA ROCHELLE, France
E-mail: Contact@logoseurope.eu

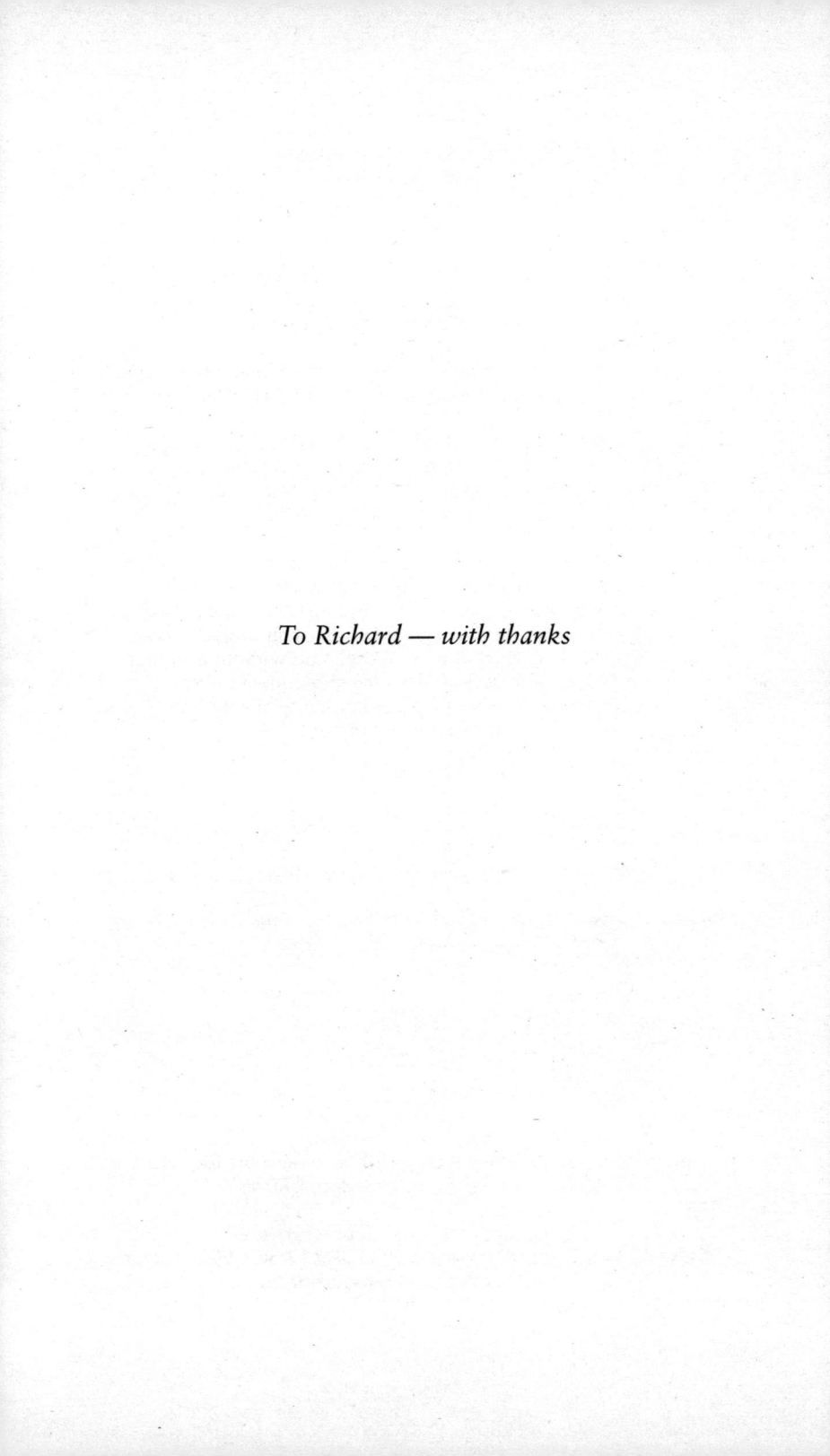

To Richard — with thanks

Chapter One

Oxford was swarming with soldiers. Airmen, too, patrolled its ancient mediaeval streets in boisterous numbers. Of undergraduates, there appeared to be very few, this winter of 1941. 'Yes, they're mostly first years nowadays – and those there are will have gone home for the Christmas holidays,' said Frederick Rowlands's companion, when the former remarked upon this. 'All except for the Indian students – too far for them to go, even during peacetime. Now they're stuck here in this beastly climate for the duration, poor devils.'

Rowlands grunted his appreciation of this fact, as he huddled deeper into his army greatcoat, which had stood him in good stead in weather like this for many years. Falling into step with his guide, as both strode briskly along the Broad, he wondered how soon he would hear a more satisfactory explanation of the summons he had received forty-eight hours ago, saying – in so many words – that he should come as quickly as possible.

There's something I need your help with – urgently.

That had been the line that had stood out most starkly from the letter Edith had read to him two nights before, and that had prompted Rowlands to drop everything – his work, his family life – and take the train from Brighton to Oxford station, where the sender of the letter, his friend and mentor, Sir Ian Fraser, had met him. 'Because it's not like the major to make a fuss about nothing,' said Rowlands, discussing this extraordinary missive with his wife – his use of Fraser's wartime rank a habit he found hard to drop.

'If he says it's urgent, it must be urgent,' said Edith, who had known Ian Fraser since her days as a VAD at St Dunstan's, the institute for war-blinded servicemen of which Fraser was the head, and to which her husband had belonged since being invalided out of the army towards the end of the last war. 'You have to go, Fred. He sounds really worried.'

Only now, instead of getting straight to the point about what was troubling him, the major was talking about anything other than that – the fact that so many students had left to join up, so that the university had virtually been emptied out overnight; the large numbers of men from all branches of the services who'd taken their place . . . 'Women, too, it might surprise you to know.'

Rowlands, with two daughters engaged in war work – one with the Women's Auxiliary Air Force – murmured that he wasn't at all surprised.

'Of course, there haven't yet been any air raids in Oxford,' the major went on, as they turned right along

Turl Street. 'The undergraduates still have to do their share of fire-watching, though. Most of the colleges – those not requisitioned by the army – have organised drills. Much as we do at St Dunstan's,' added the head of this institution. 'One has to do one's bit, I suppose.'

Rowlands felt he had heard enough. To have come all this way, in the biting cold (surely he'd felt a few flakes of snow?) only to listen to his friend ramble on about a lot of inconsequential stuff, was too much. 'Major . . .' he began, but the other put a hand on his arm, as if in warning.

'We go in here,' he said, adding in a low voice, 'I'll put you in the picture as soon as we're alone.'

They passed through a gateway, with the major's guide dog, Heidi, an Alsatian bitch, preceding them – at once attracting the attention of the college porter, who left his lodge in order to make a fuss of the animal, 'Who's a lovely girl, then?'

'Any messages for me, Dobbs?'

'No, sir . . . Least, Professor Challoner asked if you was back yet, that's all.'

'Yes, I'll be seeing him later. Put Mr Rowlands's bag in the top guest room, will you? Thank you, Dobbs. A good man,' said the major to Rowlands, as the two of them, with Heidi padding alongside, crossed the grassy quadrangle to the first of the college's mediaeval buildings. 'Lost an arm in the last show. Came out of retirement when his predecessor, Samuel Noakes, joined up.'

Rowlands nodded. It was a familiar story. Since the onset of hostilities, many such jobs had been filled by those too old to fight – or by women, in some cases. 'Can't you give me at least an idea—' he began, but again the other cut him off.

'Welcome to Brasenose,' he said, directing his friend with a touch on the arm to turn left. 'This part of it's called Old Quad.' They crossed what Rowlands sensed from the sudden quiet after the bustle of the streets to be a wide grass-covered space, and passed through another gate into the building. A few more steps brought them to a door. 'We'll talk in here. It's the senior common room. We shouldn't be disturbed until the hordes come in at teatime.'

The room, which was large, had the distinctive smell of most rooms dedicated to masculine society: a compound of stale tobacco smoke, worn leather upholstery, and the faintly musty odour of ancient tweeds. It was at least warm, with a log fire crackling in the large stone fireplace that took up much of one side of the room. 'Sit down, won't you?' said Major Fraser. 'There's a wing chair on one side of the fire – and another on this side,' he added, taking a seat. 'I think we've got the place to ourselves. Hello,' he called, raising his voice slightly. 'Anybody here?'

There was no reply to this tentative enquiry. It seemed that they were indeed alone, and so, after both had thrown off their coats, and lit cigarettes, Fraser began speaking without further ado. 'I may have mentioned at some time in the past that I knew someone in British Intelligence during the last war,' he began, then, to the dog, 'Settle down, Heidi! She's still young,' he said apologetically, but Rowlands wondered if it was more than that. Dogs were sensitive creatures, he knew. Was there someone else in the room after all? He dismissed the thought, and concentrated on what Fraser had said.

'I believe you did mention it,' he replied.

'Thought I had. Interesting chap, Challoner. Of course, we were both young men at the time,' the major went on. 'Same battalion. Thrown together – the way one was, at that time. I expect you remember . . .'

'Yes,' said Rowlands.

'Brainy chap, old Challoner, even then. Of course, they soon picked him for special duties. Listening in to the enemy's signals. All very hush-hush, you know.' He was silent a moment, as if transported back to those far-off days, when living so close to death had given life a peculiar intensity. 'Then I got my Blighty one – invalided out – as you were, too, Rowlands, and that was the last I saw of Donald Challoner for many years. Imagine my surprise when I turned up at a college reunion dinner – it must have been '38 or '39 – to find he'd ended up back in Oxford. Professor of classics, no less. Always was a clever fellow. Still acts as a kind of advisor to MI5, I gather. They're based at Blenheim Palace, would you believe? Challoner's highly regarded by that crowd, from all I hear.'

He paused, as if gathering his thoughts. Once more the dog at his feet stirred uneasily, and let out a soft growl. 'Be quiet, Heidi! Anyway, we kept in touch after that – the occasional letter, you know – although we were both pretty busy, with one thing and another.'

Rowlands smiled at this characteristic understatement on his friend's part. In recent years, Ian Fraser had combined running an organisation – St Dunstan's – catering to the needs of several hundred war-blinded members and their families, with being a Member of Parliament.

'Then, a fortnight ago, I received a letter from the

principal at Brasenose, inviting me to a reception for the "Men of 1914" – that's when I was up, you know. Never took my degree, as I joined up the following year. After that . . .' He gave a wry chuckle. 'Things took a different course for me, as they did for you, Rowlands.'

Both were silent a moment, thinking of all that had passed since the fateful day – in July 1916 for Fraser; almost exactly a year later, for Rowlands – when both had received the wounds that took away their sight, and changed their lives forever.

'Anyway,' Fraser resumed. 'The wife raised no objection to my coming up to Oxford the week before Christmas – it'd get me from under her feet, she said – and so I arrived the day before last. Thought I'd make a little holiday of it, you know. Look up a few people I used to know. Revisit a few old haunts. Only as you see,' he added ruefully, 'the whole place has been turned upside-down by this blessed war. More like a military camp than a university town.' He laughed. 'They say one should never try and revisit one's past, don't they?'

'They do.' Rowlands wondered where all this was going.

'But enough reminiscing,' said Fraser, as if he sensed his friend's impatience. 'One figure from the past who hadn't changed all that much was Donald Challoner. He and I hit it off, as we'd done long ago – only now we were both a good deal older and wiser . . . Well, certainly older, in my case. One night, we got talking, over a whisky. Most of the other fellows – you'll meet 'em shortly – had gone to bed. It was then that he told me something very queer. "I've reason to believe that there's a German spy in college," he

12

said. Could have knocked me down with a feather. Then I thought of you.'

'Me?' said Rowlands. 'I don't see why.'

'You've got form with this kind of thing, haven't you? Tracking down traitors. There was that case only a few months ago . . .'

'You know I can't talk about that,' said Rowlands hastily.

'Exactly my point,' replied Fraser. 'You're discreet. Have to be. That makes you the ideal man for the job.'

'And what job's that?'

'Didn't I say? I want you to talk to Challoner. Find out what's put this suspicion into his head. Then find the man who's been betraying secrets to the enemy. It'll be right up your street, I'd imagine.'

'But, Major—'

Rowlands's protest was cut short by the sound of voices outside the room. A moment later, a number of people entered. 'I say! Isn't it time for the tea trolley to come round?' said one. 'Must be nearly five o'clock.'

'Brr!' exclaimed another. 'Bit of a draught in here. That fire needs mending . . . Oh, hello, Fraser! Thought I saw you there.'

'Hello, Hobson. Our lecturer in modern languages,' he said to Rowlands. 'Let me introduce my friend, Frederick Rowlands. He'll be staying in college for a couple of nights.'

'Jolly good show! Are you an old Brasenosian?'

'No, just a visitor.'

'Pity,' said Hobson, taking the seat next to Rowlands's. 'We're a bit thin on the ground regarding fellows and alumni at present. This damned war, you know . . .'

Rowlands said that he did.

'Two-thirds of the undergraduates have left to join up,' the other went on. 'Quite a number of the younger teaching staff, too. Oxford's not what it was.'

'Too many women, for one thing,' said another voice. 'Last time I passed Keble, there were crowds of flappers on bicycles pouring out of the gate.'

'Most of them work at Blenheim,' Fraser reminded him. 'Doing valuable war work. I'm told they keep the whole show ticking over.'

'Yes, yes,' said the other irritably. 'But surely they could have been put up somewhere else, instead of at an Oxford college? Hobson's right. Oxford's not the same.'

'Still fulminating against the presence of our armed services, Rawlinson?' said another of the company. 'Anyone would have thought you didn't want us to win this war.'

'I never said anything of the kind, as well you know, Armstrong,' protested the man called Rawlinson. 'Only that it's changed the nature of Oxford to have all these outsiders here.'

'Speaking as an outsider,' said Rowlands, 'this place feels like a world away from the war. So calm and civilised.'

His remarks were greeted with hoots of laughter from some of those seated nearby. 'Don't you believe it!' said one – it was the jovial Hobson. 'University types can be as savage as the next man. They just hide it under a cloak of civility.'

'You disappoint me.' Rowlands smiled – although he had heard much the same story from a distinguished professor of modern and mediaeval languages in what Oxford alumni liked to refer to as 'the Other Place'. 'I'd rather thought there'd be higher standards for "Oxford men".'

'Oh, I know it all sounds very highfalutin and well mannered,' persisted the other. 'But they'll stab you in the back as soon as look at you.'

'I must say I think that's a rather extreme view,' said a man who'd just come in. His was a dry, ironic voice, with an edge of humour. 'After all, what are we fighting the Germans for if not to defend civilised values?'

'Hello, Challoner,' said Fraser, standing up to greet his friend. 'I want you to meet Frederick Rowlands. He and I go back a long way – to 1917, if I'm not mistaken.'

The two men shook hands, and Rowlands received an impression of a tall, once powerfully built man, now stooped by age and the exigencies of a scholar's life. '1917,' he said a ruminative tone. 'I was in signals, then. Trying to work out what the enemy was up to with little more than a primitive wireless set and a field telephone. Not that much has changed,' he added softly, as – distracted by the arrival of the tea trolley – the rest of the party dispersed itself in groups around the room, each caught up in its particular topic of conversation.

Challoner drew up a chair next to Rowlands's and lit his pipe. 'First time in Oxford?' he said, when it was drawing nicely.

'I was here before the last war, in my capacity as a sales representative for Methuen Books,' replied Rowlands. 'So I'm more familiar with Oxford bookshops than I am with Oxford colleges . . . although my brother-in-law was at

Worcester College,' he added, not wanting the other to think him a complete ignoramus where the university was concerned.

'I came straight from the army,' said Challoner. 'They offered me a place here on the strength of my war service. No one in my family had been to university – unlike this fellow here' – he meant Fraser, Rowlands supposed – 'I don't have generations of Oxford scholars behind me. Ah, here's tea . . .'

Over cups of this cheering beverage, the three men exchanged desultory remarks on a range of topics, none of which touched directly on the matter to which Fraser had alluded earlier. The mounting German losses on the Eastern Front, and what this would mean for the progress of the war; the victories of the British Army in North Africa; and the difficulty of getting supplies of meat and fresh vegetables for the college table, were all that was discussed – the last topic drawing in comments from other fellows, for whom it was obviously a sore point. 'We'd have more food for ourselves if we didn't have to feed the army,' said one. 'Having the officers billeted here has stretched our supplies to the limit.'

Challoner explained that, as of the previous year, they'd had the Junior Staff Officers' School in residence – replacing the Liaison Officers' School – and that he'd doubtless meet some of the military element at dinner. 'We're entertaining the commandant and adjutant tonight, as it happens. The former's a very decent sort. Plays a mean game of bridge . . . I hope you play, too, Mr Rowlands?'

Rowlands said that he did – but with Braille cards.

'Oh, don't worry, if there's a game later, we'll be using

16

my Braille pack,' put in Fraser. 'There were mutterings at first about the cards being "marked", but people have got used to it now.'

'That's settled, then.' Challoner got to his feet. 'I'm off to bathe and dress. You see we keep up some of the old standards, even in wartime. Gives people a feeling that all is not lost, in spite of wars and revolutions. I'll see you gentlemen later.'

To reach the guest room meant climbing a staircase and going along a corridor to a second, narrower, staircase that led to what was obviously an attic floor. 'What with all these army officers billeted in college, we're a bit short of accommodation for guests,' said Fraser apologetically, opening a door. 'Hope this room isn't too poky. The bathroom's across the corridor. There should be some hot water, if the army hasn't taken it all. I'll call for you in an hour. You'll need someone to show you the way to the dining hall. Place is a bit of a barracks.'

'In a very real sense, from the sound of it,' said Rowlands.

His friend laughed. 'Oh, very good! Yes, the military element is rather in evidence, just now.'

Once Fraser had left him to his own devices, Rowlands made a brief investigation of the room, which was as spartan as Fraser had intimated. There was a narrow bed, on which someone had laid out Rowlands's evening clothes; a desk and chair; a half-sized wardrobe. Here, he hung up his coat and, having undressed, put on his dressing gown. There would just be time for a bath and shave, before he dressed for dinner.

He evidently wasn't the only one to have had this idea, for he found the bathroom full of steam from someone's earlier ablutions, and the floor slippery with water. Being blind meant you had to be on the alert at all times for hazards most sighted people didn't have to consider – a door left ajar, a bar of soap dropped on the floor . . . 'Careless young blighters,' he muttered, as he lowered himself into the regulation five inches of bathwater – bathing no longer being the luxurious experience it had been before wartime restrictions, but at least, he thought, it'd wash off some of the grime of travel.

As he dried himself on the rough and threadbare towel provided, he heard the door handle rattle. 'Hurry up in there! I haven't got all night!'

'Just a minute.' Donning his dressing gown once more, Rowlands opened the door and stepped out. 'All yours,' he said.

'Oh. Awfully sorry. Thought you were one of our lot.' The young man who'd tried the door sounded abashed.

'And which "lot" is that? The army or the university?'

'Army. Lieutenant Peter Bawden at your service . . . sir,' added the other, having taken in Rowlands's obvious seniority. 'I'm with the Junior Staff Officers' School.'

'Then I expect I'll see you at dinner, Lieutenant Bawden. Take care, won't you? The floor's still wet from the last chap's bath. You wouldn't want to slip.'

'No. Thanks awfully,' said the young man. 'See you later, Mr . . . er . . .'

'The name's Rowlands. I'm a guest of Sir Ian Fraser.' Then, thinking he'd been delayed long enough, he went back to his room to dress.

Slipping on the boiled shirt and dress trousers, he did his best with the stiff-bristled hairbrush, until his damp hair was lying flat and smooth against his skull. He didn't care for the brilliantine that many of these young chaps went in for. While he fumbled with cufflinks and slung the bow tie around his neck, in preparation for tying the thing, his thoughts went to the conversation he'd had that afternoon with Fraser, and the subsequent meeting with the man who'd been the subject of that conversation.

How fantastic it had sounded – the notion that there was a German spy at the centre of British Intelligence . . . and how dangerous, if it proved to be so! He supposed Professor Challoner, himself an intelligence operative, must have good grounds for such a suspicion. Rowlands looked forward to quizzing him on the subject. Although what earthly use he could be, with regard to uncovering the said enemy agent, he couldn't imagine. It was true he had 'form', as the major had put it, when it came to smoking out traitors. But the circumstances of that affair had been exceptional – not least being the fact that his own daughter had been implicated . . . Oxford was unknown territory for him.

Chapter Two

There came a light tap on the door, and Fraser put his head in. 'Forgot to mention that there'll be a glass of sherry for us at six forty-five,' he said. 'Another tradition the college has kept up, thankfully. One good thing is the cellars haven't yet been requisitioned.' Then, becoming aware, from his friend's exasperated groans, of the struggle he was having with his tie, 'Let George – he's my scout – help you with that. He's about somewhere. Used to be a gentleman's gentleman before he joined the college staff.'

George having been applied to, and the bow tie immaculately tied, Rowlands was fit to accompany his friend – both preceded as before by the latter's dog – to the pre-prandial drinks in the SCR. This was considerably noisier and more crowded than it had been at five o'clock. The two men were greeted by a buzz of conversation from the four corners of the room. The war was the prevailing topic.

'. . . trying to finish my paper before teaching starts up again.'

'If it starts up again. How many of our undergraduates will return, do you think?'

'Oh, Oxford'll keep going, in some shape or form.'

'Glad to hear you're so sanguine. In my view . . .'

'. . . doing very badly on the Eastern Front.'

'Yes, and with the Yanks coming in at last, things will start to look very different, you mark my words . . .' The last speaker was the cheerful Dr Hobson, who hailed the two arrivals with his customary brio, 'Hello, Fraser, old man! And . . . Rowlands, isn't it? Come to join the bunfight? I warn you, the food won't be up to much – although there's still plenty of drink, thank the Lord.'

Rowlands said that he was glad to hear it. A moment later, a glass of sherry was put into his hand. He took a tentative sip. It was good stuff. 'Pre-war,' said Fraser. 'So when do you go down, Hobson?'

'Oh, I'm staying up for the Christmas vac. There's only an aged aunt left of the family, you know – and she's in Aberdeen. Couldn't get the petrol, even if I wanted to join her for the festivities . . . however festive those would be, with rationing the way it is. As for the climate up there . . .' He shuddered theatrically. 'Between you and me, I'd much rather stay in Oxford. More going on here.'

'You can say that again!' said a voice Rowlands recognised as that of one of the fellows he'd met at teatime. 'It's like living in a military camp, with jeeps tearing up and down all day, and planes flying over at all hours . . .'

'When's your paper due, Aitken?' said Hobson.

'I'm afraid it's long overdue,' was the reply. 'My publisher's having fifty fits – but what am I to do? There's a war on.'

This was irrefutable, and so they all sipped their sherry in silence, until Hobson said, 'Hello, Quine! Didn't see you there. Thought you'd gone down.'

'As you see, I'm still here,' was the dry response. 'The only time one can get any work done in this place is when the undergraduates are away.'

'Yes, and most of 'em will stay away, from the look of things,' put in another: Rawlinson, the man who'd complained about the army presence. 'If this goes on, there won't be a university to come back to.'

'Oh, but surely—' began Hobson, but just then there came an interruption from Dr Quine.

'What the devil?' At the same moment, Heidi, who'd accompanied her master into the room as before, let out a soft growl.

'Quiet, Heidi!' said Fraser, then to the man who'd protested, 'Sorry, I thought you must have seen that my dog was there.'

'It nearly tripped me up,' said the other. 'Damned irresponsible, bringing an animal in here.'

'She's usually quite good about not getting underfoot,' said Fraser mildly, but Quine wasn't to be placated.

'It's surely against regulations, having dogs in college? I hope you aren't thinking of bringing it into hall?'

'Well . . .' began Fraser; then came another voice: Challoner's.

'Sir Ian's my guest, Quine, and, as such, I think we can waive the rules a little, don't you?' His tone was pleasant, but there was an underlying steeliness that suggested he wasn't to be budged on this – or any other matter, thought Rowlands.

Fortunately, dinner was announced at that moment, and the company – having swiftly downed drinks – began to move towards the exit. 'A pity you had to witness that little outburst,' murmured Fraser to his friend, as they filed into the dining hall. 'Quine's a decent sort, really, but he does have his pernickety side – like most of us, I suppose.'

'Evidently not a dog-lover,' said Rowlands.

'No,' said his friend. 'I say, didn't you say you'd be getting a dog of your own, soon? Jolly useful for people like us, I can tell you!'

Rowlands said that, yes, he'd put his name down for a guide dog – adding that he'd given in to pressure not only from his wife, but from his youngest daughter, Joan, who had long campaigned for a dog – although as he'd pointed out to her, this would be a working dog, not a pet.

'Well, I think you'll find it a great help, having an animal to guide you,' was the reply. 'Gives one no end of independence, being able to get about without relying on another person.'

'I suppose it must,' said Rowlands, still not entirely convinced. In the ten years since guide dogs for the blind had been widely introduced, he'd been one of those who'd resisted this innovation. Because he'd managed up to now, hadn't he, with the partial sight he retained in one eye and with the aid, in more recent years, of a stick (something else he'd initially resisted). It was the fear of seeming different that made him resistant, he knew. Although Edith said that was absurd. 'Lots of men carry sticks. As for the dog, it'll make you no more conspicuous than it would any sighted person. Honestly, Fred, you make too much of these things.' She was right, of course – as she was about a lot of things.

Ahead of them in the slowly moving queue was a man to whom he had yet to be introduced, deep in conversation with another.

'. . . best if we discuss the matter later, Commandant. You're sitting on my right at high table, by the way. I've put the adjutant further along the table, with the rest of the army contingent. Challoner, you're on my left as usual.'

'Yes, Principal.'

'Professor Challoner is our classics chair,' the principal explained to his guest. 'And this is Sir Ian Fraser, one of our alumni. Good to see you, Fraser. But I don't think I know this gentleman . . .'

'This is Frederick Rowlands, my guest this evening, Dr Summerby' said Fraser. 'He and I were in the last show – although we didn't meet until afterwards. He was one of the first intake at St Dunstan's, after I took over as head in 1917. Now he practically runs the place, don't you, Fred?'

'Oh, I don't know about that.'

'Glad to have you with us, Mr Rowlands,' said the principal courteously. They took their seats at the long table, in what Rowlands guessed, from past experience of such institutions, to be a panelled hall. It would be hung with portraits of previous heads of the college, he supposed, and lit by candles in tall silver candelabra. Even in wartime such gracious niceties would hardly be foregone.

Silence fell. The principal murmured a brief Latin grace. Then the company stirred once more: adjusting gowns that had slipped off shoulders, and moving chairs closer or further away from the board, according to preference.

The wine waiter went round, filling glasses. The soup was served. Conversation broke out, in fits and starts, along the table.

Rowlands was seated next to Fraser (the dog was under the table at their feet) and, with Challoner on his right, was privy to their conversation, and also to that of those opposite: Hobson and Rawlinson. Aitken was beside the latter, Armstrong and Quine at the near end of the table. At the further end, the army predominated, with the commandant presiding over his flock, as the principal did over his. The talk, in each case, was largely 'shop', Rowlands gathered – although the principal made efforts to engage his guests from the military end in more general conversation.

'I take it your men are settling in all right?' the principal accordingly said to the commandant, who replied that the arrangements were as good as might be expected, in the circumstances.

'Wouldn't you say so, Parker?' the commandant bawled at his adjutant, who was seated across the table.

'Yes, sir, very satisfactory,' replied the other.

'Water could be a bit hotter in the mornings, what?' shouted the commandant, who was either a bit deaf, or merely used to barking his orders at parade-ground volume, thought Rowlands. 'Just as well we're used to roughing it in the army, eh?'

'Sir.'

'Speaking of which, how are the latest batch of trainees shaping up, Donaldson?' he asked another of his officers. 'Any of 'em look promising?'

'Hard to tell, sir. They've only just completed the

theoretical part of the course. We've yet to put them through the physical training.'

'Time they were out there, getting to grips with things in earnest,' said the commandant. 'No sense in filling their heads with a lot of useless facts, if they aren't seeing any action.'

'Well, of course . . .'

'Teamwork, that's what's wanted. Initiative,' said the senior officer. 'There's no better way of building it, in my opinion, than by sending a man into the field. Give him a rifle and get him attacking a target. Works wonders, with even the weaklings.'

'Yes, sir. But with its being Christmas in a few days, we're a bit short-staffed. And then there's the weather. It's coming on to snow fairly hard . . .' Donaldson's tentative objections were cut short by the commandant.

'Stuff and nonsense! "Weather" – forsooth! Why, a bit of snow never hurt anybody. You need to get the men out there PDQ. Toughen them up for what's coming.'

'Of course, sir. I only meant . . .'

Then came Challoner's voice. 'I do see what the commandant means about the necessity for action. But I'd like to think that the "theoretical part", as Captain Donaldson calls it, is as important in training a modern officer corps as the ability to strip down a rifle. Warfare has changed immeasurably in the past fifty years, whether one likes it or not.'

'I suppose you would say that, Professor,' replied the commandant frostily. 'Given that the theory side is rather your stock-in-trade. Spying and sneaking around and all that sort of caper. Dirty tricks, I'd call it. Not my idea of how a war should be conducted, but there you are.'

Plates were changed at that moment – the sole giving way to slices of rare beef – and conversation briefly lapsed, to Rowlands's regret. He'd found it an interesting debate: the man of action versus the man of intellect. But any hope he'd had of the discussion's continuing was thwarted by the principal's saying to his guest of honour, 'Do try some of the '35 Burgundy, Hastings. I think you'll find it a good year.'

The commandant's appreciative grunt seemed to bear out this judgement, and the talk moved on to other things.

Rowlands let his thoughts drift. What with the journey across London, followed by several hours in a freezing train packed with troops returning from leave (and not too happy about it), and then this drawn-out evening, in the company of a lot of men he'd never met before, and wasn't likely to meet again, it had been a tiring day. For someone for whom the usual visual clues of facial expression and gesture were absent, conversation required more of an effort than it did for most people. He'd got used to this over the years, but sometimes it was too much . . . as it was now.

And so, as he sat eating his savoury and only half listening to the talk of chairs becoming vacant, on the one hand, or the usefulness or otherwise of the forthcoming Washington Conference on the other, he was startled to hear his own name mentioned. 'Rowlands has spent some time at Bletchley Park, haven't you, old man?'

'I . . .' The visits he'd made, during the course of a murder investigation, to that most secret of government departments wasn't something he'd ever discussed – although now he came to think of it, he might have alluded to it once in conversation with his old friend. 'I have been there on a couple of occasions,' he admitted. 'But I've only the vaguest idea what they do there.'

Fraser laughed. 'Don't worry! I'm not expecting you to give away any state secrets. It's just that Challoner knows Commander Murchison.' This was the head of operations at BP, as it was familiarly known.

'Yes, Angus is an old friend,' said Challoner. 'We meet quite regularly, in fact – Oxford being a mere stone's throw from the Park.' This was another nickname for the place that lay, Rowlands knew, at the very heart of British Intelligence.

Plates had once more been cleared away and the port was circulating. Rowlands was beginning to appreciate what his friend had said about the excellence of the college cellars – and resolved to limit his intake to a single glass. What with his tiredness, and being in this strange hybrid company of dons and soldiers (to say nothing of spies), he'd need to keep his wits about him. Fragments of talk floated along the table towards him.

'. . . setting up an assault course on Port Meadow,' said a voice he recognised as that of the young man he'd run into in the corridor outside the bathroom – what was his name again? Bawden. That was it. Lieutenant Bawden.

'. . . of course, Oxford won't be bombed. Hitler's given instructions that it should be spared.' That was the man who disliked dogs. Quine. A strange fellow, thought Rowlands sleepily. Eccentric. But then, most academics were, in his experience. It was spending their lives in the ivory tower, he supposed. Not that Fraser's friend Challoner seemed especially eccentric. Unless one counted a preoccupation with German spies to be indicative of an eccentric worldview . . .

He was roused from these reflections by a touch on the arm, as, with a shuffling of feet and a scraping of chairs against floorboards, Fraser and the rest of the company rose, and began to make its way towards the senior common room. 'Reveille at oh-six hundred hours,' boomed a voice Rowlands recognised as that of the commandant – Hastings, wasn't it? 'I'll want to see you men on parade bright and early.' He himself, it became apparent, intended to enjoy a nightcap, before turning in.

'We've some pre-war whisky I think you'll like,' murmured the principal to his guest. 'Only a few cases of it left, unfortunately. The Liaison Officers' School we had billeted here last year made considerable inroads into our supplies.'

Thinking that he'd had quite enough to drink, Rowlands was about to make his excuses and retire to bed, when Challoner said, 'I'm going up to my study. Care to join me, Fraser – and Mr Rowlands too, of course? There's a matter on which I'd like your opinion.' Both said they would be happy to comply with this suggestion. 'Good show. Just give me a few minutes to change out of this boiled shirt and put on a dressing gown, would you? Never could abide these formal occasions. Can't think why we have to keep up this sort of thing in wartime.'

The three men agreed to meet up in Challoner's rooms in a quarter of an hour. 'Just time for a snifter,' said Fraser, as they entered the SCR, with the dog leading the way as usual. 'Scotch do you?'

'Just a small one.'

'Coming up.'

Already assembled around the table where the decanters were set out were what Rowlands privately thought of as the 'diehards' – men like Commandant Hastings and his entourage, determined to see the night out with yet more strong drink, as well as a few fellows of the college intent on pursuing some matter of interest only to the academic body over whisky and water. Rowlands thought he could distinguish the voices of some he'd met earlier: the jovial Hobson was one, and Rawlinson, who'd complained about the number of women in Oxford . . . and wasn't that the man who'd said his paper was overdue? Aitken. That was the one.

Sipping gingerly at his whisky (which had indeed lived up to expectations), he wondered whether he and Fraser were about to learn the name of the man at the heart of British Intelligence who, according to Donald Challoner, was betraying secrets to the enemy. His experiences a few months before, at Bletchley Park, had taught him that not only was such a thing all too plausible, but that in the search for the traitor, no one was exempt from suspicion. Even in this agreeable company of academics and military men, a renegade might be hiding.

He gave an involuntary shiver at the thought. 'Not catching a cold, I hope?' said Fraser. 'It'd hardly be surprising, given the beastly weather. Drink up! The whisky'll do you good. Perhaps I should get George to make you a hot toddy, with honey and lemon – if there are any lemons to be had.'

With a laugh, Rowlands protested that he felt fine. He touched the face of his Braille watch. It was a quarter to midnight. 'Shouldn't we be going up?' he said.

'You're right. Mustn't keep old Challoner waiting.'

Leaving what sounded like an increasingly heated debate on the merits or otherwise of the college port, and a no-less spirited argument on whether or not non-commissioned officers should be granted dining rights for the duration, the two men, with Heidi padding silently beside them, made their exit. With Fraser leading the way, they crossed the Old Quadrangle and entered a door on the far side.

'Sixteenth century, this part of the college,' Fraser was saying. 'Although there were buildings on the site – halls of residence – much earlier. It was originally set up as a quasi-religious foundation – like most Oxford colleges . . .'

Only half-listening to Fraser's account of the college's early years ('Of course after the Reformation it was handed over to one of Henry VIII's minions, who saw a way of getting into the king's favour by setting up an institution for the education of gentlemen's sons . . .'), Rowlands wondered why he felt so on edge. It was tiredness, no doubt. But, as they ascended the staircase that led to Challoner's rooms, he couldn't suppress a growing feeling of unease.

Reaching the first landing, he almost collided with a man who was coming down. 'Sorry!' he said pleasantly, aware that his physical exhaustion made him less attentive to the sounds – in this instance, the creaking of the staircase – that betrayed another's presence.

Somewhat to his surprise, there was no answering apology, as the other pushed rudely past him, his footsteps thudding heavily on the stairs as he made his escape. Not quite the manners one expected from an Oxford man, Rowlands thought. And there was something else that was peculiar about the encounter – a whiff (could it be?) of burning, which was neither the smell of pipe smoke nor of cigarettes . . . But before he could identify what it was, they had arrived at the second floor.

'Here we are,' said Fraser as they came to an outer door – the 'oak', Rowlands knew – that stood ajar. Beyond this was an inner door, on which Fraser tapped gently. 'Challoner, old man, we're here . . .' His cheerful salutation was met with silence. 'Hello, he's left it on the latch.' He pushed the door, which swung open. 'Hello?' Fraser called again. 'Anybody in?' Then, when there was no reply, 'That's odd. Perhaps he's stepped out for a moment,' he said uncertainly, as he and Rowlands hesitated on the threshold. 'Or nodded off . . .'

But then came a low groan – as of someone in pain – from inside the room. The dog growled. 'Be quiet, Heidi! I say, Challoner?' said Fraser, stepping inside. 'Are you all right?' This elicited another, feebler, groan. 'My God!' cried the major. 'I believe he's hurt . . .' Drawing nearer, he gave a cry of horror as the truth of this was brought home to him. 'There's blood . . . and something . . . a knife . . . sticking out of his back . . .'

'Don't touch it,' said Rowlands, knowing that any attempt to remove it might cause further injury. 'We must get a doctor to him – quickly!'

'Yes . . . doctor . . . hurry . . .' Challoner's voice was so faint that they could barely hear it. 'I don't . . . have long . . .'

'I'll go,' said Fraser. 'You stay with him, Rowlands.'

Left alone with the wounded man, Rowlands murmured what he hoped were comforting words. 'Hold on, old man. Help's coming.'

But it was obvious from the other's laboured breathing that he would soon be beyond help. 'Listen . . .' His voice was no more than a whisper. 'Something . . . to tell . . . you . . .'

'Don't try to talk,' said Rowlands, but the dying man paid no attention to this.

'Find . . . the . . . green file . . .' he gasped, his voice a hoarse croak like a death rattle.

'The green file,' repeated Rowlands. 'All right. I'll do what I can.'

'Find it . . .' Challoner's breathing was getting weaker now. 'Names . . .' He seemed to make a final effort, his voice no more than a sigh. 'Trust . . . no one . . .' His head fell forwards, hitting the desk at which he was sitting with a thump. Blood gushed from his mouth, spattering Rowlands. Its iron-filing smell clung to his hands. 'Professor Challoner . . . Donald . . .'

It was too late, however.

Because at that moment Fraser returned with the doctor. The latter's reaction, when he saw what had happened, put paid to any hopes that Challoner might have survived the attack. 'Dead,' he said, after a cursory examination. 'And no wonder, with that dirty great knife sticking out of his back.' He must have peered closer. 'Interesting design – handle's in the shape of an eagle's head.'

'It's a German Army officer's knife,' said Fraser bleakly. 'Souvenir of Challoner's days in the trenches. He used it as a letter-opener.'

'Well, it's done for him all right,' replied the doctor. 'Wickedly sharp, no doubt. I'll know more when I've done the PM.'

As he pronounced these words, the dog began to howl.

Chapter Three

On and on howled the Alsatian bitch, so that anyone within earshot must have heard it. And indeed, there came a querulous voice from the landing opposite. 'What's going on? Can't a fellow get some sleep?' Then, catching sight of the still and silent figure slumped at the desk, 'Good God! It's old Challoner. Who . . . who's done this?'

'That's what we need to find out, O'Halloran,' said Fraser. 'It is Dr O'Halloran, isn't it?'

'Yes, but . . .'

'We arrived a moment or so before you did,' said Fraser. 'We found him like this.'

Voices outside on the staircase indicated that the news had spread. One of these belonged to the adjutant; another was Dr Hobson's. The latter said that the principal had been sent for. 'Shocking business this, very,' he said. 'I was just turning in, as a matter of fact. Concert on the wireless I was going to listen to. Then I heard all the shouting . . . Does anyone know what happened?'

Before he could receive a reply to his question, the doctor, whose name was McIntyre, said sharply, 'I'll thank ye gentlemen to clear the way. And somebody had better assist me with moving the corpus to the mortuary.'

'Wait,' said Rowlands. 'You can't move him yet – not until the police have been called.'

'Oh, I think we should let the college authorities take charge,' said Hobson. 'After all, we've the army billeted here – and the military police – if we need to investigate further. Involving the regular police will only complicate matters, surely?'

'Not when it's a case of murder,' said Rowlands.

The fellows of Brasenose College were assembled in the senior common room, together with those members of the military contingent billeted at the college. Each of them awaited his turn to be interviewed by the police. It was half past one in the morning, and Rowlands, who had yet to go to bed, was feeling the curious wide-awakeness that extreme fatigue can bring about. Beside him sat Fraser, who seemed prone to dropping off – jerking awake every few minutes with an exclamation – 'What? Who?' – only to fall asleep again. It had been a long night, thought Rowlands, and it would get longer before any of them were released. From around the room came subdued mutterings from those fellows who hadn't yet given in to drowsiness.

'Think it'll take much longer?'

'The principal's been in there hours.'

'Wonder if old Crampton could rustle us up some coffee?'

As if by common consent, no one in the room referred

to the horrible event that had caused them to be detained there at the pleasure of the local constabulary. These – the Oxford City Police – were certainly taking their time, Rowlands thought, although it might well be that the delay was a consequence of having to wait for a higher authority – MI5 – to take charge of the investigation. Because it seemed clear to him that, had it not been for the dead man's alleged involvement with this secretive organisation, he might not now lie in the mortuary, with a German dagger in his back.

He nudged his friend awake. 'I say, Fraser . . .'

'What? Who?' muttered the other but he roused himself at last. 'Sorry! Can't think what's come over me.'

'Fancy a walk to clear your head?'

'Good idea.'

But when the two men, having navigated their way past the rows of somnolent fellows, reached the doors of the SCR, a uniformed policeman blocked their exit. 'Where might you gentlemen be going?'

'Just for a breather,' was Rowlands's reply.

'Sorry, sir, but my orders is you're all to stay in here until the inspector calls you.'

'Whatever you say, Constable.'

'Who's a nice doggie, then?' said the young man, reaching to pat Heidi. 'Good as gold, you are, ent you, my lovely?'

'A word,' said Rowlands to his friend, while the officer was thus distracted. 'I think, when the time comes, we should be circumspect about . . . ah . . . our friend's suspicions.'

'Couldn't agree more,' said Fraser, who seemed to have

shaken off his lethargy. They resumed their seats. 'Wouldn't do to . . . well, alert the wrong person that we're on to him.'

'No.'

'Although it has struck me,' Fraser went on, in a low voice, 'that somebody must already have heard something for this to have happened.'

'I was thinking the same. This "somebody" you refer to must have felt himself in danger of being exposed. Which is why our friend had to be silenced.'

'Take a seat, sir, if you please.' Inspector Dimmock of the Oxford City Police was a man in late middle-age, Rowlands judged from his voice; perhaps he, too, had been called back from retirement when the war came. He sounded far from pleased at having been hauled out of bed on a freezing December night in order to interrogate fifty or so potential suspects – most of them members of the same Oxford college – about the suspicious death of one of their number. 'All right, Mr . . . er . . . Rowlands, isn't it? I gather that you were one of the first to find the . . . er . . . deceased.'

'That's right, Inspector. Major Fraser . . . that is, Sir Ian and I had an arrangement to meet him in his rooms. When we got there, at about ten minutes to midnight, he was very near death. He died a few moments later.' He paused, to allow the sergeant who had been taking all this down in his notebook, to catch up. 'We were joined almost immediately by Dr O'Halloran. He—'

'We'll come to the doctor's statement in due course,' interrupted the inspector, who was evidently suffering from a nasty head-cold. He blew his nose sharply. 'Let's start with first things first. You say you'd arranged to meet beforehand in the deceased's rooms? When was this, exactly?'

Rowlands told him.

'So really no more than fifteen or twenty minutes elapsed between Professor Challoner going upstairs to his rooms and you and Sir Ian Fraser joining him?'

'Yes.'

'Hmm,' said the inspector thoughtfully. 'Quite a short space of time in which to seize the opportunity to kill a man . . . And what was the purpose of this meeting?'

This was the question Rowlands had been dreading. He was glad he'd had a chance to agree with Fraser what line to take. 'There was no purpose as such. Professor Challoner suggested that we – Sir Ian and I – might like to join him for a nightcap before turning in for the night,' he said. There! It was over. Even to his own ears, the lie hadn't sounded too obvious.

Inspector Dimmock sneezed, then apologised for sneezing. 'The three of you were comrades from the last war, I take it?'

'Fraser and Challoner were. I was in a different outfit. But we're contemporaries, as you can see. Ian Fraser and I met when he was the newly appointed Head of St Dunstan's, the institute for the war-blinded, and I was undergoing rehabilitation there. We've been friends ever since.'

'Yes, I spotted that you were both blind,' said the policeman, adding with a chuckle, 'The dog rather gives it away. And your stick, o' course . . .'

Rowlands smiled. If this was a sample of the inspector's observational skills, then they were in for a long night. But

Dimmock's next question showed that he was not entirely lacking in this respect. 'So,' he said in a voice thick with cold. 'Can you tell me of any reason why somebody should want to kill Professor Challoner?'

Rowlands hesitated, wondering what Fraser had said when asked this question – as he certainly would have been. 'You must remember, Inspector, that I only met Donald Challoner for the first time this afternoon. I hardly had time to form an opinion of the man – let alone to get an idea of who his enemies might be.'

'Yet you came to Oxford especially to meet him,' said Dimmock.

'It was Major Fraser I came to meet. As I said, I'd never heard of Challoner until a few hours ago.'

'Yes, you did say that,' replied the other, his tone suggesting that he didn't believe a word of it, then after a pause during which the inspector blew his nose, 'You've come up from London, haven't you?'

'Brighton. We were in London, until we were bombed out.'

'Sorry to hear it,' said Dimmock. 'Long way to come, Brighton – and in this weather, too.'

'Yes.' Rowlands wasn't sure he liked where all this was going.

'Week before Christmas, too. Are you married, Mr Rowlands?'

Rowlands said that he was.

'Only I know my wife wouldn't be best pleased if I was to travel halfway across the country to see an old army chum, a few days before the festivities.'

'Yes, well . . .'

'Long-standing arrangement, was it, this meeting with Sir Ian Fraser?'

'Not particularly.'

'That's what Sir Ian said too,' said the inspector. 'Said he'd asked you to come to Oxford almost on the spur of the moment, like. Wanted your advice on something, he said.'

'That's right.'

'And what exactly was it he needed to know that made it necessary for you to drop everything and come here?'

'It was a personal matter.'

'Funny,' said Dimmock. 'That's exactly what he said.'

'I had the distinct impression the good inspector was accusing me of something,' said Rowlands to his friend, at breakfast the next morning. He had risen at eight – late for him – and, having washed and shaved, had hurried downstairs to the dining hall, where Fraser was already making a half-hearted meal of toast and coffee. 'I felt he was within an inch of clapping the handcuffs on me.'

'Yes, lucky for us that we didn't get any blood on our clothes,' said Fraser, with a bitter little laugh. 'Or we'd have been for it.'

Rowlands was silent. His hands and shirt cuffs had, in fact, been splashed with blood; he'd been aware of trying to hide them as the inspector quizzed him. Not that this would have escaped that diligent officer's notice, he was sure. 'Look, I'm sorry about your friend . . .' he began tentatively.

'You've nothing to be sorry for. I blame myself. If only I'd insisted on accompanying him back to his rooms, instead of letting him go off to be murdered.' He pushed away his coffee with a shudder. 'Filthy stuff, this . . . What I can't get out of my head,' he went on in an anguished tone, 'is the thought that Challoner must have been stabbed only moments before we arrived. Good God, we might have passed the killer on the stairs.'

'I think we did.' Rowlands recalled the silent figure who'd hurried past him as if the devil was at his heels. At the time, he'd thought nothing of it, but now . . . That furtive movement, and that silence, spoke of culpability. Yes, if they'd reached Challoner's rooms a few minutes earlier, they might very well have caught the murderer red-handed . . . Quite literally, thought Rowlands with a shudder, remembering the smell of blood on his own hands. Along the table, the voices of other breakfasting fellows came towards him. The topic of each conversation was the same.

'Shocking business . . .'

'I mean, who's next, I wonder? Are any of us safe in our beds?'

'I've always said that there was a low element in college. Little better than hooligans, some of 'em. It's been getting worse since the war started.'

'Poor old Challoner. Who'd have thought anyone would want to kill him? A professor of classics, for heaven's sake.'

'Not that there aren't some pretty vicious disputes in the *TLS* about Greek etymology, but it hardly seems grounds for murder . . .'

'It seems fantastic that something like this should happen in Oxford.'

It struck Rowlands that those present – he detected

41

Hobson's voice, and Rawlinson's – belonged exclusively to the academic contingent; evidently the army had broken its collective fast at an earlier hour than this. He wondered if Commander Hastings's men had been subjected to the same grilling by the police as the Brasenose fellows had had to endure, or if the military police had taken care of that side of things . . . Well, it was not his concern.

Having made as poor a breakfast as his friend, he pushed away his plate. 'I think a walk, don't you?' he said. 'That's if the police don't want us for anything.'

Fraser agreed. But as they got up, and began to make their way towards the double doors of the dining hall, preceded as ever by the faithful Heidi, there came a commotion.

'What the devil is going on?' It was Dr Quine, sounding even more bad-tempered than usual. 'I arrive as usual for breakfast and find my way barred by some great lout of a policeman. It's outrageous.'

Voices from around the table hastened to put the late arrival in the picture.

'You've missed all the fun, old boy.'

'Yes, haven't you heard? There's been a murder.'

'Of course,' murmured Fraser to his friend. 'Quine's rooms are on the far side of New Quadrangle. He must have gone up to bed before all the commotion.' They had by now reached the door, where the classicist stood fuming.

'Murder? What's all this talk of murder?'

'I'm afraid it's Professor Challoner,' said Fraser. 'He was killed last night.'

'Challoner?' echoed the other. 'Killed? But in heaven's name, why?'

'That's just what the police are trying to find out, Dr Quine,' said Fraser.

But the man he addressed paid no attention to this, distracted by a more urgent concern, 'Oh do get that wretched animal away from me!'

Heidi let out an indignant growl at being thus traduced.

'Come on,' said her master. 'Let's leave Dr Quine in peace. Really, that man is impossible!' he protested to Rowlands, once they were outside. 'I'd call him a dreadful old woman – if that wasn't an insult to old women.'

'He does complain rather a lot,' agreed Rowlands. He reached for his cigarettes, extracted one, and lit it – having first offered one to Fraser, who refused it.

'Prefer my pipe, actually, old man.' The two men strolled for a while in the deserted quadrangle, their footsteps crunching softly on the frozen grass.

'So,' said Rowlands, once he had satisfied himself that they were alone. 'What do we know about Challoner, and who might have wanted him dead?'

Fraser was silent a moment, meditatively drawing on his pipe. Aromatic smoke from this hung in the cold, still air. 'Well, we know he was involved in Secret Service work.'

'Yes – and how many others knew of his involvement?' asked Rowlands. 'I got the impression at dinner yesterday that it was common knowledge.'

'I suppose you're referring to what that ass Hastings said about spies,' replied the other. 'It was just a shot in the dark. He couldn't have known for sure that Challoner was MI5.'

'Perhaps not. But somebody else – our Mr X – evidently did. More than that, whoever it was must have got the wind up that Challoner was about to reveal the name of the traitor. All we've got is the fact that the man must have been a member of the college . . . and there is one other thing,' he added. He'd yet to tell Fraser of Challoner's dying words about the 'green file'.

But before he could go on, Fraser cut across him, 'We don't know anything of the kind,' he said stubbornly. 'I for one don't believe that any of our fellows could be capable of killing another. Why, it'd be like killing a member of one's family.' He seemed more exercised by this than by the – arguably greater – crime of betraying one's country.

They had been walking around the little quadrangle that lay between the older part of the college and the newer buildings Fraser had alluded to, where Dr Quine had his rooms. The area's quaint name, the Deer Park, alluded to some long-forgotten time when those animals must have roamed within college precincts, Rowlands supposed – although the space itself seemed hardly large enough to contain a single deer, let alone a herd.

Fraser, who had been brooding on what had been said, suddenly stopped dead. 'I say, look here,' he demanded. 'Why couldn't it have been someone from outside? It's easy enough to break into college if you know the dodges. And Challoner's work – whatever that was – took him far beyond Brasenose's walls.'

Rowlands shook his head, reluctant to point out what had been obvious to him since the moment he and Fraser had stumbled across the body of the MI5 agent. Because whoever had killed Donald Challoner had done so with the weapon that lay to hand – Challoner's own knife. So, whoever had killed him must have known about the knife –

which pointed to its being someone who was familiar with Challoner's rooms. A colleague, in fact.

Then there was the matter of the green file . . .

'As I was saying,' he began – but just then there came a shout from the direction of the porter's lodge.

'Sir Ian! Hold up, will you, sir! I've a message for you.' It was the porter, Dobbs, who now panted up to them. 'Sorry, sir . . . wanted to catch you. Dr Summerby telephoned the lodge a few minutes ago to ask if you two gentlemen would join him in his study.'

Chapter Four

They found Dr Summerby in his office – a large and comfortably appointed room on the first floor, where a fire was giving out a welcome heat. 'Come in, gentlemen, come in,' he said. 'I think you know the commandant? Hastings, this is Sir Ian Fraser, one of our alumni, and his friend Mr Frederick Rowlands. They knew poor Challoner – and, I understand, were first on the scene when he was found . . .' Dr Summerby pressed a bell. 'Coffee for these gentlemen,' he said, when the manservant appeared. 'I suppose it's too early to offer you sherry?'

'Coffee will do admirably,' said Fraser, as, at the principal's invitation, he and Rowlands seated themselves on the large sofa to one side of the fireplace, while Dr Summerby and the commandant resumed their own seats opposite this. As they waited for coffee to be brought, the principal expressed his dismay at the events that had necessitated the meeting. 'Quite, quite shocking,' he said. 'That a fellow of this college should have been struck down in this savage way . . . it doesn't bear thinking about.'

'Shocking,' rumbled the commandant, adding under his breath, 'Bloody Bolsheviks. Never know when or where they'll strike next . . .'

'The worst of it is that the police evidently suspect somebody from college,' Summerby went on. 'It's preposterous. We were all there, weren't we – in the senior common room? How they think that any one of us could have been responsible beggars belief. Surely it must have been an outsider?'

'I was just saying as much to Rowlands,' interjected Fraser. 'Stands to reason it couldn't have been one of us . . . a member of college, I mean. What earthly reason could any of the fellows – or college staff, for that matter – have had for murdering poor old Challoner?'

'That's just what I was about to ask you, Fraser . . . Is there anything you – or Mr Rowlands – can add to what we know already about the night of Challoner's murder? The police haven't been very forthcoming.'

'Typical,' boomed the commandant. 'Like getting blood from a stone, getting anything out of that crowd.'

'And so I . . . we . . . were wondering, Commandant Hastings and I . . . whether you might be able to cast some light on what happened. Given that you were the last to see Challoner alive . . .'

'Not quite the last,' said Fraser. He hesitated a moment. 'As you know, Principal, Donald Challoner was engaged in secret work for MI5 – based at Blenheim Palace. He told me that he was convinced there was a German spy operating in Oxford. He said he had evidence proving who it was. But he died before he could tell us whom he suspected.'

'Damn shame he wasn't able to spit it out before he died,' muttered the commandant. 'Instead of which, a lot of good men have been left under suspicion – and not just your lot, Summerby! Judging by the grilling my men received from that oaf Dimmock and his cohorts, it's obvious that the army is as much under suspicion as the fellows of Brasenose. Which, I don't have to tell you, is bad for morale. Damn it!' he concluded savagely. 'We're trying to fight a war here. Having some of one's best young officers suspected of murder is the last thing we need! And now with all this talk of spies . . .' He broke off, as if the notion was more than he could stomach. 'Well, I call it a disgrace.'

'It's a tragedy, for all sorts of reasons – not least academic ones,' said the principal. 'Brasenose has always had very good relations with the German universities. Why, not ten years ago, we had two Rhodes scholars here – from Munich and Heidelberg, respectively. Splendid young men, both. When I last had word,' he added in a subdued tone, 'one had fled to America; the other was fighting on the Eastern Front. What a terrible world this is.'

There was a silence, perhaps in acknowledgement of this indisputable fact. To Rowlands it seemed obvious that not only was the perpetrator a member of the college, but that he had been one of those present during the conversation they – he and Fraser – had had with Challoner the previous afternoon. That this had been overheard by the man whose treachery Challoner was intending to expose seemed all too likely. It had been an opportunistic killing, carried out on the spur of the moment, with the weapon that was to hand. Yes, thought Rowlands, it had to be somebody who was in the SCR that afternoon. It struck him that the man might already have been present in the room when he and Fraser came in, thinking themselves the only ones there . . .

He thought of the man who'd passed them on the stairs to Challoner's room – the man who'd made himself scarce, without a word, when Rowlands had apologised for bumping into him. He hadn't thought it worth mentioning to the police, who were in any case much more interested in Rowlands's reasons for coming to Oxford; now he said, 'I've a feeling that Major Fraser and I might have come very close to interrupting the murderer.' He explained why.

Hastings gave an exclamation. 'You're saying that you ran into this man coming away from Challoner's rooms – and that he failed to declare himself?'

'Yes. As you'll have noticed, Commandant, I'm incapable of identifying anyone unless they speak to me – and this man didn't, even after I addressed him.'

'That does seem suspicious,' said Dr Summerby in a worried tone. 'But it might not be indicative of guilt. Some of our fellows are rather, well, absent-minded. He might just have been preoccupied with an intellectual problem.'

'Then why hasn't he come forward?' This was Hastings again. 'The man's plainly guilty of something.'

'Who occupies the other rooms on that staircase?' asked Fraser.

Dr Summerby thought for a moment. 'That'll be Dr Crawley, and Mr Playford, one of our junior research fellows,' he replied. 'But I hardly think either of them could have been involved. Dr Crawley is nearly eighty – and Playford's a very decent young fellow. Came top in Greats in his final examinations, you know. Besides which

49

he's away in Shropshire, visiting his mother. She's a widow, so he's got exemption.'

'The rooms ought to be searched,' said the commandant. 'Although it's probably too late to find any useful evidence.'

'Is there a way out of the college in that wing of the building?' This was Rowlands.

'Several,' said the principal. 'But the quickest route would be through the Fellows' Garden, on the south face of the Deer Park. There's a door into the garden on the ground floor, and a gate from the garden onto the High Street.'

Rowlands considered this. 'What seems clear is that this person was not only very anxious not to be identified, but that he knows the college well enough to be aware of the comings and goings of its inmates. Which suggests that he must be, if not a member of the college, then someone intimately connected with it.'

'You may be right,' said Dr Summerby unhappily. 'But I must say—' Before he could say what it was he had to say, the telephone on his desk rang. He answered it. 'Yes? All right, send him in. We're going to have to resume this conversation another time, gentlemen. It would appear that Blenheim Palace is taking an interest.' Which surprised Rowlands not in the least. As he and Fraser rose to take their leave, the door to the study opened and someone came in. 'Ah, come in, come in,' said Dr Summerby. 'Captain Fawcett, is it not?'

'It is,' said the man who'd just arrived, in a cool tone. 'But I understood that we were to be alone.'

'These gentlemen are just leaving,' said the principal. He did not introduce them. 'And Commandant Hastings was just giving me the benefit of his advice . . .'

'Oh, I'm off too. Know when I'm not wanted, hey, Summerby?'

The door closed behind them. 'Now that, if I'm not mistaken,' said the commandant, 'is a Grade A spook.'

The inquest on the late Donald Challoner was a perfunctory affair. Rowlands, who had been called to give evidence, had the feeling that, as far as this was possible under the stipulations of British law, the events it had been convened to investigate had been swept under the carpet. An appropriate figure of speech in this instance, he thought, since the coroner – perhaps under instructions from a higher power – had chosen to convene the court, not in a public forum, such as the town hall, but in the library of Brasenose College. Here, in an atmosphere redolent of old books and dusty furnishings (such as the aforementioned carpet), the legal formulae were swiftly gone through, with representatives of the police and medical services providing a précis of their respective findings, and a handful of lay witnesses, of which he was one, providing theirs.

By contrast with some of the inquests at which Rowlands had been present in the past, as witness or spectator, the turnout was sparse, with just a few of the college fellows who had known Professor Challoner in attendance, and a single representative of the army, in the person of the adjutant, Captain Parker, watching the proceedings. 'The old man couldn't be here himself,' he confided to Rowlands, beside whom he had seated himself, on one of the library's uncomfortable carved oak chairs. 'He's overseeing a training exercise on Port Meadow. But he'll want a full report,' he added. 'Very concerned at how this will look for the army, given that our lot are in situ, as it were.'

Behind Rowlands, several members of the college were seated – among them, he detected Dr Hobson's genial tones ('Poor old Challoner. He was a decent cove. Rotten thing to have happened.') and Dr Quine's querulous mutterings ('Why these proceedings have to be dragged out in this way, I fail to understand. Some of us have work to do.'). Although in fact the whole thing took no more than an hour, once the witnesses had been sworn in.

Rowlands's own evidence was briskly dealt with by the coroner – a laconic individual not given to the rhetorical flourishes to which some of his kind were prone. 'You were the gentleman who found the deceased, were you not?' Then, when Rowlands replied in the affirmative, 'Good, good. Can you tell us how long you had known Professor Challoner before his, ah, untimely death?' Rowlands told him that they had met for the first time that day. 'Good, good. And was there anything said at this first meeting that suggested Professor Challoner might have been in fear of his life?'

Rowlands had hesitated a moment before replying. 'I had the feeling he had something on his mind,' he said carefully. 'But he did not go into detail as to what it was.'

'Good, good. You may stand down, Mr Rowlands.'

Clearly, the powers-that-be wanted the evidence kept as vague as possible. A few more witnesses were called. Fraser (who confirmed Rowlands's account of their meeting with Challoner); Dr Summerby (who expressed his dismay at the loss of so distinguished a colleague); and

Dr O'Halloran (who added his account of the finding of the body to what had already been said) – but overall the procedure was an exercise in saying as little as possible, thought Rowlands. There was no mention of Challoner's war service, nor of his connection with Blenheim Palace.

A verdict of 'murder by person or persons unknown' was pronounced. The little gathering in the library broke up.

'Well, I'm glad that's over,' said Hobson, in Rowlands's ear. 'Hope it means that the law will leave us alone while they get on with finding the chap who did for poor Challoner. College hasn't been the same these past few days with police swarming about, and everything topsy-turvy. Bad enough to have the army taking up space, without being under surveillance from the boys in blue, eh, Quine?'

But Dr Quine, impatient to get back to his books, no doubt, had already gone.

Chapter Five

Christmas 1941 found the Rowlands family in what Rowlands still thought of as the 'new house' – although it had been over six months since a German plane, returning to base after a night bombing the Deptford dockyards, had shed its remaining load over West London, narrowly missing the Rowlandses' house but causing extensive structural damage. Moving to Brighton, where Rowlands was now in charge of St Dunstan's South Coast office, had been a consequence of this misfortune – which, he was quick to remind himself, was a relatively minor one when compared with the devastation the Blitz had brought about for many others.

Even so, it was hard not to regret the pleasant surroundings of 44 Grove Crescent, with its spacious rooms and big garden. Number 6 Dorset Gardens was a dolls' house by comparison, with no garden to speak of, and rooms that – while merely cosy when inhabited by just himself, Edith and Edith's mother – seemed cramped when, as now, more family members were in residence. This year, the return of the Rowlandses' eldest daughter, Margaret, from her war work, and of their youngest, Joan, from her aunt and uncle's house in Richmond, where she had been boarding during the school term, coincided with the arrival in Southampton of the ship on which Margaret's fiancé, Lieutenant Frank Dawson, was serving. He, too, was to join them for lunch on Christmas Day – 'Although where we're going to put everybody,' said Rowlands's wife, in mock despair, 'I haven't the faintest idea. That dining room's hardly big enough to seat four – let alone six.'

'You'll cope. You always do,' Rowlands reassured her. 'You're such a good manager.' Which she'd had to become, he reminded himself, in the years since she'd married him. There'd never been money for lavish entertaining, although things had been better when they'd moved to the Kingston house, and combined their household finances with those of Mrs Edwards, Rowlands's mother-in-law. Now that wartime restrictions were in place – as they were for the whole country – they were back to a more austere regime. Edith was particularly exercised over the fact that, with the food shortages making it likely that this was going to be a very frugal Christmas, they'd have an extra mouth to feed, 'And not just an extra girl,' she'd added, with what seemed to her husband rather poor taste. The allusion had been to last year's guest – a young woman who'd worked with Margaret at Bletchley Park. The unhappy end of that business still haunted him, and he showed by his silence how little he approved of the remark.

'I'm sure Frank will bring his ration book,' said Margaret, coming in at that moment with an armful of freshly ironed sheets. 'Mother, where do you want me to put these?'

'Top bedroom,' said Edith, distractedly counting cutlery. 'Six, seven, eight soup spoons and the same number of dessert spoons. That's a relief. I was afraid we'd have to manage with teaspoons. Of course when I married, I had a dozen of everything . . .'

Cramped as Dorset Gardens was, thought Rowlands, it still had more space than they'd had in Crofton Park. It was there that they'd lived when the girls were small – and had later been joined by his sister Dorothy and her then husband, Viktor, after the Lehmanns had been evicted from their home in Whitechapel . . . What a long time ago it seemed! Well, it was a long time, he reminded himself – nearly fifteen years.

Thinking of Dorothy, he wondered how she and Jack, to whom she'd been married for the past ten years, were getting on with running the hotel. In recent months, they'd been taking in refugees, and families bombed out of their homes after the Portsmouth air raids. It had been a while since they'd all met – Cornwall being such a long way away, and travel so much more difficult these days. Perhaps, in the spring, once the weather improved, he and Edith could go down for a few days? She'd turned forty last year – Dorothy, that was. His little sister. Even though it hadn't always been the easiest of relationships, she was still close to his heart.

'Fred, if you've nothing to do, you might bring in some more coal,' said his wife, breaking into these thoughts. 'And I'll need you to stoke up the kitchen stove, so that I can set the bread to prove and make another batch of

56

spiced biscuits . . . although what they'll taste like made with lard instead of butter and half the amount of sugar I used to use, I can't imagine.'

'I'm sure they'll taste delicious,' he said, putting on his jacket to go outside to the coal shed. It had stopped snowing, but it was still bitterly cold, with an icy nip in the air that stung his cheeks and made his eyes stream with tears. Taking care to pull on his leather gloves before starting to dig out the coal (relying as he did on the sensitivity of his fingers, he had a dread of getting chilblains), he filled the coal scuttle and trudged back across the little yard to the kitchen door. Two more trips should do it. When the kitchen range was burning merrily, and the fire in the sitting room replenished, he rubbed the life back into his hands and decided to take a turn along the seafront before it got dark.

'You might take Joan with you,' said his wife, busily rolling biscuit dough. 'She's been fidgeting about all afternoon making paper-chains and suchlike nonsense. It'll do her good to get some exercise.'

Joan was agreeable to this plan, and so they set out, both well wrapped up against the biting wind. Even though there were only two days to go before the festivities, there was little appreciable diminution in the volume of traffic – most of it military – that roared up and down the main thoroughfare. It had been one of the things Rowlands had found hard to adjust to, on moving from their quiet London street to Brighton: the constant racket of armoured vehicles passing up and down, as well as the inescapable presence of soldiers in the streets. He knew exactly what Fraser had meant when he'd said that

Oxford 'wasn't the same'. The fact was that both places – the ancient university city and the lively seaside town – had been turned into army camps for the duration.

Thinking of his friend and mentor made him smile, then frown. He wondered how the old boy was doing. In the days since his return from Oxford he'd heard nothing more about the case that had brought his visit to that city to such an untimely end. With Joan chattering away beside him about something somebody called Gloria had said at Guides the previous week, he turned along Marine Parade, into the teeth of the wind. He was still troubled by the thought that he'd missed something – some vital clue, which would turn the investigation around . . .

He recalled the conversation he'd had with Fraser and some of the other Brasenose fellows that afternoon in the SCR while they were waiting for Challoner to appear. It had been when, half-jokingly, he said something about Oxford being an ivory tower and how he'd always fancied such a life of quiet contemplation. 'Civilised' had been the word he'd used. What was it somebody had said, talking about rivalry between academics? *They'll stab you in the back as soon as look at you* . . . A phrase that had turned out to be all too horribly true. Could this be no more than a dispute between two rivals that had turned ugly? It seemed hard to believe – and yet such things did happen. Murders were committed for what seemed the most trivial of reasons. A man's dinner that had got burnt. A child's crying that wouldn't stop. A women smiling at a man who was not her husband . . . All these, or reasons like them, had often been the catalyst for murder. Professional jealousy, although perhaps harder for the average man to comprehend, could be no less bitter, he was sure.

And yet surely there had been a more fundamental reason – the fear of being exposed and hanged as a traitor – that had been the motive for the don's death? He began to review – in no particular order – the list of possible suspects . . . There was Dr O'Halloran, who'd turned up so promptly when the murder had been discovered. He'd had the best opportunity, thought Rowlands, since his rooms were across the way from Challoner's – but what possible motive could he have had? He'd seemed a gentle old boy. Then there were all the people who'd been at dinner that night, and who'd been in the SCR afterwards. Hobson, Rawlinson, Quine, Armstrong and the various army personnel. Could one of them have absented himself briefly from the company after dinner, in order to carry out the fatal attack, and then return unnoticed?

He thought of the man who'd rushed past him on the stairs, willing himself to remember what it was that had struck him as strange about the encounter, brief as it was . . . but could think of nothing, apart from the fact that the man had remained silent. Beside him, Joan was saying something about what the games mistress had said to somebody called Deanna (where did they get these names? Film magazines, he guessed). 'Deanna's awfully good at hockey. Though we had to miss the end-of-term match last week on account of the snow. D'you think it'll snow tonight, Daddy? I do hope so, because if it's a really big fall, they'll cancel the trains and I won't have to go back to school for ages and ages.'

'I thought you liked school.'

'Oh, I do. But it's a frightful bore sometimes.'

They'd reached the pier – partially dismantled, Rowlands

knew, to prevent its being used by enemy craft in the event of an invasion. The seafront, once so jolly with its rows of striped deck-chairs and its brightly painted beach huts, now wore a bleaker aspect. Quite apart from the rumble of passing army lorries, there was the sinister presence of heavy ordnance, in the shape of the Bofors guns that had been placed at intervals along the esplanade, and the tank traps and tangles of barbed wire that made the beach itself out of bounds for civilians like themselves. 'Time we were turning back,' he said. 'Your mother'll be expecting us.'

Back at the house, they found Lieutenant Dawson just arrived, with gifts of tinned ham, a box of Smyrna figs and a packet of real coffee – these delicacies considerably raising his status in the eyes of his hostess, 'I hope you can stay for supper, Lieutenant Dawson? I'm sure you must be famished after your journey.' The young man's refusal of this invitation, on the grounds that he'd be expected back at barracks, only increased his popularity with Edith, who kept pressing him to have another sandwich, or a piece of Christmas cake. 'You fighting men need to keep your strength up.' She seemed utterly smitten with her prospective son-in-law, thought Rowlands, secretly amused at this change in his wife's attitude.

Lieutenant Dawson had succeeded in endearing himself to Edith's mother, too, it seemed, 'I've always felt that the naval uniform was the most becoming,' she said, after the young officer had taken his leave.

'Granny! You sound as if you're a bit in love with Frank yourself,' said Joan, who had already voiced her approval of her sister's intended for his skills at Beggar My Neighbour and Snap.

Mrs Edwards replied mildly that, as her father had been a navy man, she'd always had a soft spot for the Senior Service. 'Rather a Ronald Colman type.'

'He's not a bit like Ronald Colman!' protested Joan. 'Much more like Gary Cooper.' Her current heartthrob.

'Would you mind awfully,' interjected Margaret, returning at that moment from seeing her fiancé off on the bus that would take him to the naval barracks, 'not discussing Frank when he isn't here to defend himself?'

Christmas lunch was a rather more austere affair than it had been the previous year, when rationing had only just started to bite. Rowlands thought regretfully of his vegetable garden at Grove Crescent, which had supplied the family table throughout the first year of the war, alleviating the food shortages most others were experiencing. Now, with no garden to speak of, and fierce competition for Kemptown allotments, the Rowlandses were reduced to what the local greengrocer's could supply: in this instance a few pounds of woody parsnips and carrots, as well as the inevitable cabbage, turnips and potatoes. Edith had managed to procure a chicken (no goose this year!) but was fretting about how it would stretch to feed six of them. The ham supplied by Frank Dawson would help to make things go a bit further, she supposed, but it wasn't going to be much of a feast.

Still, they would make the best of what they had – and be thankful for it, she said. She wondered aloud what kind of Christmas their soldiers in the desert were having. No homemade Christmas pudding for them – even if it was made with grated carrot instead of raisins. Lieutenant

Dawson – again raising his stock in the eyes of his hostess – had brought a bottle of sherry to have before the meal. There was wine, too (a decent Bordeaux Rowlands had been saving) and bottled beer for the men. And so it was a convivial party that raised its glasses to toast 'the King, and our fighting men'.

'And women,' murmured Margaret, as she took a sip.

After lunch, presents were exchanged. Edith's mother, Helen, had knitted her son-in-law a sleeveless pullover from wool she'd unravelled from a worn-out garment, steamed to remove the kinks, and re-fashioned. Margaret was presented with scented soap (a real luxury in those straitened times). Joan received a new stamp album, to display her burgeoning collection. Rowlands's present from his wife was two new packs of Braille playing cards (his old ones were greasy with use) and a gramophone record of Vaughan Williams's *English Folk Song Suite*. He gave Edith and Helen a pair of good leather gloves each. He and Frank Dawson exchanged packs of cigarettes.

All in all, it had been a very pleasant day, thought Rowlands, as he undressed before bed that night. He'd liked young Dawson, who seemed a modest fellow, with a dry sense of humour, and some thoughtful views on the present emergency. 'Ideally, Margaret and I would like to get married as soon as possible,' he confided to his prospective father-in-law, as the two of them smoked their cigarettes in the back yard. 'But with the way the war's going just now, it'll probably be months before I can get some leave. The fact is, you just can't tell how it will all turn out,' he added quietly.

Rowlands agreed that you couldn't.

'You just have to carry on, and hope for the best.'

Rowlands said that he supposed you did.

'I mean, with the Yanks coming in at last, the whole progress of the war could change . . .'

Rowlands agreed that it could.

'So we've agreed, Margaret and I, that it would be best to wait.'

'He seems a decent young chap,' said Rowlands to his wife, as the two of them got ready for bed. 'What? Oh yes,' she said distractedly. 'Nice manners.' Then, after a pause, 'I just wish Anne would find a nice boy . . .'

'Edith, she's only nineteen.'

'Girls are getting married younger these days. It's the war.'

'Yes. That was a splendid feast you put on for us,' he said, hoping to divert her from this topic.

'Was it all right? I was afraid there wouldn't be enough to go round, but it worked out in the end, I suppose.'

'It did.' He leant across and kissed her. 'Good night, old thing.'

'Good night.'

The next day was Boxing Day and Rowlands decided he'd look in at the office. There wouldn't be much doing, but he could pick up any letters that seemed as if they might need immediate attention, and bring them home for Edith to read, so as to be able to get off to a good start when Rowlands's secretary, Miss Bates, returned on the following day. But then Edith said she fancied a walk, to blow the cobwebs away, and so the two of them set off along the route that had become familiar to Rowlands during the past six months of their sojourn in Brighton. Avoiding the seafront, with its military accoutrements, he and Edith headed for the quieter reaches of Eastern Road. Here, there were no army lorries roaring up and down, no boisterous groups of off-duty soldiers, intent on avoiding the military police.

A brisk fifteen-minute walk brought them to St George's Road, and the Georgian terrace where the South Coast offices of the St Dunstan's After-Care Unit were located. As it happened, there was some post in the wire basket attached to the front door – Rowlands retrieved this, and was for returning home, when Edith said, 'Why don't I read these now? Then if there's anything that needs dealing with urgently, you can do so at once.' He said that sounded like a good idea, and they climbed the stairs to the first floor, where – both keeping on their coats, because the radiators had been off for the past two days – they sorted rapidly through the post, discarding circulars and anything non-urgent.

Fortunately, there wasn't too much that needed to be dealt with immediately: a handwritten letter requesting warm clothing for a St Dunstan's family who'd been bombed out of their home in Preston Park, which Rowlands forwarded to the appeals department in London with a typed covering note; a letter – this typed by the St Dunstaner himself – explaining that his sighted assistant (he ran a tobacconist's) had been called up, and requesting a substitute helper; and a death notice. It was one of their long-term residents, a man named Dawkins, who had died. Heart attack during an air raid. It was his sister who had written. 'When's the funeral to be held?' Rowlands asked his wife.

'Next Wednesday. St Peter's.'

'I'd better go, I suppose – or at least make sure that somebody from St Dunstan's goes.' He put the letters in his pocket for posting on the way home, and stood up. 'That's the lot. Let's get going, shall we?'

It was then that the telephone rang. 'Now who can that be? Oh . . . Hello, Major. I hope you and Lady Fraser had a pleasant Christmas?' The voice at the other end of the line made the appropriate rejoinder, then went on to give a list of instructions, which Rowlands repeated, by way of committing them to memory, 'Yes, I've got that . . . 2 p.m. in the college chapel on Tuesday . . . and Wolvercote Cemetery afterwards. Thank you, Major. Until Tuesday, then.' He hung up, and made a wry face at his wife. 'It seems to be the time of year for funerals,' he said.

Chapter Six

Oxford lay eerily silent under a blanket of snow. The heavy fall that Joan had wished for had come two days later, although it would have cleared, Rowlands guessed, in time for her return to school. It had certainly delayed his own return home by at least a day. He had only just made it to Oxford on the Monday evening, before the blizzard hit, rendering the roads impassable, and resulting in the cancellation of most of the trains. The snow continued into Tuesday, so that even the burial service that followed the funeral rites in Brasenose Chapel seemed in doubt. Fortunately, by half past two, when they were to set out for the cemetery, the snow had dwindled to a light sprinkling. It would still be hard work for the gravediggers, thought Rowlands, as the funeral party began to make its slow way back towards the cars, with the newly dug grave already half filled up with snow and the ground like iron.

There had been few mourners at the graveside – apart from himself and Fraser, and a few of the younger dons, who had braved the weather to pay their respects. Among these, Rowlands thought he recognised Dr Hobson's voice, and that of Dr Aitken. 'Dreadful business,' he heard the former say, and the latter's murmured reply, 'Yes. Not quite the sort of thing one expects to happen at Oxford.'

'Didn't Challoner have any family?' Rowlands asked his friend.

'Not to my knowledge. Parents both dead. Don't think there were any siblings – if so, they haven't kept in touch. He never married. I think,' said Fraser in a low voice, 'that college was his family. That and the service, of course.'

The SCR at Brasenose College was a good deal colder than it had been the first time Rowlands had entered the room – or perhaps it was merely that he himself felt chilled to the bone, after standing around at a graveside. Whatever the reason, he was glad of the restorative cup of tea that was offered to the mourning party, with the sandwiches and biscuits that constituted, in Fraser's wry phrase, the 'funeral baked meats'. Fraser himself sounded thick with rheum, his voice a hoarse croak. 'You shouldn't have come,' Rowlands admonished him, after one particular fierce bout of coughing. 'Far better to have stayed at home in bed.'

'I had to come,' was the reply. 'After all, it's partly my fault that Challoner's dead. If I hadn't insisted on that meeting . . .'

'That's nonsense and you know it,' said Rowlands, although he, too, had been experiencing similar feelings of guilt. 'Even if it hadn't happened that night, whoever killed Challoner would have found another opportunity. Murderers don't give up, once they're set on that course.'

'I say!' said a jovial voice Rowlands recognised as that

of Jeremy Hobson. 'That sounds as if you speak from experience. Known many murderers, have you?'

'One or two. They're usually the most ordinary of men.'

There was a startled silence; then the younger man guffawed. 'Oh, that's jolly good! You had me fooled for a minute there, old man.'

Rowlands smiled, although in truth he found Hobson's facetious manner a little wearing. But at least he'd made the effort, and turned up at the cemetery, he reminded himself. That surely meant he must be a decent sort?

'Brr!' the latter now exclaimed, blowing on his hands to warm them. 'It's perishing cold in here. Ah, here's tea at last . . .'

The rattle of the tea trolley was an unwelcome reminder, to Rowlands, of the first time he'd set foot in this room, almost a fortnight ago. Just the same chorus of voices – Hobson's, of course, Aitken's, Rawlinson's – had greeted the arrival of tea, and with it, the man Rowlands had come to meet, whose obsequies they had just been performing. He shivered at the thought. 'Hope you're not going down with this,' croaked Fraser, who was standing nearby. 'Be quiet, Heidi!' Because the dog had begun to growl softly as if she too was remembering when it was they had last assembled there. 'Don't know what's the matter with her. She's usually so good with people. Lie down, Heidi!' he ordered, as he took his seat. Tea was handed round. 'That's better,' sighed Fraser, as he took an appreciative sip. 'Nothing like the "cup that cheers" to chase out the cold. I do wonder when this snow will let up. You'll be wanting to get home, Rowlands, old man.'

'So will you, for that matter.' Although listening to the

major's rattling cough, Rowlands wondered if his friend was fit to travel. He supposed that the cold weather must have kept a lot of the Brasenose fellows away from the funeral. Dr Quine, for instance. His complaining voice had been noticeably absent. Perhaps he, too, had fallen ill? Or maybe the animosity he'd felt towards his fellow classicist had been too violent to set aside, even for death?

'I hope they give us something decent for dinner,' muttered a voice nearby, which he identified as that of Dr Rawlinson. 'That stew they gave us last night was inedible. Mostly turnips. I must say, things haven't improved in that respect since we've had the other lot imposed on us.' He meant the Junior Staff Officers, Rowlands surmised – not sure if the remark was meant for him. It seemed to him that all people talked about these days was food, or the lack of it.

Around him, the conversation rose and fell. The weather. The war. The funeral. The inadequacy of the sandwiches. Then somebody – it was Dr Aitken – said, 'Anybody know what's happened to Quine? Haven't seen him around for days.'

'No idea, old man,' said Hobson. 'He usually looks in about this time, doesn't he?'

'I should imagine he'll be in his room, writing his paper on Tacitus,' said another voice. O'Halloran's. 'I believe he said that his publisher was expecting it by the new year.' There was a general murmur of agreement with this observation; then the talk moved on to other things.

Rowlands woke next morning to a changed mood – Oxford having undergone one of the changes of personnel that were

69

increasingly a feature of these wartime years. The unearthly quiet that had hung over the snowbound streets had been replaced by something altogether more cheerful. Excited young voices funnelled up the staircase.

'Give us a hand with this trunk, old son!'

'I've got my own bags to carry, thanks very much . . .'

'Go on! Do us a favour!'

'All right, all right. Where've they put us, d'you think? Up in the attics?'

'Looks like it. What's the betting they've given the best rooms to the army?'

'Oh, quit grousing. You're lucky we haven't been put in the Nissen huts . . .'

Descending the stairs, on his way to breakfast, Rowlands encountered this noisy group on the way up. 'Need a hand, gentlemen?' he said to the two that were struggling to get a boot up the narrow staircase.

'That's awfully decent of you, sir,' said the young man who'd mentioned Nissen huts. 'If you'd just catch hold of the handle at your end, I think we can manage nicely.'

Rowlands did so, and, by judicious manoeuvring, the three of them, with the two young men heaving the boot up the stairs from below, succeeded in reaching the topmost landing. 'Phew! Quite a view you get from here,' remarked the first speaker. 'What's that extraordinary building with the dome one can see peeping over the tops of the college buildings?'

'It's the Radcliffe Camera,' said Rowlands, who had once visited the famous reading rooms in the company of his brother-in-law, an Oxford alumnus, and their respective wives. Not that he was able to appreciate the view, but he always liked to know where he stood, topographically. Landmarks such as the one he'd named were vital when it came to navigating one's way around unfamiliar territory – as Oxford was for him.

'Coo!' said the lad who'd complained about the army getting the best rooms. 'This where they put the undergrads, is it?'

'When we're not at war,' replied Rowlands drily. 'Most of those that haven't already joined up have been moved into rooms in Christ Church. That's the big college across the way, with the very tall bell tower – it's called Tom Tower.' He made a move towards the stairs. 'Well, I'll leave you to settle in.'

'Wait.' It was the man who'd asked about the Radcliffe Camera. 'You've been an absolute brick. Name's Holifield. Pilot officer, RAF. And this reprobate is Flight Sergeant Andrews. Our lot are just moving in, as you'll have gathered, Mr . . . er . . .'

Rowlands supplied his name.

'Well, Mr Rowlands – or is it "Professor" or "Doctor"? One never knows, round here . . . we're very grateful for your help, aren't we, Andrews?' The other muttered an agreement. 'Buy you a drink in the bar sometime – that is, if there is a bar.'

'Oh, I think you'll find there's no shortage of bars in Oxford,' said Rowlands with a smile, as he left them to it. He'd look in on Fraser before going into breakfast, he decided. The poor old fellow hadn't sounded at all well when they'd parted company the night before. To get to Fraser's rooms meant crossing Old Quad to a staircase diagonally opposite his own. This proved less straightforward than

71

it had before, since Old Quad was now a hive of activity. Crowds of young men – no doubt the fellows of those he had just met – were busy unloading luggage, and hurling imprecations at those unwise enough to get in their way. Evidently, the RAF was moving in.

'Watch yer backs!' shouted someone in Rowlands's vicinity; a moment later he found himself being hauled unceremoniously out of the way, as a handcart propelled at speed came lumbering towards him. 'Sorry, sir, our chap couldn't see you over all these mattresses,' said another voice, adding, in a rougher tone, to his subordinate, 'Look where you're going, can't you, Prescott? You nearly had the gentleman over . . .'

'I think I was as much to blame,' said Rowlands. 'I wasn't paying attention.'

'Be that as it may, sir,' replied the man who'd called out – presumably an NCO – 'we can't have our lads turning the place into a bear garden, can we?'

Rowlands smiled his agreement and went on his way, taking care to skirt the noisier groups of arrivals. Already agreeable smells of breakfast being prepared were issuing from the kitchen block. The clock was just striking eight as he climbed Fraser's staircase. He found the latter still in his dressing gown. 'That you, old man? Come in, do,' he croaked. 'Just getting m'self dressed. Won't keep you a moment . . .'

'I hope you're not thinking of getting up?' said Rowlands. 'You sound a good deal worse than you did yesterday. Lady Fraser won't be very pleased with me if I send you home in this state.'

'Fiddlesticks,' was the reply. 'I'll be right as rain when

I've had some fodder . . .' This brave statement was lost in a fit of coughing.

At last, Rowlands persuaded his friend to stay where he was. 'I can ask George to bring you up a tray,' he said. 'You oughtn't to be venturing out in this cold.'

'All right, all right . . .' Another fit of coughing. 'I say, Rowlands, do me a favour, will you? Take Heidi out for her walk. She oughtn't to be cooped up indoors all day.'

After breakfast, Rowlands accordingly collected the dog, and set off in the direction of the railway station. He wanted to find out if any trains were running that day, or, failing that, whether they'd be running the next day. Having made the journey to and from the station several times already, he was confident that he could find the way; the porter's directions confirmed this feeling, 'Turn right along Turl Street, then left onto the Broad, left at Magdalen Street and right onto George Street. When you get to Hythe Bridge Street, keep going straight on, and you can't miss it. Reckon there won't be any trains today, mark you, sir – not with all this snow about.'

It was certainly icy underfoot, with last night's heavy fall trampled into slush by passing traffic, and re-frozen into a hard, slippery surface – the kind Rowlands dreaded above all. One false move, and he'd be flat on his face, he thought. Fortunately, the dog was a stabilising factor, provided as she was with a harness, to which a handle was attached. This, although a cumbersome arrangement for the poor beast, made it easier to get along, Rowlands had to admit. It took him a few minutes to get accustomed to letting the dog lead him, as the two of them threaded their way through the swarm of RAF men just then besieging the college.

Emerging onto the Broad, he recalled that Blackwell's Bookshop was across the way – he'd last visited that august institution, beloved of all Oxford alumni, a couple of years before the last war, when he'd been working as a sales representative for Methuen. How long ago it seemed! He'd been twenty-two then, and eager to make his way in the book trade. The Blackwell's visit had been a successful one, with plenty of orders following. If he kept this up, his manager – old Wilkes – had said there'd be a promotion in it for him . . . His mind still dwelling on that far-off time, when life had been full of promise, and the shades of war had not yet closed in, he wasn't paying full attention to what was going on around.

'Look out!' There came a furious ringing of a bicycle bell, as the machine came hurtling out of a side street towards them. If it hadn't been for Heidi's stopping dead – thus forcing her master to do the same – there would have been a collision. The cyclist – a young woman – must have dismounted from her bike a moment later, for she came hurrying up, saying breathlessly, 'Crikey! I . . . I nearly hit you . . . I'm so sorry . . . I thought you must have seen me . . .'

'That's just it – I can't see,' he confessed, adding, with a rueful smile, 'But the fault was mine. I was wool-gathering, I'm afraid. Fortunately, my dog was more alert than I was. So no harm done. Come along, Heidi.'

He made as if to go on his way, but the girl said, 'Wait. I believe we've met . . . ages ago. You're that detective, aren't you? I recognised you at once.'

'I'm afraid I . . .'

'We met in Cambridge – or should I say, "the Other

Place"?' She laughed. 'It must have been six . . . nearly
seven . . . years ago. I was at St Gertrude's,' she added shyly.

Now he knew her. 'Miss Thompson,' he said. 'Of course.
It was at the end-of-term garden party that we met, wasn't
it? You were in the college dramatic society – putting on
scenes from Shakespeare, as I recall.'

'Oh, I only helped out backstage,' she said. 'But you're
right. I was a member of SGDS . . .' She sighed. 'It seems
such a long time ago.'

It so nearly echoed his own thoughts of a moment ago,
that he smiled. '*Tempus fugit*,' he said.

'What? Oh yes. It does rather. It's hard to believe . . .'
She broke off. 'I mean, all that – the garden parties and
going punting and all the rest – seems like a hundred years
ago.'

'Another world,' said Rowlands.

'Yes.' Perhaps a memory of the dreadful events that
had happened soon after that famous garden party came
back to her, for she shivered slightly – which was hardly
surprising, thought Rowlands. It had been a bad business.

'Well, it was very nice to meet you again,' he said,
thinking that she might be lingering out of politeness.
'I'd better let you get to your tutorial . . . or lecture,' he
improvised, realising that she couldn't possibly be a student
here. Why, she must be twenty-four or -five. She probably
had a teaching post at one of the women's colleges – St
Anne's or Somerville.

'Oh, I'm not an academic,' she said, as if she guessed his
thought. 'I finished with all that a long time ago. Besides
which,' she added kindly, 'term hasn't started yet, so there
won't be any tutorials. I was just on my way back to

Keble—' She broke off suddenly, as if she'd said more than she meant to.

'I'd better be off, too,' he said, refraining from asking the obvious question as to what she was doing at a men's college. 'This has been something of a flying visit to Oxford. I hope to be going home tomorrow – if they haven't cancelled all the trains.'

'A pity. We could have met for tea,' she said. 'Another time, perhaps?'

Then she was off, with a merry ringing of her bicycle bell. He realised that she hadn't asked his name. Perhaps, he thought wryly, he would remain 'that detective' to her – a reminder of an episode in her past she'd rather have forgotten.

At the station, it was as the porter had predicted: all trains cancelled until the line could be cleared. 'It looks like another night in Oxford for us, Heidi,' he said, as they began the slow trudge back to the college. He'd better ask if he could telephone Edith from the porter's lodge to let her know he'd be delayed. Although he wouldn't have felt comfortable about leaving Fraser in the state he was in – even if the trains had been running as usual.

Since it was still early, he decided to take the longer route back, via the High, Catte Street and Brasenose Lane. It seemed a shame to be in Oxford, a city renowned for its architectural beauty, and not explore a little further, he thought. Even though he was, perforce, oblivious to that beauty, he still retained a memory of what was there. This was thanks to those earlier visits – the first when he'd still had his sight; the second, after the war, when his wife's brother had shown them around with proprietorial pride.

For here was the handsome façade of Balliol College; the Martyrs' Memorial in St Giles; the Trinity College gateway, with its elegant Palladian chapel; the Sheldonian theatre, the Bodleian Library and, rising superbly above it all, the glorious dome of the Radcliffe Camera. On both occasions – especially the first – he'd been entranced by all these . . . now reduced to shadowy impressions in his memory.

But he could still enjoy the physical sensation of walking though Oxford – the crunch of his footsteps in the snow as he passed from narrow street to narrow street of the mediaeval quarter. The sound of voices – youthful, excited – carrying further in that snowbound quiet. The crisp smell of the air was pleasant, too, as was the smell of freshly baked bread wafting from a baker's shop, the smell of tobacco from a newsagent's. With Heidi's aid, he found he could stride confidently along (keeping a sharp ear out for passing bicycles), and had reached Christ Church just as the clock in Tom Tower was striking ten, before deciding to turn back.

Turning in at the college gates around five minutes later, he was surprised to find Old Quad as silent as the grave. Having stowed its bags and baggage, the RAF must have made itself scarce for the time being, he thought. The porter, too, appeared to have deserted his post. 'Hello?' called Rowlands, to confirm this. 'Anybody there?' But there was no reply – which was odd.

He was making his way along the flagstone path that led to Fraser's room, when there came the sound of hurrying footsteps coming towards him. 'My Gawd! My Gawd!' gasped a voice: the porter's, as it happened. 'Come quick, sir. There's been another one . . . Oh Gawd . . .'

'What do you mean, "another one"?' demanded Rowlands.

But the porter seemed to have run out of words. All he could do was mutter, 'My Gawd, my Gawd,' over and over.

Rowlands tried again. 'Mr Dobbs? What is it that's happened?'

'I'll telling you, aren't I?' cried Dobbs. 'Another one. Dead. Horrible, it was . . .' He gave a shudder. 'Walked in, I did, an' found 'im. Throat cut from ear to ear.'

Further questioning of the agitated man revealed that the dead man was Dr Quine. 'Thought as I 'adn't seen 'im for a while,' said Dobbs. 'But I didn't think nothing of it . . . Only reason I went to 'is rooms was because some letters 'ad come for 'im . . . 'E likes 'is letters delivered prompt, does Dr Quine. Give me a rocket, 'e did, 'cause I kept one of 'em back till the afternoon post one day – we being short-staffed, you see . . .' His voice tailed off, as if he'd just realised that the irascible Quine would no longer be able to give him – or anybody else – a 'rocket' for dereliction of duty.

'You'd better take me to his rooms,' said Rowlands, then, as the two of them set out across the quad, 'On second thoughts, I think we should leave Sir Ian's dog in the porter's lodge. Is there somewhere we can tie her up?' He recalled how distressed the animal had been in the presence of death. With Dobbs's assistance, he tethered her to a chair in the porter's lodge. 'Come on,' he said to the man. 'We'll go first to Dr Quine's rooms. And then,' he added grimly, 'you'd better call the police.'

Chapter Seven

Quine's rooms were in the newer part of the college, across the quaintly named Deer Park. It was here, the porter said, that most of the Junior Staff Officers' contingent were billeted – 'seeing as the rooms are a bit more modern, like.' Rowlands privately thought that the college authorities might have preferred not to have the sixteenth-century buildings around Old Quad knocked about by a lot of boisterous young army officers, but kept this thought to himself. Although the fact that the RAF had been allocated rooms in the older part of Brasenose indicated that there was now a shortage of space in the new. ''Course, Dr Quine weren't too happy when he was offered rooms in this building,' said Dobbs. 'But Dr Summerby thought it would be a good idea to have one of the fellows keeping an eye on things, as it were. Didn't much fancy it, though, didn't Dr Quine.'

Rowlands could well imagine.

'Say, you don't think . . .' The porter's voice assumed

a horrified tone. 'That 'e done it 'cause o' that? Topped 'isself, I mean.'

'It seems highly unlikely. And we don't know for certain that he killed himself.'

'You don't mean . . . murder?' said Dobbs.

'I don't mean anything. That's for the police to decide.'

Entering Quine's sitting room – one of two rooms that made up the 'set' – Rowlands was glad that he'd followed his instincts in leaving the dog behind. Even though it was icy cold, the room still smelt of blood, of which a copious amount had been spilt, according to Dobbs. 'All down 'im, sir – 'is shirt-front's soaked,' said the porter with a shudder. 'The 'earth-rug, too. That'll take a mite o' cleaning, that will.'

'How long has Dr Quine been like this, do you think?'

''Ard to say, sir. Could be three days – maybe four. Must've been Boxing Day – evening of – last time I last saw 'im. Didn't speak to me, mind. Just nodded, as 'e went by, on 'is way to 'is rooms. D'you think 'e was planning it, then, sir? To do away wi' 'isself, like?' His voice broke on the last phrase.

'Pull yourself together, man. You were in the last war, weren't you? You'll have seen worse than this.'

'That's true, sir,' said the other in a subdued tone. 'But somehow I never thought to see it at Oxford.'

'No, indeed. Now listen to me, Mr Dobbs. You're to touch nothing, you understand? That's very important. But I want you to use your eyes. Take your time looking around. Can you see anything resembling a file – the kind you keep documents in, I mean, not the other sort?'

Dobbs took a minute to reconnoitre. 'No, sir,' he said.

'You're absolutely sure? This particular file would be green in colour.'

'There's nothing like that, sir. I mean, there's papers, sir – lots of 'em. Books, too – piles an' piles, on 'is desk. But no files as such, that I can see.'

'All right. Now I want you to check the desk drawers, if you will. Are you wearing gloves, by any chance? If not, you can have mine. We don't want to contaminate the evidence . . . if there is any evidence.' He handed the gloves to the porter, who put them on.

As Rowlands stood there, trying to contain his impatience, the former began his search, his stertorous breathing audible in the intense quiet, as he pulled out the first drawer. 'Nothing in this one, sir . . . Jus' papers and suchlike. No green file.'

'Keep going.'

'An' this one's the same . . . Pencils, paperclips, old examination papers . . . 'Ello! Someone's been up to something here. The lock's broken on the right-hand drawer. Looks as if somebody'd forced it.'

'Let me see.' Wrapping a handkerchief around his hand, Rowlands pulled open the drawer.

'Empty, sir.'

Except that it wasn't entirely empty. A smell arose from the drawer – one that Rowlands recognised. An acrid, ashy smell, as of burnt paper and card. It was the same smell he had smelt on the stairs, the night of Challoner's murder. When the man he now believed had killed Challoner, and Quine, too, had pushed past him – carrying the green file.

'Good,' he said. 'It's what I thought.'

'I don't get it, sir,' said Dobbs, in a puzzled tone. 'There's nothing there.'

'Exactly. Now cast your eyes towards the fireplace. Is there anything there that looks as if it has been burnt? Letters, say? Or documents?'

'No, sir. Nothing that sort.'

'Hmm. All right. Then we'd better lock this room, and telephone the police. I'll let Dr Summerby know what's happened.'

He found the principal in his study, giving a tutorial to one of his students. 'Ah, Mr Rowlands. I won't keep you a moment. Mr Arkwright and I were just concluding our discussion. Thank you, Mr Arkwright. A creditable effort. We will make an advocate of you yet . . . Although it's unlikely the lad will finish his studies – this year, at any rate,' he confided to Rowlands, when the student had gone. 'He intends to join one of the services as soon as he is of age – as so many of our young men are doing. Oxford has indeed become a "university of first-year students". And with our teaching staff so reduced – just myself and Dr O'Halloran, and Dr Crawley . . .' He broke off. 'But I see you have something to tell me.'

'Yes. I'm afraid something terrible's happened.' Rowlands gave Dr Summerby as succinct an account as he could of the discovery of Dr Quine's body.

When he had done so, the principal was silent for a moment. 'Poor unhappy man,' he said at last. 'To have been driven to such measures . . . You are saying it was suicide?'

'It looks that way,' said Rowlands. 'But the police will

no doubt confirm matters, one way or another, once they have carried out their investigation.'

'The police . . . of course, of course.' Summerby sounded as if he had only just realised the implications of this. 'Such a dreadful thing for college,' he murmured. 'As if we haven't already had our share of death and destruction during these past months, with so many of our young men having made the ultimate sacrifice . . . I suppose,' he went on, in a firmer tone, 'this . . . this incident is not unconnected to what happened before? Dr Challoner's death, I mean.'

'I couldn't say without more information, Principal.' A thought occurred to Rowlands. 'I don't suppose you could give me a bit more insight into Dr Quine's state of mind during the past few days? I mean, did anything about his behaviour strike you as out of the ordinary?'

Summerby thought for a moment. 'I can't say that it did. He was the same as ever, you know. A little . . . ah . . . eccentric in his manner . . . But that's not unusual in Oxford.' Dr Summerby attempted a laugh.

'When did you last see him?'

Another pause for thought. 'He was in hall for our Christmas lunch,' said the principal. 'There were only a few of our fellows – Dr Quine, as I've said, Dr Hobson, Dr O'Halloran, Dr Rawlinson and myself – and some of our undergraduates . . . those unable to return to their families for one reason or another,' he added. 'Foreign students, mainly. We've one or two from India and the colonies – young Arkwright being one such. His people are in East Africa, and so . . . But that has no bearing on the matter. Yes, Dr Quine was in hall that evening. We exchanged a few remarks about the weather, and . . . let me think . . . about a series of lectures he was to give on the Punic Wars. Yes, yes. I remember now. He was anxious that the numbers of attendees would be down . . . because of the weather, you know . . . and the war.'

'And that was the last time you saw him?'

'Well, to speak to, you know. I saw him at breakfast next day – but we exchanged no more than a "Good morning", as I recall. Dr Quine,' added the principal sadly, 'disliked conversation first thing in the morning.'

'I see.' That tied in with what Dobbs had said about having seen Quine cross the quad on his way to his rooms on Boxing Day, thought Rowlands. Unless anyone else could be found who would admit to having seen him, it would appear that that sighting was the last time he had been seen alive.

'What I don't understand is why,' Dr Summerby was saying. 'Why now – with all that's been happening in college. Unless . . . unless . . .' He seemed unable to finish the thought.

'Unless the two deaths are connected, as you suggested just now,' supplied Rowlands. 'What was the relationship between the late Professor Challoner and Dr Quine, would you say? Were they on friendly terms?'

'I would have said not,' was the blunt reply. 'You might say they were rivals. Both classicists, you know. But of course Challoner was offered the chair, whereas Quine . . .' His voice tailed off. 'You don't think,' he went on in a horrified tone, 'that Quine murdered Challoner because of that?'

'It would certainly be a reason why he decided he couldn't live with himself – if he had murdered Professor

Challoner, I mean. But we'll have to see what emerges from the police investigation.'

Because at that moment there came the sound of heavy boots on the stairs, and the rumble of male voices. Dobbs had evidently done what Rowlands had asked, and summoned the authorities. 'Thank you for coming to inform me of this news, terrible as it is,' said the principal, as he rose to face this latest invasion of his private space. 'It will enable me to face whatever questions the police have to ask with equanimity.'

'Mr Frederick Rowlands. You were the gentleman who found the body of the other gentleman,' said Inspector Dimmock. Rowlands agreed that he was. 'Coincidence, wouldn't you say – you stumbling across the deceased on that occasion, and now this?'

'Not really. As you'll recall, Inspector, Major Fraser . . . that is, Sir Ian . . . and I had an arrangement to meet Professor Challoner on the night he was killed. It was to attend his funeral that I returned to Oxford two day ago, so . . .'

'Still seems like a bit of a coincidence that you were first on the scene when this Dr Quine's body was discovered,' said the policeman.

'I was one of the first – but yes, it does seem like a coincidence,' agreed Rowlands, knowing an idée fixe when he heard one.

'You didn't touch the deceased when you entered the room, I hope?' went on the inspector in a severe tone.

'Certainly not. I merely stood in the doorway of Dr Quine's room, while Mr Dobbs – whom I gather you've

85

already spoken to – described what he could see.'

'Since you couldn't see it yourself, I suppose?'

'Exactly so, Inspector. He described it, as I've said, and—'

'Why don't you tell me what he said?' said Dimmock slyly.

He's hoping to catch me out, thought Rowlands – *but why? The man surely can't think I murdered Quine?* 'All right,' he replied. 'He – Dobbs – said that Dr Quine was sitting in a chair in front of the gas fire. The fire was off, and the window was ajar. The room was very cold,' he said, adding, 'I could feel that for myself. I wonder if—'

'Just the facts, if you will, sir. You can leave speculation to the police.'

'As you wish. His – Dr Quine's – throat had been cut. There was a lot of blood, which had stained his shirt-front and formed a pool in front of his chair. The razor with which it was done had fallen down beside the chair.'

'On which side?' demanded the policemen sharply.

'On the right-hand side.'

'All right. Anything else?'

'Dr Quine was wearing a tweed suit and a flannel shirt with a soft collar. No tie. He had discarded his overcoat and hat. His academic gown was hanging on a hook behind the door. There was an empty glass, which might have contained sherry, on the occasional table beside him.'

'Hmph,' said the inspector at last. 'You're very particular with your evidence.'

'I've learnt to be.' Rowlands didn't say how it was he had learnt, and the other didn't ask. 'May I ask a question?' he said, when it seemed as if the interview was over. 'Did Dr Quine leave a note?'

'Ha! What makes you ask that?'

'It's usual in such cases.'

Again, there was a silence – as if the other were taken aback by the remark. 'There was,' said the inspector grudgingly, 'a note, as you say. We're having it tested now, for fingerprints.'

'I don't suppose you'll find any but Dr Quine's,' said Rowlands. 'But then, you wouldn't expect to.'

'No, indeed,' said Dimmock, exhaling noisily. 'In a case of suicide, which this appears to be, you wouldn't expect any fingerprints but those of the deceased, on the note or on the glass.'

'Or indeed on the razor.'

'Quite so.' There was a brief silence. 'I think that's all for now, Mr, er, Rowlands,' said the inspector at last. 'My sergeant'll type up what you've said and I'll ask you to sign it, if you will.'

'Of course, Inspector,' replied Rowlands meekly.

If he felt a pang of guilt about not mentioning the green file, and how he had come to know about it, he consoled himself with the thought that there was really nothing to tell – since the file itself had been missing from both Challoner's rooms and Quine's. The smell of burning had been the only indication that it had ever been there. And what kind of evidence was that? A smell. If he'd said anything, the inspector would have thought he'd taken leave of his senses.

It was getting on for lunchtime by the time was able to put the whole case to his friend, who had been waiting anxiously in his room since he had heard the news of

Quine's death from the porter. The latter had taken the opportunity of returning Fraser's dog to her master to put him in the picture, with the gloomy relish with which he'd first informed Rowlands of the catastrophe. 'This place is beginning to resemble a slaughterhouse,' complained Fraser, from his seat by the fire. 'Dobbs did his best to make my flesh creep with his talk of throats cut from ear to ear . . .' He shuddered. 'Ghastly way to do it. A gun's much cleaner.'

'Yes, it couldn't have been a pretty sight,' said Rowlands. 'Dead how long, do you think?'

'Hard to say, until they do the PM. But the last time he was seen was four days ago – the morning of Boxing Day.'

Again, Fraser shuddered. 'Poor blighter. Forgotten about all that time. Did nobody think to ask where he was?'

'Evidently not.'

Both were silent a moment, then Fraser said, 'D'you know, in spite of what we've got to put up with, you and I – being blind, you know – I'd rather have the life I've got, with a decent home to go to, and a loving wife to look after me, than the desiccated existence of these poor academics.'

Rowlands said he felt the same.

'There was a note, you say?'

'That's right. I've no idea what it said, however.'

'I don't suppose we'll be told – or at least not until the inquest,' said Fraser. 'Perhaps it'll prove to be a confession.'

'Perhaps.'

'Wouldn't that please our Inspector Dimmock! To have his case nicely tied up for him . . . It'd please that other chap, too – the one from MI5.'

'Captain Fawcett,' said Rowlands, who had been thinking the same. Yes, it would certainly be a gratifying development as far as the Secret Service was concerned, to be able to close the case, and forestall any further questions about the death of Donald Challoner.

It was the strangest New Year's Eve Rowlands could remember – and there'd been some strange ones in the past. 1914 had been one of these, he recalled – when they'd thought the war that had started that summer would be over by Christmas, only to find that the new year found them all still on the battlefields of the Western Front. Nor did the outlook for this new year seem any less bleak. After the horrors of 1941, with battles raging in North Africa and in the North Atlantic, massacres in Lvov and Kyiv, and God only knew what other atrocities being perpetrated at that very moment by the Nazi regime, it was hard to feel any sense of optimism about the future.

Then to be stuck here in this . . . charnel house, thought Rowlands – because what, after all, could one call it but that? Two brutal killings in as many weeks had brought a flavour of the morgue to what had seemed a realm of ancient peace. Although even as he had the thought, Rowlands dismissed it. The truth was harder and colder, with the cloistered tranquillity of these time-worn foundations having been bought at the cost of much blood and suffering. Hadn't he walked, only that morning, past the Martyrs' Memorial in St Giles – where three men had been burnt alive for professing their faith?

Be of good comfort, Master Ridley, and play the man; *we shall this day light such a candle by God's grace in* *England as shall never be put out.* He had always admired the casual bravery of the words.

Closer to home and to the present day was the bravery of the young men joining up in their tens of thousands to fight the enemy in their fighters and bombers, their tanks and armoured cars, and on the decks of their destroyers and aircraft carriers. He thought of young Dawson, to whom he'd taken such a shine at Christmas, 'The trouble is you just can't tell how it will all turn out,' he'd said. 'You just have to carry on, and hope for the best . . .' Yes, there were many kinds of bravery.

This reminded him that he had still to telephone Edith – although, given the state of the weather, it seemed unlikely that she'd be expecting him back tonight. When he eventually got through to her, he found that she had been up to the railway station (a steep and slippery climb, in snowy weather) to ascertain for herself the state of the trains. 'So I gather you won't be back until at least tomorrow, if not Friday,' she said.

'I'm afraid not. Look, Edith . . .'

'Don't tell me – something else has happened to keep you in Oxford.'

'I'm sorry to say you're right.' Without going into detail, he put her in the picture.

'How dreadful,' she said, when he had finished. 'I don't like this, Fred. I wish you'd never got involved.' It was not what she'd said in the first instance, but he didn't remind her of that.

The remaining two minutes of the call were taken up

with what had been happening at home. Frank Dawson had gone back to his ship, and Margaret was back at work (both were careful not to mention where this was). There'd been a letter from Anne saying that the WAAFs at her station (wherever that was) had been served Christmas dinner by the officers. Joan was pining to get back to school – 'She's changed her tune,' said her father.

'And Mother's well,' concluded Edith, as the pips began to go. 'Look after yourself, won't you, Fred?'

'You too,' he said.

He'd one more call to make – this time on Ian Fraser's behalf. Fortunately, it didn't take too long for the operator to connect the call; he had been conscious of a certain restiveness on the part of the porter as he was talking to Edith. Well, let him stew. This was important. 'Lady Fraser?' he said, as the call was put through. 'Frederick Rowlands here. I'm phoning to let you know that Sir Ian won't be back today.'

'Trains, I suppose?'

'That's right.'

'How's his cold?'

'Not a lot better. I think it's best if he stays put.'

'Tell him to get well soon, or I'll have to come up there – trains or no trains.'

'I'll tell him.'

'I'm glad he's got you with him,' she said, as the call ended.

Dinner that night in hall was a surprisingly jolly affair, with the newly arrived contingent of RAF men competing with the incumbent army officers in seeing how much noise they could make. As the evening wore on, with each side proposing more and more extravagant toasts to the other, the Brasenose fellows, reduced as they were in number, found themselves overwhelmed as if by an invading army. 'Rowdy young scamps,' muttered someone in Rowlands's ear – it was Dr Aitken. 'Acting as if they owned the bally place.'

'They're just letting off steam,' said Rowlands, as a chorus of 'Run, Rabbit, Run' resounded from the rafters. He didn't add, because it seemed at odds with the festive mood of the occasion, that for most of them this would be the first and last taste of conviviality before the rigours of training took over. Some of these RAF lads, he thought – and then brushed away the thought – would barely outlast their training. Six weeks was the average survival rate for a fighter pilot – which most of this lot were destined to be. He recalled Dr Summerby's bleak words, during their meeting earlier that day, 'We're losing so many of our good men to the air force. They seem to favour that branch of the services particularly. It accords with the Brasenose ethos only too well – we're renowned for our sporting prowess, you know. Our type of young man – athletic, courageous, intensely loyal and light-hearted – is exactly the type they're looking for.'

Well, the 'light-hearted' element was certainly in evidence, thought Rowlands, as the laughter got louder and the singing more raucous. For himself, he was glad of the distraction from what had been an otherwise grim day. He supposed he'd be expected to attend the inquest on Dr Quine, and wondered when this would be – not tomorrow, surely? Perhaps the day after that. He thought,

92

If the Major's right, and the note Quine left is a confession, then that solves the mystery of who killed Challoner. It all seemed too neat, somehow.

He'd drop in on Fraser after dinner, he decided, having little taste for the revelry that would doubtless follow in the SCR, where the Brasenose fellows would be joined by their counterparts in next-door Lincoln College – as well as by senior army and RAF personnel. But when he got to Fraser's room, he found the latter already asleep, having left most of his supper untouched. He thought, *All this has hit him hard* – and it wasn't just the flu he meant. Fraser was restless, tossing and turning in his sleep, and muttering under his breath. Rowlands guessed he was in that state between sleeping and waking that fever can induce.

His eyes were closed, and he made no response when spoken to, but a stream of words – some clear, some unintelligible – issued from his lips.

'Put out that light! They'll see us . . . Good God! Ceiling's caved in . . .' Then came a wordless muttering, of which Rowlands could make out only a word or two. '. . . can't see . . . so dark . . . dead men . . . careful! . . . one false step . . . no, no . . .'

'Major,' he said softly, not wanting to shock the man out of his dream. 'It's all right. The patrol's here. We've come to take you back.'

After a while, Fraser's anguished muttering subsided, and he fell into a deeper sleep. When he was quiet, Rowlands left him. On the stairs he met someone coming up. 'Who's there?'

'Only me, sir.' It was George Perkins, the scout. 'Just wanted to see how Sir Ian was doing.'

'Not well – but he's asleep now. You might bring him a hot drink – or some water, in case he wakes. He was quite feverish when I got here.'

'Right you are, sir. I'll see to it. He didn't ought to have gone out in all this snow,' said the servant. 'Risked catching his death, I'd say.'

Chapter Eight

New Year's Day dawned bright and cold. There had been no more snow overnight, and when Rowlands went to see how Fraser was, he found him up and dressed. 'Thought I'd come down for a spot of brekker,' he said, in spite of Rowlands's effort to dissuade him. 'Can't be doing with staying in bed all day.' It was still an effort for him to walk across the quad, however, and after breakfast – a cheerful meal, enlivened by the presence of the RAF contingent – he was more than ready to retire to the SCR for a smoke and a warm in front of the fire. He was sure, he said to Rowlands, that he'd be fit enough to make the journey back to London the following day. 'I expect you'll be required to attend the inquest on poor old Quine,' he said. 'Have they said when it will be?'

'Not yet,' replied Rowlands. 'Inspector Dimmock isn't very forthcoming with his information. I'm glad you're feeling better, Major,' he added, privately wondering if the other wasn't being over-optimistic. He'd been quite delirious last night, and his chest still sounded bad. All of those, like himself and the major, who'd been in the last 'show', tended to suffer from bronchial complaints, the result of being exposed to mustard gas. With what he hoped wasn't too obvious a display of tact, he said, 'I wondered if I might take Heidi out for a walk again this morning? It's been rather good for me to have the chance to practise what having a dog of my own would be like.'

The major readily assented to this plan, saying that if Rowlands didn't mind he'd stay by the fire and enjoy his smoke. 'I know Heidi'll keep you out of mischief. She's got a sixth sense about danger – haven't you, my lass?'

The clock was striking the half-hour when they set out into the crisp, bright morning. With no particular destination in mind, Rowlands let the dog lead him out of the college gates, straight down Market Street, and then right into Cornmarket Street, along Magdalen Street, and thence into St Giles'. Balliol and St John's Colleges were on his right, he knew, the Ashmolean Museum on his left. This time, his senses were alert for passing traffic – bicycles especially. He wasn't going to be run over a second time, he thought wryly.

Even so, as he walked his thoughts kept coming back to Challoner's dying words about the green file. Surely that was the key to the whole affair? If so – and given that his investigative skills were necessarily limited – he must do his utmost to find it. 'Trust no one,' Challoner had said. A second death had proved that his warning had not been an idle one.

Another five minutes' brisk walking brought Rowlands and his canine companion to the gates of another college.

He would have passed it, oblivious to this fact, if a vehicle –
a motorbus, to judge from the throbbing of its engine in low
gear – hadn't chosen that moment to pull up in the street
outside. The driver stuck his head out of his cabin. 'Bus for
Keble College,' he shouted – at which summons, a crowd of
what turned out to be young women started pouring out of
the gates.

'Come on, Madge!' cried one of them to another. 'You
can finish putting on your lipstick on the bus.'

'Don't rush me,' was the reply. 'Bus doesn't leave till
a quarter to. We've plenty of time before we're due at the
palace.'

It was then that something clicked in Rowlands's mind,
like the pieces of a kaleidoscope falling into place. It was
something somebody had said – Fraser, he remembered
now – about the 'Blenheim Girls' . . . 'Doing valuable war
work,' he'd said. That was it. And just at that moment,
there came another shift of the kaleidoscope . . . Because a
young woman, evidently the last of the group that had been
boarding the bus as he stood there, lost in these reflections,
came hurrying out of the gates, cheered on by her friends.
'Good old Angie! Cutting it fine, as ever . . .'

The latecomer had just reached the bus and was about
to mount the steps when Rowlands seized his chance. 'Miss
Thompson. It's Frederick Rowlands. We met yesterday, if
you recall. Might I have a very quick word?'

'Come on, Angie!'

'Bus won't wait forever.'

Angela Thompson hesitated. 'I'm really in an awful
hurry . . .'

'I won't keep you a moment. As it turns out, I'll be

staying in Oxford for another day or two. I was wondering if we might meet later – perhaps for tea?'

'Well . . .' She sounded doubtful. 'I finish work at five-thirty. So I should be back in Oxford by six.'

'Splendid. I'll call for you then, shall I?'

He wasn't sure if she'd replied or not, but a moment later the bus roared away. 'Well,' said Rowlands softly, bending to pat Heidi. 'It's a long shot, but it just might work.'

The back bar of the Eagle and Child in St Giles' was quieter than the public bar when Rowlands and Angela Thompson arrived, with Heidi (once more borrowed from Major Fraser, with his compliments) leading the way. True to his word, Rowlands had been waiting outside the gates of Keble when the Blenheim Palace bus returned at six o'clock. It had been Miss Thompson who'd suggested the pub – 'as it seems a bit late for tea' – with which suggestion Rowlands had thankfully concurred. The Bird and Baby (as it was known by Oxford aficionados) with its low-ceilinged panelled rooms and well-stocked coal fires offered a welcoming refuge from the chill of the streets.

Now they sat on either side of a narrow oak table, whose surface, polished smooth by the hands and elbows of those who had sat there before him, spoke to Rowlands of the many past conversations that had taken place in that room. Their own conversation, he guessed, would be inaudible to anyone but themselves, owing to the cheerful commotion issuing from the crowded 'public', where a crowd of undergraduates, servicemen and locals kept up a continual banter. As it was New Year's Day, there was a good deal of hilarity, and loudly boastful talk about this being the year they'd 'beat the Hun, on land, sea and in the air'.

'I'll drink to that,' said Rowlands, raising his glass. 'And to all those engaged in beating Hitler – in whatever capacity.'

His companion echoed his toast, but did not respond to his last remark. Their conversation, up to that point, had been general: whether the snow would lie, or if a thaw had set in at last; what a well-behaved dog Heidi was; and the relative merits of Oxford compared to Cambridge. 'I seem to have moved from one Victorian Gothic establishment to another,' observed Miss Thompson wryly. 'Given that Keble is a year younger than St Gertrude's, and displays the same fondness for red brick.'

'That's interesting to know,' replied Rowlands. 'I don't think I ever had reason to go to Keble when I was here before the last war – so I've only the vaguest notion of what it looks like.'

'Some people might say that was a blessing,' laughed his companion. 'It's certainly not one of the more beautiful colleges, but I'm fond of it, none the less . . . Why did you really want to see me?' she demanded suddenly. 'It wasn't to hear my views on Victorian architecture.'

'No.' He took a sip of his beer and thought how best to put what he had to say. 'I did have an ulterior motive. You see . . . it so happens that I've become a witness in a murder case in Oxford. I can't tell you much more than that, except to say that the murder victim worked at Blenheim Palace. It occurred to me that if I'm to get any further with regard to finding out who's responsible, I'd need to extend my search to Blenheim.' Her silence was not encouraging. 'I thought, as you go there every day on the bus, you might—'

She cut across him. 'You're suggesting I should try and smuggle you onto the bus? You must see that's impossible, surely?'

'Yes, yes, I do see that. And I wasn't asking for a lift to Blenheim! But since you're on the spot, as it were, I wondered if you could look out for something for me – it's a file, with a green cover. Concerning a particular individual, about which the man I'm referring to had suspicions.'

'I couldn't possibly. I mean, you're asking me to divulge confidential information. People have been sent to prison for less . . . How did you know about this file, anyway?'

He lowered his voice, although with that racket going on next door, he was sure they couldn't be overheard. 'The man who was killed told me . . . just before he died . . . that there was a file. He'd been about to divulge a name when he was killed – the name of someone he believed to have been betraying secrets to the enemy. I think,' he added, when she said nothing, 'that was why he was killed – to stop him giving away that name. There's been another death since. So you see, Miss Thompson, it's a matter of great urgency to find that file, and report its contents to the authorities.'

'And just how would I explain my sudden interest in the contents of this particular file – always supposing I can find it?' she said. 'Why, it might take weeks. You've no idea how many files we—' She broke off, as if she'd said too much.

'I know it's a lot to ask,' he said. 'But if you did find it, you could simply tell me the name . . .'

'What? And get myself shot? I've signed the Official Secrets Act, you know. I'm risking my neck even talking to you like this.' She pushed back her chair, and was on her feet before he could reply. 'Thanks for the drink.'

'Miss Thompson . . . Please . . .'

But she was already on her way out, pushing past the crowd of young men in the public bar. 'I say, where's the fire?' said a voice Rowlands thought he recognised; a moment later, he was joined by its owner. 'Thought I saw you hiding in here,' said Peter Bawden cheerfully, leaning to pat Heidi. 'Who's the young lady in a hurry? Not your daughter, is she?'

Rowlands said that she was just a friend. 'Although I do have a daughter about her age,' he said, thinking that Margaret, then working for another top secret branch of British Intelligence, might well have taken him to task as fiercely as Miss Thompson had for trying to corrupt an employee of MI5.

'You look as if you need another drink,' said Bawden. 'Same again?'

Rowlands shook his head. 'Thanks, but I ought to be on my way.'

'No need to rush off! I was just about to get them in.'

'Yes, what about it, old man?' came a voice from the doorway. 'Some of us are dying of thirst here.'

'All in good time, Ginger . . . Now, what'll it be? Pint of Morrell's, unless I'm much mistaken.'

'Well, all right – thanks,' said Rowlands.

Having given his order to the barmaid, the young man sat himself down in the place so recently vacated by Angela

Thompson. 'So,' he said, 'I don't suppose you'll tell me your friend's name?'

Evidently Bawden didn't believe in wasting time, thought Rowlands. 'It's Thompson,' he said. He took a sip of the beer that had just been placed in front of him – a not very subtle bribe, he saw.

'Does she have another name?' persisted the lieutenant. When Rowlands supplied it, the young man cried, 'Angela! Angel by name and angel by nature . . . Where can I find this divine creature?'

'I don't think you'll get very far if you take that line,' said Rowlands. 'Angela Thompson's a sensible young woman, with her feet firmly on the ground. As to where she lives, I'm sure you can find that out for yourself.'

'I suppose I'll have to trek round all the women's colleges in Oxford, asking for a Miss Thompson,' grumbled Bawden. 'Since you won't be a sport and tell me.'

'Bet she's one of the Keble crowd,' shouted somebody – the thirsty Ginger – from the bar next door. 'Chap I know says you can see 'em pouring out of the college first thing in the morning. There's a bus that comes for 'em. Some of 'em are still in their dressing gowns and pyjamas, this chap says . . .'

'That's quite enough of that sort of talk!' said Peter Bawden. 'I only want to ask her to tea,' he added to Rowlands. 'It's so difficult to meet nice girls in Oxford. Those that aren't locked up after 10 p.m. in Somerville or Lady Margaret Hall are confined to Keble. Although what they're doing there, I can't imagine.'

'Don't try,' said Rowlands. 'They won't tell you.'

'That's rather what I thought,' said the young man disconsolately.

Fraser was a little better next day – or so he said – and was once more talking about going back to London, as soon as he could get a train. 'I really don't want to be away any longer than I can help,' he said to Rowlands. 'There's a great deal to do in the office' – whether it was his office at Westminster he meant, or St Dunstan's head office, wasn't clear to Rowlands – 'and the sooner I get on with it the better.'

'I see that, but . . .' Rowlands broke off as his friend once more succumbed to a spasm of coughing.

'I'm all right,' he said irritably, when he could speak. 'It's just this wretched cold. It'll pass off soon.' Rowlands wasn't so sure, but he said nothing more. Useless to argue when the major was in this mood – one with which Rowlands could sympathise. He hated giving in to illness, too.

The two of them were sitting at one of the long trestle tables in hall, over a frugal lunch of what one of Rowlands's neighbours – it was the jocular Hobson – described as 'dishwater soup, boiled potatoes with the eyes left in, and reheated Spam'. Encouraged by the groans and laughter this elicited from some of the other fellows, he enlarged on his theme, 'I honestly don't think we'd be fed worse if we were in the army. Bully beef and carrots would be a feast compared to this.' It occurred to Rowlands that Hobson had probably never been near an army mess. It was true that the food at Brasenose was of uneven quality, but the country was fighting a war, damn it! Everyone had to put up with the food shortages.

One of the older dons – Rowlands thought it was the elderly Dr Crawley – seemed to be of the same opinion, for he said severely, 'Young man. When you have lived as long as I have, you will learn to be grateful for whatever the Lord has thought fit to provide for you. Good, plain food such as this would indeed seem a feast to the starving of Europe.'

Hobson subsided at this reprimand – but Rowlands heard him mutter something under his breath that was evidently not very complimentary to Dr Crawley.

At Fraser's suggestion, he and Rowlands took a turn around Old Quad after lunch. 'Good to get a breath of air,' said the former. 'Never could abide frowsting away in front of the fire, the way some of these old chaps do.'

Rowlands forbore from pointing out that 'old chaps' such as the pious Dr Crawley had managed to live well into their eighties by just such means as he described, while the major himself, although a good twenty years younger, was already showing signs of decrepitude. But then, he reminded himself, the good Dr Crawley hadn't had to fight a war that had left him blinded and missing half a lung. Although the major would have been the first to say he was one of the lucky ones.

As they walked briskly – or as briskly as they could – around the snowy quad, Fraser seemed to reflect on what had passed between them at luncheon. 'Sorry for being a bear, old man,' he said at last. 'It's just that, having got you into this mess, I feel that I'll be leaving you in the lurch, what with this wretched inquest looming. It won't be until Monday at the earliest, I'm afraid . . . and the worst of it is, you'll have to do without Heidi.'

'I'll manage,' said Rowlands. 'But I honestly think—'

What he thought remained unexpressed, for at that moment, there came the sound of a car pulling up in the street outside, followed by car doors slamming, and voices coming from the direction of the porter's lodge. 'Who on earth can that be?' said Fraser.

He didn't have long to wait before finding out.

'Hello, darling. I see you've disobeyed my orders by getting out of bed. Really, I sometimes wonder if you've any common sense at all!'

'Iris, my dear,' replied Major Fraser to his wife – for it was she. 'Just taking a little stroll in the fresh air, you know. Never did anybody any harm.'

Iris Fraser gave a snort of disbelief. 'So you say. You're wheezing like a steam engine. This freezing air can't be doing you any good. As for you, Frederick,' she went on, with mock severity. 'I'm surprised at you, letting him wander about in the cold like this, with every chance of his getting pneumonia.'

'I'm sorry, Lady Fraser—' he began.

'Bosh,' she said. 'You're not sorry a bit. Now, for goodness' sake, lead me to a nice warm fire, where I can thaw my hands and feet, before we have to make the journey back. I've left Patchett having a cup of tea and swapping war stories with the porter,' she added, referring to the chauffeur, Rowlands supposed. 'Both in the Mons "show", apparently. I must say,' she went on, slipping a fur-clad arm though Rowlands's, as the two of them, with Fraser and Heidi leading the way, crossed the quadrangle. 'I rather like your Brasenose, Ian. Pretty, isn't it, with all that mediaeval flummery? I didn't know any Brasenose

105

men when I was up at Somerville. Only Balliol and St John's types. So it's rather nice to see it from the inside at last.'

This seemingly inconsequential chatter did not disguise the anxiety Lady Fraser was evidently feeling about her husband's health. 'He looks dreadful,' she said to Rowlands, when the major had gone to order tea to be brought to the senior common room. 'Grey and drawn – and as for that cough! I haven't known him this bad since that "go" he had with the influenza after the war.'

'I'm sorry . . .' Rowlands began again, but she put a hand on his arm to forestall further self-recrimination.

'I'm sure you did your best to convince him to stay in bed. Ian can be very stubborn at times – don't I know it! It's what's got him through, I suppose,' she added softly, as the subject of these remarks returned. 'I hope you've ordered your bags to be brought down?' said his wife. 'As soon as I've had my tea, we'll be off. I'd like to get back to London before dark. The roads are treacherous – and with no street lighting, we'll be lucky not to end up in a ditch.'

Chapter Nine

Rowlands went to the gate to see them off. With him was Heidi – the major having insisted on leaving her behind, after all. 'She'll be more use to you in Oxford than she will be to me,' he said, adding ruefully, 'Especially if Iris has her way . . .' By which Rowlands understood that any thoughts the major might have had about resuming his Westminster duties had been shelved, for the time being. Since the air raids of the previous May, which had caused so much damage to the Palace of Westminster, MPs had been meeting in Church House; more recently, a temporary Commons Chamber had been set up in an undamaged section of the House of Lords. 'It's rather a makeshift affair,' Fraser had confided to Rowlands. 'But it seems important to carry on – bomb damage or no bomb damage.'

Now he outlined his plans concerning Heidi from his seat in the back of the Bentley, where he had been installed by Patchett, the chauffeur, with a rug over his knees, 'I've arranged it all with Dobbs. He's to feed her and let her sleep in his quarters, and you're to take her out whenever you want to.' He chuckled – the laugh ending in a wheeze. 'If my dear wife has anything to do with it, I won't be venturing far beyond my garden gate for the next few days.' Although since the Frasers lived 'over the shop' in St John's Lodge, the St Dunstan's HQ, Rowlands guessed that it wouldn't be long before his friend resumed at least some of his duties as head of that institution.

Rowlands thanked him, and said he would be grateful for Heidi's continuing assistance. And it had been useful, having a canine guide, in a place that was largely unfamiliar to him. It made him impatient for the day when he'd have his own 'seeing eye' dog. Stupid to have resisted this for so long, because of some groundless fear of being seen to be different.

'So, Heidi old girl, it's just the two of us now,' he murmured, reaching to pat the animal's head, as the sound of the Bentley's engine died away. Iris Fraser was right: it wouldn't be long before it would be getting dark, in this bleakest of midwinter months. Not that it mattered to him one way or the other, but he knew it would be foolhardy to risk going out into the blacked-out streets, even with the cautious Heidi to protect him. It wasn't so much that he'd run the risk of walking into people he couldn't see, as that they might walk into him.

With the idea of taking a walk around Christ Church Meadow, he directed the guide dog towards the High, and thence along St Aldate's. The porter had assured him that the great open space, bordered by the Cherwell and Thames – here called the Isis – was still open to the public during daylight hours. 'They've not requisitioned it for the army yet,' he said. 'Reckon it'll take more'n a few parachutists dropped from Jerry planes to make 'em do that.' This last remark referred to a rumour that had been doing the rounds, Rowlands gathered, of enemy agents using such methods to invade Oxford's hallowed purlieus. It struck him that there were other, more insidious ways of achieving the same end – not least by planting a 'sleeper' in the very heart of the university . . .

Preoccupied with these thoughts, he and Heidi had entered the gate into the War Memorial Garden (Rowlands reflecting sadly that the war whose dead it commemorated had already been overshadowed by the present conflict) and were walking along the Broad Walk, intending to turn right along the path that led to the river. It was a circular walk, the porter had said, that would take them about half an hour, at a brisk pace – although with all this snow about, he'd added, the going might be harder. Rowlands calculated that they should manage it comfortably. He was looking forward to striding out (always difficult in the more populous city streets) and to filling his lungs with the cold, clean January air. Space and silence – these were what he craved. A brief respite from the incessant demands of the outside world.

Before they had gone a hundred yards along the broad avenue, whose towering elm trees would be leafless now, Rowlands knew, their branches weighed down with snow, the world asserted itself. 'Halt! Who goes there? Friend or foe?' A youthful voice, trying to sound deeper and gruffer. Rowlands guessed that its owner was about sixteen.

'Friend,' he replied, wondering if he was expected to put his hands up. 'Who's asking?'

'Private Stanley Harris. LDU,' was the reply. Again, the voice seemed about to shift into a treble register.

'That stands for Local Defence Unit, doesn't it?' said Rowlands. So they were recruiting children now, were they?

'Yes, sir. Just started my patrol. Sorry if I've held you up, sir, but you're not one o' the regulars and so I thought . . .'

'That's quite all right,' said Rowland. 'You were only carrying out orders, I imagine.'

'That's it, sir. Captain Farrell said as we're not to let anyone pass without we challenge him. Might be a spy, sir, you see.'

'I do. And these spies are being dropped by parachute, I'm told?'

'Yes, sir. They can come up the river in submarines, too,' said the lad eagerly.

Rowlands thought this seemed even more unlikely than the parachute theory, but wisely said nothing. 'Well, Private Harris, I'll leave you to it. Time I got on with my walk.'

'OK, sir. I say, sir . . .' Suddenly the boy sounded younger than his probable sixteen years. 'Mind if I pat your dog, sir? He's a nice one, isn't he?'

'She,' said Rowlands. 'Yes, you can pat her. She's very friendly. She won't bite.'

Having concluded this little exchange, Rowlands set off once more, smiling to himself at the earnestness with which young Harris had spoken. It was a cold afternoon for marching up and down with a .22 rifle over one's shoulder, keeping an eye out for 'spies'. He hoped the lad was at least getting some fun out of it. No doubt as soon as he was of age, he'd join one of the regular services, as so many of his fellow Oxfordshire men had done.

With Heidi padding noiselessly beside him, Rowlands strolled on, past the Dean's Ham, and Boathouse Island (from the silence, he guessed there were no boats on the river just then) and along Cherwell Path, his footsteps squeaking softly on the hard-packed snow, while from the branches of a nearby tree, snow that had gathered there slid to the ground with a suddenness that made him jump. He thought, *I've got to talk to people . . . It's the only way.* But quite what he meant by that, he would have found it hard to say. There were few others about – another man walking a dog, with whom he exchanged a terse greeting, and a pair of lovers, muttering sweet nothings to one another by the river. It seemed the wrong season for a romantic stroll; perhaps they had nowhere else to go, he thought.

Following the directions the porter had given him, he reached the end of the circular walk at last, by way of the sinister-sounding Deadman's Walk. As he and Heidi passed out of the gate that led back onto Aldate's, he checked his watch. It was four o'clock. He knew that the bells for which Oxford was famous had been silenced, as a wartime precaution – as church bells had been across the rest of the country – but even so, he fancied he could hear them ringing out through the crystalline air, as they had done on that long-ago first visit to the city, when he was young, and war was still a remote shadow on the horizon.

It would be getting on for teatime, he realised. They'd all be assembling in the SCR within the next half-hour. If he were to carry out his plan – he saw it as 'filling in the gaps' of his investigation – his best opportunity would be now. He accordingly left Heidi in her new quarters at the porter's lodge, deciding that, after more than a week at Brasenose, he was familiar enough with the layout of the place to find his way without her. With the little sight that remained to him, and his excellent hearing, he had managed to get about almost unaided for the first few years of his blindness, relying sometimes on aural clues (voices, traffic sounds) and sometimes on simple tricks like counting steps. In recent years, and at the urging of his wife, he'd resorted to using a stick – although he drew the line at the white-painted variety. Now, it seemed, he was ready (if not quite ready) to rely on the assistance of a dog.

Even so, he felt a small glow of satisfaction when he reached the SCR, guided there as much by the buzz of voices as by his mental map of the college. The rattle of the tea trolley told him his instinct had been correct: this was the hour of congregation, when any fellow of college not otherwise engaged would descend from his solitary rooms to the general meeting-place. As Rowlands went in, an agreeable waft of heat from the fire – a large one, built on sixteenth-century lines, although with a modern grate and fireguard – drew him towards it. Here, a number of fellows were already gathered; he was hailed by one of them – Jeremy Hobson – as he approached.

'Ah, here's Rowlands. He's a man who knows his own mind. What d'you think of this Declaration by United Nations that's just been signed in Washington – that no country is to make peace with Germany, or any of the Axis powers, without the say-so of the others? A bit much, wouldn't you agree?'

Rowlands wouldn't agree, as it happened, but as he opened his mouth to say so, someone else cut in, 'You surely can't think we should try and negotiate a separate peace with Hitler? Chamberlain tried that in '39 and look how that went!' The speaker wasn't familiar to Rowlands; he guessed it must be one of the Lincoln College fellows, who shared the SCR facilities from time to time.

'I wasn't asking your opinion, Marston, old boy, but that of our guest,' replied Hobson, apparently unruffled by this blunt rebuttal of his own view. 'You strike me as a sensible man, Rowlands. Surely you can see how impossible it will be to get every country presently at war with Germany to agree when to call it off?'

'That will be when we win the war,' said Rowlands quietly. 'Not before. And I imagine that, when the time comes, there'll be a treaty drawn up that all the parties concerned will sign – just as there was at the end of the last war.'

'I suppose you mean Versailles?' said Hobson in a scoffing tone. 'Hardly a shining example of how to ensure a lasting peace.'

'With hindsight, Versailles wasn't perfect, but it was the best the Allies could come up with, under the circumstances,' said someone else. Rawlinson, thought Rowlands.

'Exactly my point.' Hobson wasn't about to concede the argument. 'It was an imperfect treaty, which gave rise to the mess in which we now find ourselves. A case of too many cooks spoiling the broth, if ever there was one.'

Rowlands, who could only remember the enormous relief he'd felt when the Treaty of Versailles was signed in

1919, and the war that had devastated so many lives – his own included – was officially over, said nothing more, not wanting to be drawn into what seemed to him a pointless discussion. Having collected a cup of tea from the trolley, he found himself a vacant seat by the fire, and settled down to doing what he'd intended to do when he entered the room, which was to pay attention to what was going on around him. It was one of the things he was good at – listening. Without Fraser there to talk to, he'd have more scope for forming an opinion of the members of college he'd yet to get to know.

There was the thoughtful Rawlinson, for instance, who occupied the armchair next to his. What did he know, if anything, about Rawlinson? That he was tutor in philosophy; that he had been a rowing blue; that his manner was pleasant and unassuming . . .

'I gather Fraser's gone home?' Rawlinson said to Rowlands, who admitted that it was so. 'Glad to hear it,' was the reply. 'Poor feller sounded as if he was at death's door. You're staying on for a few days, I take it?'

Rowlands explained about the inquest.

'Ah yes, of course. Rotten bad luck for you, stumbling across poor old Quine like that . . .' A longish pause ensued. 'Wonder what drove him to it? Don't suppose we'll ever know.'

Rowlands murmured something that sounded like agreement, although in point of fact he knew he wouldn't rest until he'd found an explanation for Maurice Quine's death – and indeed, a perpetrator, if his suspicions that this was not a suicide were confirmed.

On the far side of the fireplace, he could hear the

vice-principal, Dr Ponsonby-Smythe, booming away – his orotund tones well-suited to the lecture theatre, Rowlands guessed. By contrast with the self-effacing Summerby, whose passion for the minutiae of jurisprudence was matched only by his love of the sporting life, Ponsonby-Smythe was something of an aesthete, in a college not renowned for its intellectual prowess. It was in his rooms – famously decorated in blue and orange – that the monthly meetings of the Pater Society were held. It struck Rowlands that there could have been no more incongruous an alumnus and fellow of 'BNC' than the author of *Marius the Epicurean* . . . but then, as he was beginning to understand, such incongruities were what Oxford was all about.

'I see no reason at all why we shouldn't bring out the college silver for the feast, as we've done since time immemorial,' the vice-principal was saying, addressing the group on his side of the fire. 'There's not the slightest justification for breaking the tradition now, just because there's a war on. Fact is, the men expect it, and I'd be the last to deny 'em a touch of splendour, when so many of 'em are having to face so much.'

'You're not of the opinion then, Vice-Principal, that it might be of greater benefit to college to sell the silver, given the nature of the times?' This was Hobson – ever the mischief-maker, thought Rowlands – although it was often hard to tell how much of it was bluff.

Ponsonby-Smythe refused to dignify this with any reply, apart from a disgusted snort; but someone else – it was Aitken, the lecturer in chemistry – said in a speculative tone, 'I wonder just how much it would fetch? Thousands,

I should think. Some of those pieces – the candlesticks, and that enormous silver platter, and those goblets – must be worth a fortune.'

'I say, are there any more of those muffins?' said Marston, the Lincoln fellow. 'I've got a paper to write and I can't do it on an empty stomach.' The plate with the muffins was handed across, and conversation turned to the forthcoming term's arrangements. There was speculation about how many of their students would be returning.

'I happen to know that young Jackson won't be back,' said Aitken despondently. 'He was one of my prospective Firsts. But he's chosen the RAF over a career in science, worse luck.'

'What'll happen to Quine's students?' said Rawlinson. 'I suppose they'll be distributed amongst the rest of us . . . or farmed out to other colleges.'

'I wonder who'll have Quine's rooms?' said Hobson. 'Think I'll put in a word with the principal when he comes to re-allocate them. Mine are so cramped, I can barely turn around.'

There was a brief silence at this – perhaps of disapproval at the history don's presumption. 'The police have got them sealed off, surely?' said Aitken. 'They won't let anyone back in until after the inquest, I'd say.'

'Mr Rowlands can probably tell us,' said Hobson slyly. 'I gather he's got form in these matters.'

'A little,' he admitted, reluctant to be drawn on this point. The last thing he wanted was to alert the perpetrator of what he now believed to have been a double murder to the fact that he was under suspicion. There was no escaping it, he thought – any of these people could have murdered

Quine, and Challoner before him. And that was before you took account of the others – army officers, college staff and guests – who'd been present in college when the deaths had occurred. He realised that he was no nearer establishing a comprehensive list of suspects who'd been at dinner on both nights – that of his arrival at Brasenose, and on Christmas night. If he could discover that, he'd be closer to finding the man that Challoner was hunting. The spy within Oxford's ancient walls.

Chapter Ten

Dinner that night was an unexpectedly pleasant occasion. In the absence of his friend, Rowlands had considered avoiding formal hall altogether, in favour of having a tray in his room, but – mindful of his self-appointed mission of 'filling in the gaps' – decided to brave it after all. He accordingly presented himself at the appointed hour for pre-prandial sherry in the SCR, intending to make himself as unobtrusive as possible. He had once again decided against taking Heidi with him, since after a few days in residence, he could find his way about the college perfectly well; the dog's usefulness was as a guide (and protector) in the less familiar Oxford streets. Yes, being invisible was his aim this evening . . .

And so he was disconcerted to be hailed, almost as soon as he entered the room, by the principal. 'Mr Rowlands! It is Mr Rowlands, is it not? Faces are rather a blur to me these days, even with these strong glasses . . . Do tell me how Major Fraser is getting on. I was so sorry to hear that he was unwell. I hope he is no worse?'

Rowlands was able to reassure Dr Summerby on this point, adding that, as his friend had now returned home, he hoped it would be all right for him to stay in college until Monday, on account of the inquest. 'But of course, my dear chap!' was the reply. 'Consider yourself our guest for as long as you wish to remain. The vice-principal and I were just saying that one of us ought to attend the proceedings on behalf of the college. Poor fellow,' he murmured, and it was obvious from his tone that it was Quine he meant. 'What a waste. What a sad waste of really quite a brilliant mind.'

'Not perhaps the most emollient of characters,' said the vice-principal. 'But sound enough where his subject was concerned . . . Are you an Oxford man, Mr Rowlands?'

Rowlands said that he was not.

'Ah, then you are an outsider! Always the best kind of observer,' said the other. In spite of his florid manner, Ponsonby-Smythe was no fool, thought Rowlands. 'I believe,' the vice-principal went on, as the three men sipped their sherry, 'you have worked with the police before, in an advisory capacity?' Then, as Rowlands made a deprecatory gesture, 'Beryl Phillips, the mistress of St Gertrude's College, is a cousin of mine. She speaks very warmly of you, and of the assistance you gave the college during that dreadful affair . . .'

The case he was referring to, which had indeed involved that distinguished Cambridge women's college, dated from six years before. Groaning inwardly, Rowlands said that it was kind of Miss Phillips to remember him, but that he'd done no more than anyone who'd found himself on the spot would have done. This wasn't strictly true, but he'd really rather not have advertised his role as a sleuth to all and sundry.

But any hope he had of remaining incognito was scotched by Ponsonby-Smythe's saying, in his richly penetrating tones, 'Yes, a murder in college is something one would really rather not have to confront, as head of an institution – wouldn't you agree, Principal?'

To which Dr Summerby could only murmur an affirmative, adding that it was all 'most distressing – the very last thing one would expect to happen at Oxford'.

'What price our civilised values now?' murmured Ponsonby-Smythe, as the company began to make its way towards the dining hall.

The principal made no response to this, but went on, as if his deputy had not spoken. 'Something that's been puzzling me, Mr Rowlands, is how you manage to conduct your, ah, investigations, in the absence of sight? I myself am partially blind – not, I should add, as a consequence of the last war, but as a result of debilitating disease . . .' Talking all the while, he guided Rowlands to the place next to his at high table. 'And so I wonder – knowing the difficulties as I do – how you cope with the obvious challenges of, ah, being unable to see what is in front of you?'

'It's quite straightforward, really.' Before Rowlands could expand on this, he became aware that a silence had fallen across the room, as its ranks of fellows and scholars filed in, each taking his place behind his appointed seat. Those undergraduates that remained – first years for the most part – stood at long oaken trestle tables, arranged in rows along the length of the hall, from whose barrel-vaulted ceiling even the smallest sounds (coughs, shuffling of feet) reverberated. At right-angles to the body of the hall stood high table, with its rows of carved oak chairs – 'museum pieces', Fraser had called them; it was to him that Rowlands owed these details of the room.

The principal murmured a Latin grace, and the company – consisting also of the Junior Staff Officers' contingent and the RAF men who'd lately joined them – sat down, with a scraping of benches against floorboards, and a sudden increase in the volume of conversation. 'You were about to tell me,' said Dr Summerby courteously, picking up the thread of their conversation amid the general roar, 'how you are able to get a sense of what places and people look like.'

'I merely ask questions,' said Rowlands, as the soup course – a vichyssoise – was set before him. 'People are generally quite happy to supply one with visual information. For instance I know from Major Fraser – who of course relies on his memories of life as an undergraduate at Brasenose – that this room was an eighteenth-century addition to the college, that its walls are panelled in English oak and that there are portraits of former principals and benefactors hung around the room. There is an ornamental fireplace on the side of the room opposite the doors, and large stained-glass windows depicting Biblical scenes on both sides of the hall—'

'Ah,' interrupted the vice-principal. 'There you go wrong. The windows have not been visible since September 1939, when the blackout was imposed. The portraits, too, have been removed and stored in the undercroft.'

'I stand corrected.' Rowlands smiled. 'But you see I

can only rely on what others tell me . . . modified by my own observations, which are mainly aural. I can tell, for example, that this room has a high ceiling. The echo tells me that. And of course I don't need to be told that it is full of people – many of them young, and full of high spirits.'

'Very good,' said the principal. 'If only I could persuade my students of the value of empirical evidence! But I fear they are too willing to take others' experience as gospel – and to reproduce the same second-hand information in their essays.'

On Rowlands's right-hand side sat the college chaplain, the Reverend Allbright, whom he'd met for the first time that evening, as the clergyman was, by his own account, more often to be found at Christ Church than at his alma mater. 'I take turn and turn about with Mr Osgood at the cathedral,' he explained to Rowlands – referring to the Christ Church chapel, which had been elevated to that status by Henry VIII, he added. 'Most of my undergraduate flock are now housed in Meadow Buildings – that is Christ Church too, you understand – so it makes it more convenient for them to attend services there, now that our own chapel is closed up, you know.'

Rowlands murmured some reply, his attention more engaged with the discussion that was taking place on the other side of the table between Dr Crawley and Dr Hobson. As far as Rowlands could make out, from the snatches of conversation he caught between the chaplain's drawling tones and the livelier bursts of talk and laughter emanating from the 'army' end of the table, this was on the question of whether 'history was at an end' – in the words of Hobson – or whether civilisation would rise again from the ashes of war, as it had done in the past. The history don was evidently of the opinion that the 'old order', as he put it, was finished. Only when all the moribund institutions and outdated notions had been swept away would a new world emerge.

It seemed to Rowlands, nodding politely as the Reverend Allbright described a recent rugger match between the two colleges in which, he was glad to say, Brasenose had proved the victor, that Hobson, usually so genial, was being unusually vehement. Gone was his facetious manner, which often made it hard to tell whether or not he was being serious. Certainly the elderly classics don appeared to take him at his word, 'You young men are such Bolsheviks,' he remarked, taking a sip of water (he alone, among the BNC fellows, did not drink wine). 'Always wanting to tear things down. And yet, you know, it will all seem remarkably trivial in a hundred years' time.'

Perhaps realising that he had allowed himself to become overly heated, Hobson laughed. 'You're absolutely right, sir. I was forgetting myself – behaving as if I were at a public meeting, instead of at dinner with my elders and betters.'

It was gracefully done, and Crawley seemed to take it in good part. 'You are far from being the first young feller with whom I have broken a lance,' he said. 'And you will not be the last, to judge from the present intake.' Rowlands guessed he was alluding to the noisier element in hall – whether undergraduates or servicemen he was unable to tell – who were even now exchanging cheerful banter across the tables.

'Bet you a quid I can do it in half the time.'

'Careful! I might just take you up on that.'

'Now, now gentlemen! You must know that betting is forbidden within college precincts . . .'

'Oh, boil your head!'

The legendary exploits of a former alumnus and member of the Oxford University Air Squadron – recently killed in action – were being related by an admirer, 'Jack Brady. Hell of a nice chap. No nerves at all. We were on a training exercise in Scotland, few months back. Visibility terrible. He was in the lead plane. Halifaxes, you know. One of the crew shouts, "Look out! That looks like a mountain ahead." Jack pulls back the stick just in time or the whole crate would have been a goner . . . Missed it by inches. "You were right, it was a mountain," he calls back. Hell of a chap.'

The fish course was taken away and the meat course substituted. Rowlands tasted little of either, intent as he was on what was being said around him. Further along high table sat the commandant and his officers, one of whom was Peter Bawden. He heard the latter say, 'B-but, sir, I thought I was to lead that exercise, not Jerningham. I'm ready for it, sir. I know I can do it . . .'

'All in good time,' was the reply. 'Jerningham's two months your senior. Can't have you promoted over his head. Wouldn't do.'

'I see that, sir, but—'

'No buts,' said the commandant. 'Your turn'll come soon enough. Ah, here we go . . .' Because the gong had sounded, signalling the end of dinner and the removal of the high table party to the Principal's rooms for coffee and dessert.

Rowlands rose with them, but, as he turned to follow his hosts out, he felt a touch on his sleeve. 'Mr Rowlands.' It was young Bawden. 'I must speak to you. 'S urgent . . .' From the other's excited manner and slightly slurred speech, it seemed to Rowlands that he was a bit tight. Hardly surprising, given the amount of wine they'd all drunk.

'It's late, Lieutenant Bawden,' he said. 'Can't it wait until tomorrow?'

'Leaving at five tomorrow. Training exercise. One I was s'posed to be leading,' he added bitterly. 'So it'll have to be now.'

'Very well. Fire away.'

They were standing at the foot of the staircase that led to the principal's rooms; a few stragglers from high table ascended this, continuing conversations started at dinner. Rowlands heard someone say, 'If you'll let me have that paper first thing . . .' and someone else's yawning reply, 'Right you are, old man. Pop it in your pigeonhole, shall I?'

'I've seen her,' blurted out young Bawden. 'Angela, I mean. She's one of the Blenheim Palace girls, as we thought.'

'I'm not sure you ought to be advertising the fact,' said Rowlands. 'It's confidential information.'

'I know that!' said Bawden indignantly, then, in a crestfallen tone, 'She wouldn't talk to me – even though I went all the way out there . . . Said she was too busy.'

'There you are, then,' began Rowlands, but something the young man had just said caught his attention. 'What do you mean – you went there?'

'What I said. I waited until the bus came, and then I

followed it out there – to Blenheim. I've a motorbike,' he added with a touch of pride. 'Norton WD 16H. Took me twenty minutes, door to door. Opened her up.'

'Mr Bawden—'

'I thought,' interrupted this irrepressible young man, 'you might put in a word for me. Tell her I just want to talk to her. Take her for a drink . . .'

'Really, I—'

'You're my only hope,' interrupted the young man. 'Angela knows and trusts you.'

'We didn't exactly part on good terms,' said Rowlands. 'But it's true that I've known her for a while . . . All right,' he said after a moment's thought. 'I'll try and talk to her, for all the good it'll do. In return, I'll need a favour from you.'

It had been twenty-five years since Frederick Rowlands had last been on the back of a motorcycle – and that had been in midsummer (not that you'd have guessed it, from the amount of rain that had fallen that month over Belgium). The despatch rider had had a message from brigade headquarters to deliver to their OC, Captain Willoughby, and it seemed quicker to take him to the battery rather than to give directions. 'Hop on, then, chum,' the messenger had said – Rowlands had never learnt his name or rank – and the two of them rocketed over the scarred and rutted ground, avoiding the flooded shell-holes by a miracle, as the powerful machine (a Triumph, Rowlands recalled) tore along the lines.

Speeding along the Woodstock Road was a rather different experience – a lot smoother-going, for a start –

although that, too, was not without its hazards, given the iciness of the roads. And it was very cold. Rowlands was glad of the leather jacket and helmet Bawden had lent him, as he clung on for dear life. How could he ever have thought this mode of transport enjoyable? All but the most rudimentary conversation proved impossible over the roar of the motorbike's engine and the scream of the wind. They came at last to a skidding halt in front of what was evidently the main gate to the property. 'This is it,' said Bawden. 'The jolly old barracks itself. Not that I'd want you to picture it in that way – it's a very grand affair indeed. Bigger than Buckingham Palace – and a lot more imposing.'

'So I've heard,' said Rowlands. 'Thanks for dropping me off.'

'The thing is,' Bawden went on, 'I don't see how you're going to get inside. I mean, there are already a couple of MPs giving us dirty looks from the gatehouse, and you've no authority here, any more than I have.'

'I'll think of something,' said Rowlands. 'You head back to Oxford. I'll find my own way back.'

'But . . .'

'Don't worry, I'll talk to Miss Thompson. Although I doubt very much if she'll be willing to see me here.'

Further conversation was curtailed at that moment by the arrival of a very large – and no doubt heavily armed – military policeman. 'Hi, you! Move along there!' he said without preamble. 'This is government property. The public ain't allowed.'

'If we're being strictly accurate, this is the public highway,' retorted Bawden – perhaps unwisely, for the

MP said, with no change of tone, 'I'll have your name and number, Sonny Jim. Seems to me you must be AWOL from your unit, this time o'day . . .'

'You mind your own business!' Bawden snapped; Rowlands put a cautionary hand on his arm.

'The lieutenant was just giving me a lift on his way back to Oxford,' he said addressing the MP. 'He's got nothing to do with my visit to Blenheim.'

'Ho! So you admit your destination was the palace?' demanded the guard. 'What are you – some kind of spy? I think you'd better come with me.'

'Willingly,' said Rowlands, then, to Bawden, who was hovering nearby, evidently unsure of whether he should go or stay, 'Thank you for the lift. It's saved me a long bus journey.'

'I—'

'Goodbye, Lieutenant. You'll be expected back in Oxford. I've taken you far enough out of your way already.'

When the motorbike had roared away, Rowlands turned once more to the policeman. 'I'd like to speak to Captain Fawcett,' he said. 'I've some information he might find interesting.'

But Fawcett, it turned out, was not so easily found. It was true that, after Rowlands had made his request, the attitude of his custodian changed from one of deepest suspicion to one of wary regard. 'You'd better come along o' me, then – sir,' he remembered to add. As Rowlands, following the direction from which the voice had come, took a tentative step towards where he supposed the gate to be, holding out his hand in order to feel where it was and thus avoid walking into it, the MP exclaimed, 'Why, you didn't say as you was blind!'

'It isn't usually how I prefer to introduce myself,' replied Rowlands wryly. 'But, as you've observed, it makes me rather an unlikely spy.' He didn't add that this last was an epithet that had been applied to him on a number of occasions in the past, when his sleuthing activities had brought him into conflict with some of those he was investigating.

'No . . . I do see that,' admitted the MP sheepishly. 'All the same, sir, I'll have to ask you to step inside . . . carefully does it!' – as, successfully navigating the gatepost, Rowlands found himself at the entrance to a gatehouse. 'I'll need to telephone the house before I can let you go any further, see? It'd be more'n my job's worth to allow you or any other unauthorised person to go wandering about unsupervised, like.'

Rowlands said that he quite appreciated that, and had expected nothing less. Inside the gatehouse, Rowlands was ushered into a room he guessed must be some kind of lock-up, while the policeman consulted his colleague on the ticklish matter of this unexpected visitor. Through the door between him and the outer room, he could make out only a few words. 'Tricky . . . can't let 'im go . . . never hear the last of it . . .'

A few minutes elapsed, at the end of which someone – the man to whom he hadn't yet spoken – put his head around the door. 'Care for a cuppa?'

'Thanks, but I was hoping to speak to Captain Fawcett.'

'He can't be found just at present.'

'Then . . . is there anyone else I could speak to? It's

rather urgent.' But the door had already closed.

Another twenty minutes went by. The tea had been brought and drunk. 'I really do need to speak to someone at MI5,' said Rowlands to his kindly gaoler. 'Captain Fawcett for preference – but if he's not available, then anyone in a senior position would do.'

''Fraid it don't work like that,' explained the man Rowlands had privately christened 'Cuppa Tea'. 'You can't just waltz in and ask to see the top brass. There's protocol to be observed.'

'I realise that,' began the exasperated Rowlands. 'And I'm not asking for special treatment – only to pass on some information that might prove useful.'

His pleas fell on deaf ears, however. Left alone once more in the windowless room, he wondered how much longer he'd be detained there. He'd committed no crime. Could he really be kept against his will? He knew that the answer wasn't a simple one. The country was at war, and this was the headquarters of British Intelligence – one of the most secret places in England. Of course they weren't just going to let him go. He'd been foolish to suppose it.

It was then that he heard the car's engine – a throaty purr that spoke of the finest British engineering, of wealth and privilege, of pre-war glamour. A Bentley. Rowlands was certain of it. He got to his feet then, as he heard the vehicle slow down, so that its driver (or owner – who might be one and the same person) could be identified by the sentry, before being waved through. Seeing his chance, Rowlands took a deep breath and shouted, 'Let me out!' at the same time banging on the door with all his might. 'Let me out! Let me out, I say!'

A moment later, two things happened: the door opened and a voice – the MP's – said sharply, 'Now then! That's quite enough of that!'

Then a second voice – a cultivated voice, with an authority that suggested the speaker was accustomed to deference – said, in tones of mild astonishment, 'Good heavens! Who've you got locked up in here, man? He doesn't *look* like a German spy.'

'Well, no . . . The fact is, sir . . . I mean Your Grace . . .'

'I should let him out at once, if I were you. I'll take charge of him. I hope,' he went on, now addressing Rowlands, 'these men haven't been too rough with you?'

'Not at all. They were only doing their duty.'

'Then there's no harm done,' said the other. 'Name's Marlborough. Military liaison officer with the United States forces in Oxon – that is, I will be, once they get here. And you are?'

Rowlands gave his name and offered his hand, which the other shook. From this brief contact, Rowlands realised that the owner of the hand was well over six foot tall, and of a military bearing – an assessment confirmed when Marlborough said, 'Old soldier like myself, aren't you?'

'Yes, Your Grace. Royal Field Artillery, 1914 to 1917 – year I was invalided out.'

'Where did it happen?'

'Passchendaele.'

'Ah. Bloody business, that. I was in Belgium and France, too.'

They had by now exited the gatehouse and were standing by the waiting Bentley. 'Hop in,' said the Duke, in a near-echo of that long-ago injunction from the despatch rider on the Menin Road. 'We'll go straight to the private quarters, Saunders,' he said to his chauffeur. 'Should be in time for a spot of tea. I expect you could do with it,' he added to his guest.

Chapter Eleven

'It's rather a pity you can't see the old place,' observed the owner of it in a reflective tone. 'It's rather a fine example of the English Baroque style . . . not to everybody's taste, of course, but one comes to admire it. Built by Vanbrugh in the seventeen hundreds for my six-times-great-grandpapa.' He chuckled reminiscently. 'That is, until my six-times-great-grandmama took against him – Vanbrugh, that is – and hired somebody else to finish it off . . . Luckily, he wasn't a bad architect, either. Name of Hawksmoor.'

'I know his London churches,' said Rowlands.

'Yes. Rather bizarre, most of 'em, in my opinion. Here we are.' Because the car had now pulled up. A moment later, the driver got out and opened the door for the Duke and his guest. 'We're in the east wing these days,' said the latter. 'Suits us quite well. The fact is, this place is far too large for one family. Do you need me to take your arm?' he added, as the two of them began to walk across the granite setts that lay in front of the building.

'Thank you, Your Grace – but I can manage all right by following the sound of your voice and footsteps. Although I'd be grateful if you'd mention any obstacles before I discover them for myself,' said Rowlands with a smile.

'Very well. Couple of steps here,' said his host. 'Door in front of you.' This proved to have already been opened by the attentive butler, who stood aside to let them pass.

'Her Grace said to tell you that tea is being served in the Bow Window Room, Your Grace.'

'Thank you, Crawford. It's this way,' said the Duke to Rowlands. 'Straight across the hall – about ten paces – and then the second door on the right. Ah, there you are, my dear!' he cried, on entering this room – which had a pleasant smell of fresh flowers (gardenias, thought Rowlands), beeswax and apple-wood from the fire that was burning merrily in the grate. 'As you see, I've brought a guest. This is Mr Rowlands. He's just spent a rather disagreeable couple of hours in our gatehouse, so he'll need reviving with a good strong cup of tea and some of Mrs D's excellent scones. Rowlands, do let me introduce my wife. She's sitting on the sofa just in front of you. There's another sofa at right-angles to it.'

The unusual specificity of these instructions must have told the Duchess all she needed to know about her guest, for she merely said, 'How do you do, Mr Rowlands? Do sit down. As my husband says, the sofa adjacent to this one is nearest – and closest to the fire. I should imagine you must be chilled to the bone after being cooped up in that freezing gatehouse.'

Rowlands thanked her and sat down. She poured out a cup of tea from the silver teapot on the tray in front of her and passed it to him. It was hot and freshly made, and he drank it gratefully. It had indeed been chilly in the gatehouse.

'Rowlands was at Ypres, around the same time as I was,' remarked the Duke, who had seated himself next to his wife. 'Royal Field Artillery, you said, didn't you, Rowlands? The men in charge of the big guns. My outfit was the Life Guards.' Marlborough was silent a moment. 'It wasn't a war for horses – as we soon found out. Poor beasts stood no chance at all against shells and tanks.'

'No.'

'It was supposed to be the "war to end all wars" – but it didn't work out like that, unfortunately. Now it's the next generation who'll pay the price . . . although thankfully,' he added, 'our two boys are too young to be part of it . . . yet.'

'Do you have children, Mr Rowlands?' asked the Duchess. She had an agreeably low voice, and a gentle manner, that made Rowlands warm to her.

'Three,' he said. 'All girls.'

'How nice. We've three daughters, too – and two sons, as Blandford said. The youngest is only two. He's rather a darling, although I say so myself.'

'You spoil him,' said her husband indulgently.

'Only as much as he deserves,' was the reply. 'Ah, here's Nanny with little Charles, now' – because the door to the sitting room had opened. But it wasn't the nanny and her charge who entered, but somebody else.

'Am I too late for tea?' said a voice Rowlands knew, then, 'Hello, Mr Rowlands. This is a pleasant surprise!'

Rowlands, who had risen to his feet, was momentarily lost for words. But then he thought, *Of course she'd be here. It's just where I'd have expected to find her.*

'Good afternoon, Miss Barnes,' he said. 'How very nice to see you again.'

It had been six months since they'd last met, at the end of a case that had drawn Rowlands into the secret world in which he found himself caught up once more. This was Iris Barnes's milieu – he knew enough about her previous activities to realise that she must be involved, at some level, with the present case – the one that had started, for him, with the major's letter. And yet in these surroundings, as the guest of the Duke and Duchess, it hardly seemed appropriate to broach the subject that had brought him to Blenheim. Fortunately, the social awkwardness of the occasion was deftly overcome by the Duchess, 'Iris, my dear, you seem to know everybody. Come and sit down, while I pour you some tea, and tell me where and when you two met.'

Miss Barnes flung herself down on the sofa next to Rowlands. 'I believe it was in London – or was it Berlin?' She helped herself to a scone. 'Too long ago to remember exactly when . . . Mr Rowlands and I have worked together on a number of different cases,' she went on, taking a bite.

'How interesting. Are you with the service too, Mr Rowlands?' The Duchess again.

'Mary, my dear, I really think . . .' began her husband, in a warning tone, but Rowlands saw no harm in replying.

'I'm not with the Secret Service, Your Grace. Miss Barnes is referring to some help I was once able to give the police, during a murder case.'

'Several murder cases,' put in Iris Barnes. 'If we're being precise. Mr Rowlands is a detective – and a very good one,

136

I might add. You'll remember the Castleford murders, Bert?'

'Good Lord, yes. Poor Neddie Swift very nearly got it in the neck over that affair. Don't tell me it was you who put the police straight, Rowlands?'

'The police would have got to the truth eventually,' replied Rowlands, feeling as uncomfortable as he always did when attention was drawn to his sleuthing activities.

'Yes, but maybe not in time to save Ned. I know I shouldn't ask,' Marlborough went on, 'but are you here at Blenheim in a similar capacity?'

'Indirectly,' admitted Rowlands. 'I have some information that I hope might be of use to MI5. It was Captain Fawcett I wanted to speak to – but I gather he's not available.'

'Oh, Reggie's around somewhere,' said Miss Barnes vaguely. 'But you can talk to me.'

'I think,' said the Duchess, 'that I'd better go and see what's keeping Nanny. She promised to bring Charles in to see me, before his bath-time.' She got up. 'It was very nice to meet you, Mr Rowlands. It's not every day I can say I've entertained a detective to tea.'

When she had gone out, the Duke, too, got to his feet. 'I've things to see to, as well,' he said. 'I'll be in my study if anyone wants me.'

'Dear Bert,' said Iris Barnes, when the door had closed behind him. 'Always the soul of tact. Although he'd have been quite within his rights to stay, given his present military role. But he tends to stay out of intelligence business. Doesn't care for "spooks", as he puts it.'

This reminded Rowlands of something he'd heard

recently, from just such another bluff soldier – Commandant Hastings. He smiled. 'What I've got to tell you isn't very much in itself,' he said. 'Just a couple of things that might, or might not, add up to something . . .'

'And what have they "added up to?" No, don't tell me – let me guess. Murder.'

'It seems you're already ahead of me,' he said wryly. 'Yes, that is what I suspect – and it isn't one murder, but two.'

'You'd better put me in the picture,' she said. 'Cigarette?'

'Thanks.'

She lit one for both of them, and put his between his lips. 'Go on.'

He did so, sketching in the events of the past few weeks as succinctly as possible. She listened in silence, until he had finished.

'It sounds as if there's no hard evidence that Dr Quine's death wasn't suicide,' she said in a thoughtful tone. 'Although I've a feeling you're about to tell me something that points to its being murder.'

'Yes. You know, of course, that I was one of the first to find Donald Challoner, the night he was killed – and there's no doubt that that was murder.'

'None,' she agreed, adding quietly, 'Poor Don. I liked him. A very fine agent, too . . . Sorry, you were saying?'

'I was alone with Challoner for a few minutes, while Fraser fetched the doctor. During that time he – Challoner – spoke to me.'

She gave a little gasp. 'So he was still conscious?'

'For a short time, during which he managed to say two things. He was dying, of course, so it was hard to make out anything very definite . . . If I hadn't been leaning over him, to see if I could detect a pulse, I'd have missed what he did say. "The green file" was the first thing. Then, "names". I took this to mean that the information contained within the file must include the name of the traitor Challoner had intended to reveal to Fraser and me when he'd summoned us to his rooms.'

'Yes, that makes sense. He didn't say anything more about what was in it?'

'No. The only other thing he said was, "Trust no one." Those were his last words. So you see, I've been cautious, up to now, about who I have told.'

'Not the police?'

'No. Not even Ian Fraser. Although I hardly think *he'd* have been involved in anything dubious,' he added, with a laugh in which there was a shade of unease. 'But he fell ill, soon afterwards, with a fever . . .'

'Was he delirious?'

'Yes. I couldn't risk trusting him with what Challoner had said in case he let it out inadvertently. People were in and out of his rooms, all the time. College servants, bringing food. Doctors. Visitors. I'd trust Fraser with my life,' he said. 'But it would have been expecting too much of a sick man to burden him with what I knew.'

'You said there was something else . . .'

'There was. I didn't think anything of it at first. It was only after Quine was killed that I remembered what it was that had first struck me about the earlier case, and started to put two and two together.'

'What was it you noticed?' she said quietly.

'Nothing much in itself. A smell of burning. Specifically, of burnt paper . . . or . . . or cardboard.'

'Burnt paper or cardboard,' she echoed.

'I told you it wasn't much. But I'd noticed it first on the stairs to Challoner's rooms. Someone coming down as Fraser and I were ascending pushed past me. The smell clung to his clothes. It was faint – but unmistakeable. Scorched paper. The obvious thing was the green file – although I didn't realise that until afterwards. It was when I smelt the same smell again, in Quine's rooms, the day we found him – Dobbs and I. He's the Brasenose porter,' he added in case this wasn't obvious. 'There was the same acrid smell – burnt paper and cardboard – in one of the desk drawers in Quine's room. It must have contained the green file, although it was empty when I – or Dobbs, rather – searched it. Quine must have taken it from Challoner's rooms, as he lay dying, and then put it in the desk for safe-keeping.'

'But you didn't find the file . . .'

'No. It was nowhere to be found. I asked Dobbs to search the room, but he found nothing. So either Quine destroyed it himself, because his was the name in the file – the name Challoner had meant to give me and Fraser that night – or somebody else destroyed it, having killed Quine, to prevent him from revealing what he knew . . . It all hangs together.'

'It does,' said Iris Barnes, stubbing out her cigarette in an ashtray that was to hand. 'It hangs together beautifully – except that it's all wrong. Quine didn't kill Challoner – although it seems likely that he did steal the green file from Challoner's rooms. But he didn't burn it. It was already burnt.' She stood up. 'Come with me. There's something you should see.'

* * *

140

Exiting the library, they went along a corridor, which brought them to a door. Miss Barnes unlocked this. 'If you haven't already worked it out, we've just left the private quarters,' she said, re-locking the door behind them. 'I usually go the long way round, but this is quicker – and I'm sure Bert won't mind. He's such a dear. He and my father knew one another when Daddy was in the diplomatic service. Since Daddy died, Bert's looked out for me.'

Rowlands nodded, knowing that that was how it was in the circles in which people like Iris Barnes moved. You looked out for your friends – and the offspring of your friends. It was, he supposed, a world in which everyone knew everyone else.

More corridors followed. 'This place is a labyrinth,' Miss Barnes went on. 'One really needs a map to find one's way about. I still take wrong turnings, sometimes . . .' He wondered if her remark alluded to something more than just the difficulties of navigating the building. He, too, often found himself adrift in the unfamiliar territory of the secret world. It was a hall of mirrors, which threw back images designed to mislead.

They passed through a series of rooms, each larger and grander than the last, it seemed to him: the echo such apartments gave back was one clue to their size; another was their chilly temperature. Uncarpeted floors and enormous windows (however efficiently blacked-out) didn't give one a feeling of cosiness. From one such vast room came the rattle of typewriters. 'The Long Library,' said Rowlands's companion. 'It's where most of the "Blenheim Girls" work – those that aren't in the registry. And it is one of the longest rooms of its kind in Europe, I believe. Very grand in its heyday, no doubt – with those fluted columns, and all that elaborate stucco work on the ceiling and around the bookcases. Hawksmoor's finest room, they say. Not looking quite its best these days, with government-issue chairs and desks cluttering the space, and the windows shrouded in blackout blinds. Thankfully, they've left some of the pictures up.'

They cut across one end of the enormous room, which Rowlands pictured as long gallery and library in one – an ideal refuge, for previous incumbents of the palace, on wet days when no hunting was to be had, and the prospect of tea by the fire might be enlivened by glancing through the latest novel by Miss Yonge, or idly turning the pages of the stud book. He marvelled at the ingenuity that had turned a space designed for purely recreational purposes into a hive of industry. This, Miss Barnes informed him, was Section F, dealing with Russian affairs. 'Of course, since they are now our allies, we need only keep a watchful eye, to make sure they are not getting above themselves . . .'

They came to a doorway, flanked by marble pillars. 'We go in here,' said Rowlands's companion. 'The Great Hall. Another room that lives up to its name. It's where we've housed the registry, so it's full of filing cabinets. But even that – and the ugly matting we've had to put down to protect the magnificent stone floor – doesn't detract from the splendour. It's sixty-seven feet from floor to ceiling,' she added, but he had already registered the vast size of the place from its echo, and the volume of air over his head.

'Impressive,' he said.

'Oh, it is. A much nicer place to work than the last one.'

She must have nodded, or made some other sign to one

of the women seated at a nearby table, who at once got up and came over. 'Yes, ma'am?'

'Unlock one of these filing cabinets for me, would you?' said Miss Barnes. 'Any one of them will do.' Then, as she and Rowlands, accompanied by the girl, crossed the room to where the metal cabinets stood in a long row, 'I take it these are the files salvaged from the prison?'

'They are, ma'am.' She unlocked one of the cabinets. 'These are G to H. We haven't gone through these ones yet,' she added apologetically. 'We're still working on E to F.'

'All the better, for my purposes,' replied her superior airily. 'You can leave the key with me. I'll lock up when we're done.'

When the young woman had returned to her desk, Iris Barnes slid the drawer of the filing cabinet open. At once, and before she could draw his attention to it, Rowlands got a whiff of the unpleasantly acrid smell arising from the files that were stored within. A smell of burnt paper and cardboard.

'You see?' said Miss Barnes softly. 'Your instincts have been proved right again, Mr Rowlands. That green file is important – and it is one of ours. They all smell like this – those that survived the devastation. A German bomb crashed through the glass ceiling of the workshop at Wormwood Scrubs prison, where the registry was housed before it was moved to Blenheim Palace. This was in September 1940. Luckily no lives were lost, but a lot of valuable research went up in smoke – quite literally. The damage was compounded by the fact that the half-burnt files were then thoroughly soaked by the fire brigade's efforts to douse the flames . . . which accounts for the disgusting smell . . . Phew!' She slid the drawer closed and turned the key, but even so the smell of scorched paper lingered.

'The task these ladies at Blenheim have is to salvage what can be salvaged from the paperwork that escaped the worst of the fire, and to recreate what didn't. No easy job, as you might imagine.'

'No indeed,' he said. It seemed obvious to him now that the green file, with its incriminating evidence, had been in Donald Challoner's rooms the night he was murdered, and had then been purloined – for what purpose he could only conjecture – by Maurice Quine. What had become of it afterwards was now the question. 'Do you think the missing file has been destroyed?' he asked – for once careless of who might be listening. In a room such as this – a vast repository, he gathered, of hundreds of similar files containing confidential information about hundreds of suspected enemy agents – his question would seem unremarkable. Around him, in the hushed atmosphere of the Great Hall, young women, such as the one Iris Barnes had conscripted to do her bidding, sat diligently working away at just the same question he had put to her: had a file and its contents been destroyed or not? Was there anything that could be salvaged?

Ignoring his query, Miss Barnes remarked in an amused tone, 'You seem to have attracted the attention of at least one of our young ladies. That pretty fair-haired girl over there can't stop looking at you, Mr Rowlands.'

He had a good idea who this might be. 'I'm sure she's just surprised – whoever she is – at seeing an unfamiliar face at her place of work,' he said hastily. 'Don't your "Blenheim Girls" have to sign the Official Secrets Act?'

'I believe they do. You seem very well-informed about it all, Mr Rowlands.'

He knew she was teasing him, but refused to rise to the bait. 'I feel I should go. I've disrupted things quite enough.'

But there was still one further encounter to come. As they quitted the Great Hall, this time by way of the ante-room that stood between it and the main entrance, someone came hurrying down the stairs. 'Might I have a word, ma'am?' It was a voice Rowlands knew from somewhere. A dry, somewhat colourless voice. Now where had he heard it before?

'Reggie. This is Frederick Rowlands. You'll remember he gave evidence at the Challoner inquest.'

'Ah. Mmm. Yes,' was the MI5 man's only response.

'Mr Rowlands, this is the elusive Captain Fawcett. Mr Rowlands has been trying to get in touch with you all day, Reggie.'

'Mmm. Been a bit tied up,' was the reply. 'Couldn't get away before now.'

'Well, it's good to catch up with you at last,' said Rowlands, holding out his hand. After a perceptible pause, the other shook it. From this brief contact, Rowlands received an impression of a man of average height and unathletic build. A desk man, he rather thought – somebody more at home orchestrating the action than participating in it. In this, he was to discover, he was mistaken.

'Mr Rowlands has some information for us regarding the night of Donald Challoner's murder,' said Miss Barnes. 'He was also one of the first to find Dr Quine's body . . .

after Quine's apparent suicide. He has information about that, too.'

'Mmm. Perhaps,' said Fawcett, 'we should find somewhere more private to talk?'

There was a small sitting room to one side of the entrance hall, where a fire had been lit. Tapestries on the walls added a further layer of warmth – as they did elsewhere in the palace, Miss Barnes pointed out. 'Can't have government employees freezing to death,' she quipped. In these relatively comfortable surroundings, the three of them sat down.

'So, Mr, ah, Rowlands,' said Captain Fawcett. 'You believe you can help us find Challoner's murderer?'

'Before we go any further,' interrupted Iris Barnes. 'I think a drink is called for – and not tea, this time. Whisky and soda do you, Mr Rowlands?'

He said that it would. She accordingly poured drinks for the three of them from one of the decanters ranged on a sideboard – presumably for the use of senior intelligence officers only, Rowlands thought. Thus refreshed, he repeated his account of the night of Challoner's murder, and his conviction that the famous 'green file' had not only been present in the room just before it, but had been taken away soon afterwards – presumably by Maurice Quine. 'It wasn't in Dr Quine's rooms when I went there with the porter,' he concluded. 'So one can assume it had been removed – and probably destroyed – by the man who killed them both.'

'Not necessarily destroyed,' said Miss Barnes. 'You see, the information it contains might well be of significant value to our perpetrator – call him X. His name might not

146

be the only one listed there.' She paused a moment, to take a sip of her whisky, and (thought Rowlands) to decide how much to tell him. 'Agents – even the double kind we're dealing with here – don't work alone, Mr Rowlands. At the very least, the file on X will contain details of those with whom he's worked in the past. Handlers. Cut-outs. Contacts of various kinds. All of whom might conceivably give him away, and are therefore a danger to him. So you see . . .'

'He'll want to eliminate anyone whose name is in that file,' said Rowlands.

'Precisely,' was the reply.

Chapter Twelve

It was Captain Fawcett who offered to drive Rowlands back to Oxford. 'Least I can do, having kept you hanging around for so long,' he said – Miss Barnes having put him in the picture about Rowlands's earlier detention in the guardhouse. The latter privately wondered whether this suggestion – that the dour Fawcett should act as their guest's chauffeur – hadn't come from Miss Barnes, whose brisk manner towards the MI5 officer was rather that of a superior towards a subordinate than otherwise.

As Rowlands took his seat beside Fawcett in the Vauxhall, he speculated as to what her actual role in all this might be. In the dozen years since he'd first met her, she'd played a number of different parts – journalist, writer, socialite – and had shown herself to be at home in a range of milieu, many of them in foreign parts. This chameleon-like quality, combined with a proficiency in languages, and (as he could attest) an adeptness with firearms, would have made her a considerable asset to British Intelligence, he thought;

although it seemed to him that she was a bit too much of a maverick to fit in comfortably with the old-school tie and gentleman's club set.

'You seemed to be of the opinion, during our conversation just now, that Dr Quine's apparent suicide was in fact murder,' said Fawcett, breaking into these musings with characteristic bluntness. He skilfully navigated the car past a row of Nissen huts ('why they had to plonk them just here I can't imagine') and joined a queue of army lorries, rumbling its way out of Great Court and onto the main drive. 'Had you any particular reason for doubting that the man killed himself?'

'Nothing concrete,' replied Rowlands. 'Of course, the fact of Quine's having taken the green file from Challoner's rooms put him in rather a suspicious light, initially. The suggestion that he'd committed suicide out of remorse for having killed Challoner only made sense if the file had been found in his rooms. That it wasn't indicates that someone else took it – having killed Dr Quine in order to do so.'

'Mmm,' said the MI5 man. 'I can see that you've thought this out. Any ideas on who the culprit might be?'

'None. And it is only a supposition. Quine might have destroyed the file himself – although we found no evidence of this . . .'

'"We"?' queried the laconic Fawcett.

'The porter, Dobbs, and myself.'

'Of course.' Fawcett reflected for a moment. 'One does wonder,' he said at last, 'why – having gone to so much trouble to make Quine's death look like a suicide – the perpetrator should have made such an elementary mistake.'

'I'm afraid I . . .'

'No, of course you wouldn't have been in a position to notice such a thing,' said the other. 'Confound these icy roads! One has to crawl along at a snail's pace. Yes,' he went on. 'He – whoever he was – went to great lengths to delay the finding of the body, since if Quine was killed on Christmas night, or early on Boxing Day, he would have lain undisturbed for at least a couple of days, as Boxing Day was a holiday for the college staff, you know. But he – our perpetrator – slipped up. It happens all the time. A small but obvious mistake, which casts doubt on the whole thing.'

They had by now reached the outskirts of Oxford, Rowlands guessed, from the increase in the volume of traffic. 'Damn this blackout,' muttered Fawcett. 'One can't see a foot in front of one with these masked headlights . . . When a man cuts his throat,' he continued, as if there had been no change of subject, 'he usually makes a couple of tries at it, first. Getting his nerve up, so to speak. In this case, there were no "practice cuts" . . . and Quine was left-handed. The police got on to that right away. But the cut was from left to right. An elementary mistake, as I said.'

'Was Quine an enemy agent, too?' said Rowlands. 'He seemed like a harmless academic, to me.'

'Oh, people can seem to be anything at all,' said Fawcett. 'But to answer your question, I rather think not. Dr Quine had quite a different reason for wanting to get his hands on the green file.'

'Blackmail?'

'Just so. You know, you interest me, Mr Rowlands. You're rather . . . dogged, if I might say so. Most men in your situation – forgive me if I seem impertinent – wouldn't even attempt to grapple with the kind of situations you seem to get yourself into. Murder. Suicide. Blackmail.' He gave a short, rather mirthless laugh. 'One would hardly expect an old soldier like yourself to interest himself in such police court stuff.'

'It's been remarked before that my blindness doesn't make me an ideal detective,' said Rowlands drily.

'And yet you're rather a successful one, from what I can gather,' was the reply. 'What is it that drives you to get involved in these cases?' Fawcett sounded as if the answer to this question was of real interest to him.

Rowlands smiled. 'I imagine it's much the same as whatever drives you to do your job,' he said. 'Call it a passion for truth. Or justice.'

Another few minutes brought them to the porter's lodge. Refusing Rowlands's offer of a drink, Fawcett said he had to return to Blenheim. 'Truth and Justice are hard taskmistresses,' he said, with another of his dry laughs.

In the lodge, Rowlands found Dobbs about to give Heidi her supper, having just returned from walking her around Radcliffe Square. 'You went out so early this morning,' he said reproachfully, 'that I'd no chance to ask what arrangements you wanted to make for the dog.'

Rowlands, who was starting to feel the weight of the past few hours, muttered that he'd been unexpectedly detained. What he wanted right now was a bath – always supposing there was any hot water left – and then dinner, if he hadn't already missed it. He remembered that the next day was Sunday. 'I'll be by bright and early, to take Heidi for a walk before church,' he said. The inquest was at two on Monday. After that, he and Heidi would shake the dust of Oxford off their feet (or paws) and take the train to London. It would be a relief, he thought, to leave Oxford, for all its seemingly civilised values. In the past few days, he had started to find it claustrophobic. A definite aura of Bluebeard's Castle hung over the mediaeval quads and 'dreaming spires'.

He wished Dobbs goodnight, patted Heidi, and made for the door. Perhaps he'd ask for a tray in his room, after all. He wasn't sure if he could face high table.

'Almost slipped me mind,' said the porter. 'There was a message for you. From a young lady.'

'Did she give a name?'

'Said as you'd know,' said Dobbs. 'Fair-haired young lady. Said as she'd meet you in the usual place. Eight o'clock. It's a quarter to, now.'

A wintry Saturday night in Oxford. The Bird and Baby was packed to the rafters with a noisy, cheerful rabble of young men and women, whose allegiances – whether Town or Gown, military or civilian – were not always easy to discern. As Rowlands shouldered his way through the crowd around the door, using Heidi as a canine 'advance guard', he caught snatches of the flirtatious banter going back and forth between a group of RAF men and some local girls.

'Well, you're a cheeky one, and no mistake!'

'I say, old bean, I think the lady likes you.'

'Don't flatter yourself. Think yourselves God's gift, you glamour boys . . .'

Further into the long, narrow pub, an earnest young man was explaining to another earnest young man that Schopenhauer was 'bunk'. Rowlands pressed on. In the back bar, he found Angela Thompson, nursing a half of bitter. When she saw him she got to her feet. 'I didn't know if you'd come.'

'I've only just got your message.'

'I . . . I want to buy you a drink.'

'Thanks, but I'm afraid, as my daughters will tell you, that I'm horribly old-fashioned when it comes to buying drinks. Now, what'll you have?'

Ignoring her muted protests, he retraced his steps to the bar, returning, after an interval, with a pint of Morrell's and a half of the same for her. He found her talking to the dog – 'You're a lovely girl, aren't you? A lovely girl . . . I've saved you a seat,' she said, as Rowlands set down the drinks. She took a gulp of hers. 'I saw you earlier today.'

'I guessed you must have done.'

'I didn't realise . . . that is . . . I want to apologise . . . for the things I said.'

'Think nothing of it. You were quite right to warn me off. I might have been anybody.'

'Yes, but I ought to have known I could trust you – after what happened before. That time in Cambridge, I mean.'

Trust no one, thought Rowlands, but he merely smiled. 'Was there anything particular you wanted to say to me – apart from what you've just said?'

Angela Thompson hesitated. At one of the other tables in the cramped little room a genial argument was in progress concerning the merits or otherwise of the local football team; at another, the discussion was of which of the films on offer at the local 'flea pit' – *49th Parallel* or *Quiet Wedding* – would make it worth leaving the warmth and comfort of the back bar. No one was paying them any attention, it seemed. 'It's just . . .' she began. 'You were right . . . I mean about what you told me.'

'Tell you what,' said Rowlands. 'Why don't I walk you back to Keble when we've finished these, and you can tell me what's on your mind then?'

Miss Thompson agreed that would be best. 'In the meantime,' said Rowlands. 'I've got something to ask you. Are you engaged to be married?'

'No!'

'Then what is your objection to going for a drink with a perfectly nice young man?'

'Oh! I suppose you mean Peter Bawden?'

'Don't you like him?'

'It's not that . . . I mean, I do like him. It's just . . . Following me all the way out there, on that silly motorbike of his, when I'm supposed to be at work . . .'

'Coming on a bit strong, eh?'

'Something like that.'

'Understood. I'll tell the young jackanapes to keep his distance in future.'

'No. Don't do that. Tell him I wouldn't mind going for a drink – after work.'

On the walk back to Keble, she said, without preamble, 'You were right. One of the files is missing – a green one, as you said. There are several other colours – buff, grey, blue – depending on . . . well, what's in them. They're all numbered, too, so it was just a case of checking to see if any of the sequence of numbers was missing. We've already been through the first few batches, so it was the ones that hadn't been checked that I looked through.'

'G to H,' said Rowlands softly.

'What? Oh, I see. Yes, it wasn't long after I started going through the filing cabinets that I saw it . . . the space where the missing file should have been.'

'Any idea what was in it?'

'I'm afraid not. I suppose it must be something important, if senior officers like her are looking into it.' He guessed it was Miss Barnes she meant.

'I think it is pretty important,' he said.

Sunday was uneventful. An early morning walk with the dog around Christ Church Meadow, followed by morning service at the cathedral, presided over by the affable Reverend Allbright, set the tone – a welcome relief from the troubling events of the previous few days. The collect for this second Sunday after Epiphany had a resonance for Rowlands, and doubtless for other members of the congregation, as they sat beneath the lofty fan-vaulting of the four-hundred year-old building, whose site had been a place of worship for a thousand years. 'Mercifully hear the supplications of Thy people, and grant us peace all the days of our life . . .'

Thus intoned the Reverend Allbright, as his predecessors in earlier times of war had done before him. 1941 had been a bloody year, at home and abroad, thought Rowlands – with those fighting the enemy on land, sea and in the air suffering grievous losses, and civilian lives at risk from aerial bombardment and other horrors too appalling to contemplate, if one believed the reports that filtered back from occupied Europe. Listening to the beautiful words of Psalm 23 being sung by the cathedral choir, he wondered what 1942 would bring, and feared it was nothing good.

* * *

The inquest on Maurice Arthur Quine was not a lengthy affair. Once Inspector Dimmock had told the court what he had found at the scene ('the body of a man in his late fifties, with a severe wound to his throat') and both Rowlands and William Dobbs had given their corroborating evidence, there was little more to add, beyond the medical officer's report on the cause of death – self-evident in such a case – and the absence of any suspicious substances revealed by the post-mortem examination of the body. 'He means he weren't drugged,' hissed Dobbs in Rowlands's ear – the porter having appointed himself the latter's guide and interpreter, something Rowlands would gladly have gone without.

As he had anticipated, after his conversation with Captain Fawcett, the police had requested an adjournment. Which meant they were regarding it as a suspicious death, he guessed, wondering how much – or how little – the MI5 man had imparted to the inspector of the likely connection between Donald Challoner's murder and this one.

Well, he for one was glad to be out of it. Let the police and MI5 get on with their respective investigations – he was for London and (once he'd delivered the faithful Heidi to her master) for Brighton and home. It had been over a week since he'd last seen his wife and family. The couple of telephone calls and one exchange of letters didn't make up for Edith's company, nor her sound common sense. He'd often had recourse to this in the past, when a case was proving troublesome, and looked forward to talking over the 'Oxford Murders' with her now.

He accordingly picked up his bag, packed that morning,

and collected Heidi from the porter's lodge. Dobbs, who seemed to have taken a shine to both the dog and her human companion, insisted on accompanying them both to the gate. 'You look after yourself now, sir,' he admonished Rowlands. 'Sure you'll be all right getting to the station? It's right along Turl Street, remember? Then left onto the Broad an' keep going left . . .'

Rowlands assured him that he had the directions clear in his mind, and said farewell to Dobbs and to Brasenose College with a light heart. 'Come along, girl,' he said to Heidi. 'If we step out, we should be in time for the quarter to.'

But as he set off along the familiar street, now cleared of the snow that had made walking so treacherous, a car pulled up alongside, and a voice said, 'Good. I've caught you.' It was Iris Barnes. He wondered why he wasn't more surprised. 'As it happens, I have to be in London tonight. Thought I'd save you the train journey. Not a pleasant prospect, at this time of year . . . Well, don't just stand there – get in! The dog can go in the back.'

The car – a Jaguar SS100 roadster – made short work of the seventy-odd miles between Oxford and London, and were passing through the Chilterns, when Miss Barnes said, 'I gather Reggie Fawcett brought you up to speed with the Quine affair?'

'If you mean that he intimated that Quine was killed because he was a blackmailer – then yes.'

'Excellent. Then what I'm about to tell you won't come as a surprise. We've reason to believe that the man who killed Challoner – and was being blackmailed by Quine – has been passing information to the enemy about one of our most secret operations. He – whoever he is – is a very dangerous man, Mr Rowlands.'

'Do you know who he is?'

'We have our suspicions, but there's nothing definite, as yet – except to say that he must have a connection with Oxford.' This seemed so obvious that he didn't think it needed a reply. Then she said, 'Yes, it's the one thing that all those concerned have in common – that they were all, at one time or another, members of Oxford University . . . including the man we're on our way to see,' she added casually.

'Miss Barnes . . .' He'd known all along that she must have an ulterior motive for offering him a lift to London. There was always a reason for everything she did. 'You realise that I have to deliver Major Fraser's dog to him at Regent's Park?'

'Don't worry. I'll make sure you and Heidi arrive there safely,' was the reply. 'This shouldn't delay us long.'

'I was also rather looking forward to seeing my wife,' added Rowlands glumly, resigning himself to a further delay, even as he spoke.

'Oh, you'll see her very soon, I promise you that,' said Miss Barnes. 'You know it's funny,' she added, apropos of nothing. 'To be working together again, I mean. I think we make rather a good team.'

The miles sped past. The steep hills and winding country roads of Oxfordshire and Buckinghamshire gave way to a more urban landscape. From the increase in the volume of traffic, Rowlands guessed they must have entered the outskirts of London, and the dreary reaches of Acton, Hammersmith and Notting Hill. Now their progress was impeded by traffic lights along the Edgware Road, Oxford Street and Park Lane. 'Not far to go now,' said Miss Barnes, after another stop-and-start interval. 'Here's Birdcage Walk. Next stop, the Air Ministry.' Although why she was taking him there, and what it had to do with the grisly happenings at an Oxford college, he'd no idea. Well, he'd find out soon enough, he thought.

Having pulled into one of the parking bays outside the ministry – which Rowlands guessed was one of those anonymous white stone edifices put up since the last war – they were ordered by a sentry to state their names and purpose. Barely checking her stride, Miss Barnes brandished her pass, and the RAF officer drew back, muttering apologies.

'This way. We'll find him in his office, no doubt. He never seems to leave it. God knows where or when he sleeps . . .' She led the way across a slippery marble floor to a bank of lifts. 'Fifth floor,' she said to the lift attendant. 'We're expected.'

Disgorged onto the fifth floor, they traversed a linoleum-lined corridor, then another at right angles to it, and came at last to a door. Without knocking, Miss Barnes opened it, and went in. 'Hello, Victor,' she said to the man whose office it was. 'I've brought someone to see you. This is Frederick Rowlands. He's the one I told you about, who's been looking into the Oxford murders.'

'Ah, yes,' said a voice – a young man's voice, thought Rowlands, surprised at this. 'Poor Don Challoner. Beastly way to go. Pleased to meet you, Mr Rowlands. I'm VR Smith. I've been taking an interest in the case myself.'

Chapter Thirteen

'Take a pew,' said Victor Smith – or 'VR' as he evidently preferred to be known. 'They haven't given me the most luxurious of quarters, but there are chairs, as you can see . . . I'd offer you coffee, only Dolly – that's the boss's secretary – isn't here to make it. I've some Scotch, though, if you'd care for a snifter? There's just the one glass, so we'd have to share.' When both his visitors declined the whisky, he poured what was left in the bottle into the glass, and took a swig. 'Just as well neither of you drink,' he said cheerfully. 'There's only enough left for one, as it is . . . Now, what were we saying? Ah yes. Murder most foul. One man stabbed in the back, the other with his throat cut from ear to ear. Horrid sanguinary stuff. You'll be asking yourself, I imagine,' he went on, addressing Rowlands, 'what all this has to do with me – a mere scientist, or "boffin", as I believe we're called by the man in the street, damn his eyes.'

Rowlands was indeed starting to wonder what

connection the Oxford murders could have to this excitable young man, who sounded as if the drink had already gone to his head, when the latter said suddenly, 'What do you know about radiographic beams, Mr Rowlands?'

'Absolutely nothing.' Rowlands smiled. 'But then I'm not a boffin.'

'Ha ha! Very good, Fred! I may call you Fred, mayn't I? It might surprise you to know that your ignorance is shared by many of the most eminent men in the land – some very big cheeses indeed – including the air minister, the chief of air staff, the leaders of Fighter Command and Bomber Command . . . not to mention the big cheese himself, our very own, best-beloved PM . . .'

'Victor!' said Iris Barnes sharply.

'All these important men, as well as others too numerous to list – members of the scientific fraternity, political bigwigs, chiefs of staff and the rest – know as little about the matter as our old friend "the man on the Clapham omnibus". At least,' concluded Smith, whom Rowlands was beginning to realise had a high opinion of no one but himself, 'he has an excuse for his ignorance! When I tell you, Fred, that all these fellows I've just mentioned sat around the table in the Cabinet Room at Downing Street and simply goggled at me, when I tried to explain a few basic facts pertaining to the defence of this country, you will realise what depths of stupidity we are up against.'

'I do wish you'd stop preening yourself in this unlovely fashion, and get to the point,' said Miss Barnes. 'We haven't got all night.'

'I was just about to,' was the reply. 'However,' he went on, picking up his narrative as if there had been no interruption, 'one man in that room had the good sense or vision to realise that what he was hearing from me wasn't just some fantasy of Mr Wells's – but the plain truth.' He was silent a moment, as if contemplating that fact. 'We are fortunate to have such a leader in times like these. He – Winston – saw at once that what I was proposing might turn the tide of war in England's favour. The uncomfortable fact was that our enemies were already using the beams to pinpoint targets across the British Isles and so—'

'You still haven't explained how these "beams" work,' put in Miss Barnes impatiently.

'Haven't I?' VR Smith gave a chuckle. 'I forget who I've told and who I haven't told, sometimes. Well, it's very simple. The beams are radio beams, projected from two different sources – radio transmitters, located in, say, northern France or . . . or western Germany. The beams form a kind of pathway in the sky, along which the Luftwaffe can fly its planes in the certain knowledge that, where the two beams intersect to form an X, there they can drop their bombs, and those bombs will hit the target. X marks the spot, in a very real sense!

'To make matters worse,' went on Smith in a cheerful tone, 'the Germans didn't stop at having two beams – they now have three, which gives them greater accuracy, with consequent greater loss of life. You'll remember Coventry . . .'

'Of course.' The bombing of that city, a little over a year before, was something that Rowlands, along with the rest of the country, would never forget.

'We could have prevented Coventry,' said Smith, 'if the

circumstances had worked in our favour. Unfortunately, they did not. Manchester was another failure. But we are getting better at doing what we set out to do.'

'Which is what?'

'Jamming the radio frequencies,' was the reply. 'Thus rendering the beams ineffective. In common with most of the British public, Fred, you doubtless think that it is the efforts of our gallant RAF night-fighters in the air, combined with the action of anti-aircraft guns on the ground, that protects our cities from being pounded into dust. But it isn't so. It is in fact the counter-measures that we in what might laughingly be termed the "scientific community" – the boffins, if you like – have put in place against the beams that have protected us and saved lives.

'Now,' he said, 'we face another challenge. You are blind, aren't you, Fred? I noticed it as soon as you came in.' He laughed. 'The dog was a clue, of course! Anyway. Imagine, if you will, the crew of a German night-fighter – a Dornier, say. How do you, the pilot, spot your target – call it a British Wellington – in the dark? You are blind (forgive my labouring the point). What can you do? Then imagine that your plane is fitted with a radar system that acts as a kind of seeing-eye dog . . . What is the dog's name, by the way?'

Rowlands told him.

'Heidi! A good German name. Almost as good as Freya . . .'

Iris Barnes made a warning sound in her throat.

'All right, all right. I'll be good,' said Smith. 'Yes,' he went on. 'Suppose that you, the pilot of the Dornier, can now rely on his "Heidi" device to see in the dark, and be guided to his target . . .' His voice had assumed a dreamy quality. 'Can't you see what a difference that would make to the war in the air?'

Rowlands said that he saw that perfectly.

'Of course you do. You're an intelligent man,' said the other. 'So you will also see how essential it is that we get hold of one of these German radar transmitters and take it apart.'

Rowlands was reminded of a small boy, enthusing about the properties of his new crystal set. He wondered how old VR could be – he sounded about twenty-five, although he was probably nearer thirty. Not a great deal older than the Oxford undergraduates now marking time at the university before signing up for their own share of military glory.

'We'll have to capture one, of course – they're dotted all along the French coast.'

Another admonitory sniff from Miss Barnes.

'Which brings me to the crux of the matter,' Smith went on. 'If we're to get our chaps into France – and don't ask me how we're going to manage that, because I don't know – then it's vital that news of the operation, which is likely to take place within the next six to eight weeks, doesn't become known to our enemies. Iris here has told me that you've been doing good work, Fred, tracking down the fellow who killed Don Challoner . . . and the other bloke. Not that I care two hoots about him – dirty little blackmailer! So it stands to reason that you must keep up the good work, and find this man – whoever he is – who's been selling British secrets to the Germans. I can't tell you how catastrophic it would be for the war effort, if he were to get wind of Operation B—'

'Victor! That's enough,' said Iris Barnes sternly. 'I think you've told Mr Rowlands all he needs to know.'

'You may be right,' said Smith. 'It doesn't do to confuse people with too much information, I've learnt. Just keep your ear to the ground, Fred, and sing out the minute you come across anything untoward—'

'But what kind of thing?' interrupted Rowlands. 'I've only just heard about these "beams" of yours, and I don't know the first thing about radio transmitters. The only thing I discovered while I was staying at Brasenose College was that someone is very anxious to suppress the fact that his name may be one of those listed in a certain green file.'

'Precisely,' was the reply. 'Find him, and you've found our traitor. I don't doubt that he'll be keen to impress his masters by passing on a juicy bit of intelligence. That can't be allowed to happen. As for what to look for – or listen out for, in your case – any mention of France, or French place names, however casually, should be regarded as suspicious. Ditto references to "radar", "Freya" or "Würzburg", or any talk of secret operations.'

'Mr Smith . . .'

'VR, please!'

'VR, then. I don't know what Miss Barnes has told you about me, but I'm not a member of the Secret Service, just an ordinary civilian. My blindness means that people sometimes confide in me – and often underestimate me – but it doesn't give me any particular advantage when it comes to finding things out . . . rather the reverse, in fact.'

'I don't agree. How was it that you identified this

famous green file – which I gather is still missing?'

'It was the smell that alerted me. It was one of those rescued from the fire at Wormwood Scrubs. It smelt of burning. But that doesn't mean . . .'

'My dear Fred, it means everything! A man who can – quite literally – sniff out a secret document, and then realise that it's the clue that will lead him to a murderer, is the kind of man I want working for me.'

Iris Barnes gave a cough. It was enough to bring the excitable Smith back down to earth.

'All right, I get the message. Fred here is a free agent. But I do want to be kept informed if he "sniffs out" anything else that has a bearing on the case.'

'You can trust me for that,' said Miss Barnes. 'We'll be on our way. I'll be in touch. Till then, do try and stay out of mischief, Victor. You don't do your cause any good by antagonising the very people you need to support it.'

'Oh, you know me,' laughed VR Smith. 'I get on with everybody. It's the others that don't always get on with me. It was good to meet you, Fred,' he added, vigorously shaking Rowlands's hand. 'I see what Iris means about your being a man she can trust.'

In the lift on the way down, Rowlands was silent, thinking about what he'd heard; nor did his companion break the silence. It was only as they left the building, emerging into the chill January night, that Miss Barnes spoke at last. 'Well,' she said, with a little laugh in which admiration was mingled with exasperation. 'That was the great VR Smith! You might not think it, but he'll probably win us the war.'

* * *

166

It was a twenty-minute car journey from Whitehall to Regent's Park – a journey extended only slightly by their having to avoid certain streets that were still unsafe due to bomb damage. 'They've done a pretty good job of clearing up, after the raids last May,' said Iris Barnes, as the Jaguar sped along Charing Cross Road. 'Of course, a lot of the buildings are still boarded up . . . those that aren't damaged beyond repair. But on the whole,' she went on, as they turned along Oxford Street, 'it all looks a lot better than one might have expected. Even dear old John Lewis has got its window displays up again.' She laughed. 'It really was rather an uncanny sight, seeing it after the bombing, with all the plate-glass windows blown out, and mannequins scattered across the pavement. They looked like dead bodies. Rather grim. Although not as grim as the real thing, of course. You'll remember how badly the East End was hit . . .'

'All right,' said Rowlands. 'I get the message. And I do want to be of help. But I still don't see what I can do that I haven't already done. I mean, I don't have any reason for returning to Oxford. As for tracking down documents relating to some top-secret military operation, involving beams, or radar, or whatever you call it, I haven't the first idea how to go about it.'

'Don't worry,' said Miss Barnes. 'I'd no intention of asking you to go back to Oxford. You've already done us some valuable service. Time to let the younger generation take over. How well do you know Angela Thompson?'

'Not very well,' replied Rowlands guardedly. The last thing he wanted was to drop his young friend 'in it'. 'We've had a drink once or twice, for old times' sake. We met years ago in Cambridge – when Angela was an undergraduate. I was caught up in a case, then . . .'

'Yes. The St Gertrude's murders,' she said. Was there anything she didn't know?

'That's right,' he said. 'I haven't seen her in all that time – until now.'

'You know that she works for us?'

He admitted that he did.

'Of course she was there that day in the registry, when I was showing you around. Naturally you didn't see her, but she recognised you all right.'

'What's she got to do with all this? You're not telling me you're going to ask her to spy for you?'

'She's proved herself to be very competent,' was the reply. 'Nearly there, now. Here's Portland Place. You know, I still can't get used to seeing Broadcasting House surrounded by sandbags. It took a direct hit during the Blitz. Nine people killed.'

'It's too dangerous,' said Rowlands, ignoring this last remark. 'She's just a girl.'

'She's a capable young woman. We've been keeping an eye on her for a while, now. She's wasted doing routine clerical work. Time she was given a chance to spread her wings.'

'He's killed two people already. He won't stop at a third, either.'

'There's always an element of risk in this game,' said Iris Barnes. 'Ah, here we are! St John's Lodge. I expect you'll be glad to see your old haunts again, Mr Rowlands.'

Returning to the St Dunstan's HQ – where Rowlands had been an inmate for the first two years of his blindness, and which had become his place of work for ten years after that – was always a pleasure, not least because it meant seeing his old friend Ian Fraser again. Now, however, that pleasure was mingled with anxiety, as he thought how ill the major had been – knowing only too well how often, for men of their generation, a seemingly minor illness could turn into something worse. He'd lost too many friends of late – some, like himself, still in their early fifties – worn down by chronic ill-health, made worse by the exigencies of wartime.

But when the housekeeper, Mrs Britcher, ushered them in – exclaiming at how perishing cold it was, and how they'd better come in quick if they didn't want to catch their deaths – there was a surprise waiting. Sitting opposite the major in his place by the fire was someone else who had been occupying his thoughts for the past few days. 'Hello, Fred.'

'Edith! Well, this is grand!'

'We felt, Iris and I, that as you'd been detained in Oxford so long – for which I'm largely to blame – the very least we could do was to invite you to break the journey here – and get your good lady to come and meet you,' said the major. 'Hello, Heidi old girl,' he said, patting the dog. 'I hope you've been good for my friend Rowlands?'

'She's behaved impeccably,' said the latter. 'Major . . . Lady Fraser . . . I don't know if you've met Miss Barnes?'

'Oh, we're old friends, aren't we?' said the major's wife, coming forward to greet the other woman. 'We Irises must stick together. A very floral generation, wasn't it, with all its Roses, Poppies and Lilies? Although of course we're hardly the same generation, are we, my dear? I suppose flower names have always been popular . . .'

'It's lovely to see you again,' said Iris Barnes. 'You, too, Uncle Ian.' She kissed them both. 'Although I ought to be quite cross with you, for neglecting your health so badly.'

'I've been scolding him, too,' said Iris Fraser. 'He knows he's not budging from that fireside until he's completely better. Now then. Who's for a sherry before dinner?'

As the five of them sat over their drinks, while the estimable Mrs B put the finishing touches to the meal, Rowlands reflected wryly on how small the secret world turned out to be. It shouldn't have surprised him that the Frasers knew Iris Barnes, nor that the major, one of his own closest friends, should be 'Uncle Ian' to her, just as the Duke of Marlborough was 'Bert'.

'What's so funny?' said Edith in an undertone.

'Oh, nothing,' he said. Having touched on Lady Fraser's recent visit to Brasenose ('Those mediaeval quadrangles – quite lovely, but frightfully chilly'), the conversation had turned to a spirited discussion of the merits or otherwise of an Oxford education.

'Of course, I read classics,' said Iris Fraser. 'Much good it did me when it came to rolling bandages and making beds as a young – and very green – VAD.'

'It's given you a fine head for crossword clues, however,' put in her husband. 'Not that my own MA in history had benefitted me particularly . . . You were at the Sorbonne, weren't you, my dear?'

This to Iris Barnes, who replied with customary insouciance, 'Yes, I was there for a year or two, during Daddy's posting to Paris. I don't think I learnt much – apart from how not to get on in polite society.'

'Your French is no worse for it,' said her 'Uncle Ian' fondly. 'Always a useful thing to have, languages.' With which Rowlands could only silently concur, having also had evidence of Miss Barnes's proficiency in Spanish and German.

'All this talk of our undergraduate days is very dull,' said his hostess, perhaps realising that two of her guests, not having had the advantage of a university education, were barred from joining in the conversation. 'How are your delightful daughters getting on these days, Edith? I gather Margaret's doing very well . . .'

Edith said that her eldest child was certainly working very hard. Nothing was said about what it was that Margaret was actually doing – nor where she was doing it – although Rowlands was sure that everyone in the room had at least a fair idea. But that was the secret world for you, he thought. Everything was known – or guessed at – and nothing was said. 'Anne seems to be settling in nicely to her job, too,' he said. 'I must say, when I had daughters, I never expected that I'd have to see them take such an active role in the war effort.'

'Times have changed, since our war,' said Ian Fraser. 'The women are just as much a part of things as the men, now.'

Chapter Fourteen

Two weeks had passed since that cosy fireside chat with his old friends, and all that had been said – and left unsaid. Back in the office, Rowlands was soon immersed in the day-to-day routine of work, with little time to dwell on what might be happening in Oxford. Just then, he was preoccupied with organising the training programme for some of the new generation of St Dunstaners – young men recently blinded in action, and about to be discharged from the purpose-built St Dunstan's building at Ovingdean, now requisitioned as a hospital.

Men like Flight Lieutenant Bob Simmons, who'd been flying his Hurricane over enemy territory when a Heinkel coming the other way had shot out his windscreen, shattering the Perspex. A fragment had taken out his left eye; the other, although damaged, had since been saved by the surgeons. Half-blinded and in pain, Simmons had managed to fly the seventy miles back to base, and to land the plane, before losing consciousness. 'I was bloody lucky,' he'd said, describing this incident from his hospital bed. 'If I'd blacked out any sooner, I'd have landed in the drink, instead of on terra firma.' He was hoping to go back to the RAF – 'when these bandages are off' – to a desk job, if they'd have him.

Then there was seventeen-year-old Joe Horrocks – blinded when an incendiary bomb went off in the street where he was patrolling with the Home Guard. 'I'd a month to go before I turned eighteen,' he'd said, unable to keep the bitterness out of his voice. 'I was going to join up – Royal Sussex Regiment – now I never will.'

Rowlands, recalling his own anger and pain after he'd been invalided home, when the realisation of his own 'uselessness' had hit him, knew that no consoling words would make the lad feel better. 'Oh, we'll put you to work, never fear,' he said briskly, keeping any trace of sympathy out of his voice. There was nothing worse than being pitied. 'I learnt Braille and typewriting when I wasn't much older than you are. There are jobs you'll be fit for – good jobs, too – if you apply yourself and get down to it.'

Nor was it just the young that needed help and support. Some of the veterans of the Great War – Rowlands's contemporaries – had enrolled in the Home Guard, doing guard-room duties, looking after armouries and carrying out other essential tasks not restricted to the sighted. Others were proving their worth as roof-spotters, listening out for the distinctive sounds of approaching enemy aircraft, when visibility was poor – the blind having trained their hearing to better effect than those who relied solely on their eyes. St Dunstan's men manned stirrup-pumps, when the incendiaries were falling like a terrible rain on

British towns. 'If you've lived through being shelled by the Hun, a few sticks of incendiary bombs are nothing,' said Alf Foster, another of Rowlands's charges, now in his late sixties. He, along with many of the older generation, had a wife and family to support. Alf's day job was as a market gardener – essential in these days of food shortages.

Although it wasn't the season for growing vegetables, thought Rowlands, as, walking stick in hand, he trudged along the icy streets to get to the office. As ever, he avoided the seafront, which was becoming more and more like a military encampment, with its barbed wire and gun emplacements. He wondered when the day would come when the town returned to its earlier, happier, incarnation as a seaside resort. It was hard to believe – with both the piers half-dismantled and the beaches out of bounds. There was always the sea, he reminded himself, drawing in a deep breath of the cold, salt-tasting air. That, at least, was unchanged, even if its recreational aspects – bathing, sailing – had been superseded in the past two-and-a-half years by its function as a barrier against the foe.

In the St George's Street office he found Miss Bates, busily typing up some letters from her shorthand notes. He greeted her, and hung up his coat and scarf. 'Anything new?' he asked.

'Well it looks as if the Russians are doing awfully well,' she said. 'They've beaten back the Jerries outside Moscow.'

'That's good news. But I meant the Home Front.'

'Oh! Nothing much. I think that John . . . that is, Mr Harvey . . . said he'd pop in and see if we needed anything done.' She sounded faintly embarrassed.

'Good. You can ask him to move those boxes out of the

office,' said Rowlands. 'I keep tripping over them. How's his telephony training going?'

'Quite well, I believe,' was the demure reply. Rowlands smiled to himself. John Harvey was one of their recent recruits – having been invalided out of the army following an accident during training that had left him blind. At Rowlands's suggestion, he'd started learning to use a switchboard – which had been the former's own job when he'd first left St Dunstan's. In between classes for this and other necessary skills, young Harvey had been 'popping in' to the office on a regular basis. Might as well make himself useful, he'd said, given that there wasn't much else he was fit for except manhandling packing cases. He hated being idle. This was doubtless true, but Rowlands thought that the presence of the cheerful Mavis Bates might be another reason for the young man's frequent visits to St George's Street.

They worked on, in companionable silence. After a fortnight back at work, Rowlands felt as if he had never left. 'Have the orders come in from the War Office for those camouflage nets?' he asked the secretary – the manufacture of such nets being one of the tasks for which St Dunstaners' manual dexterity fitted them.

'Yes, Mr Rowlands. They came in this morning. I'll just look them out . . .'

The telephone rang. 'I'll answer it,' he called, since she was busy going through the order book. 'St Dunstan's After-Care. May I help you?'

'That Frederick Charles Rowlands?' demanded a gruff voice he couldn't place at first.

'Speaking,' he replied.

'Ah. Your wife said as I'd find you there.'

'Who is this?'

'Inspector Dimmock, Oxford City Police. I'd like a word with you, sir, at your earliest convenience.'

It felt strange to be back in Oxford. Most of the snow had disappeared, but it was still bitterly cold – an icy wind whistled along the High, as Rowlands arrived at the Mitre Hotel, where he had booked a room for the night. He reflected wryly that his impression of the university city was far from being the rose-tinted idyll of popular perception. There'd been that visit to Blackwell's before the last war – that had been a broiling hot day all right! He remembered how uncomfortable he'd felt in his dark suit and stiff collar, among the dawdling undergraduates in their white flannels and blazers. Oxford itself had been at its most beautiful – a fairy-tale city, built of golden stone. Recent experience had shown him a very different place – cold, dark and full of secrets.

Collecting his key at the hotel desk, he decided to leave his overnight bag in his room, and have a quick wash and brush-up, before making his way to his appointment. It was getting on for lunchtime when he descended the stairs from the second floor of the rambling old building, and he decided he'd time for a pint and something to eat, before presenting himself at the police station. From the bar to one side of the lobby, he could hear the jovial conversation of those already installed there. Some of them, he judged, were commercial travellers, of the type that, in the not-too-distant past, kept such establishments going. He wondered how much the demand for fancy goods had diminished in recent times, knowing how the war had affected sales of items that had previously been St Dunstan's stock-in-trade: the pen-wipers, needle cases, raffia baskets and containers for pipe-cleaners manufactured in their thousands by their home workers.

Here in Oxford, there was evidently still a market for such domestic goods – at least if the two men standing at the bar were to be believed. 'Six dozen best quality pillowcases . . . and a further six dozen to follow if they sell 'em,' said a voice rich and throaty from beer and cigarettes. 'Call that a nice morning's work, I do!'

'Mine wasn't so dusty, neither,' said the other man, with a wheezing laugh. 'Twenty-four pairs of satin cami-knickers at nineteen-and-eleven the pair. Sold the lot to Boswells in Cornmarket Street . . .'

Rising above the general murmur were the voices of servicemen – whether RAF or army, Rowlands couldn't tell.

'Make mine a double, will you? I've had a rough day . . .'

'Rough night more like! What time did you get in this morning?'

'Never you mind, old boy.' Raucous laughter followed this sally, which was evidently a satire on the Oxford manner, for other – even less convincing – impersonations ensued. 'Frightfully, frightfully sorreah, old chep . . .'

'I say, let me pass, won't you?' said someone else – this one with a genuinely 'Oxford' accent. 'I've been trying to get to the bar for the past five minutes.' The voice was familiar. As Rowlands was trying to place it, the speaker must have noticed him, for he said, 'Well, blow me down! If it isn't the very man I've been wanting to see!'

'Hello, Lieutenant Bawden. Yes, I've just arrived.'

'What'll you have?'

'No, let me get them. I owe you a drink.'

'Nonsense. The debt's all on my side.'

From which Rowlands gathered that Peter Bawden's courtship of the lovely Angela Thompson had met with some success. 'Ginger! Jumbo! Over here!' called the young man. A moment later they were joined by the aforementioned officers – respectively, Second Lieutenant Robert Jarvis ('Ginger' to his friends) and Lieutenant John Barker (alias 'Jumbo'). All, Rowlands surmised, members of the Junior Staff Officers' School, currently billeted at Brasenose.

'So what brings you to Oxford?' said Bawden, as the four of them sipped their pints. Knowing it might be his last chance to get any lunch, Rowlands had also bought himself a meat and potato pie, which seemed to consist mainly of potato. 'Don't tell me you're investigating another murder?'

Rowlands swallowed a mouthful of pie. 'What makes you ask that?'

'Oh, just a wild guess,' was the reply. 'After all, you were the man who found the other bodies and so I thought . . .'

'You're letting your imagination run away with you, Lieutenant Bawden.'

'But you are a detective, aren't you? Angela said . . .'

'Whatever Miss Thompson may have told you about me has no bearing on the present case,' said Rowlands firmly. 'It was pure coincidence that I happened to be on the scene when Professor Challoner's and Dr Quine's bodies were found.'

'But that's not—'

'Bodies? What's all this about bodies?' interjected Ginger Jarvis, cutting across his friend's protest. He guffawed. 'Sounds like something out of Mrs Christie's latest.'

'I say,' put in Jumbo Barker. 'Are you really a detective?'

But Rowlands, having disposed of his pie and pint, was now on his feet. 'Good to see you again, Lieutenant Bawden. Perhaps I'll see you around. Give my regards to Miss Thompson, won't you?'

It was a ten-minute walk from the High to the Oxford City Police Station in St Aldate's, and Rowlands was there by two o'clock. Having presented himself to the sergeant at the desk, he was directed to take a seat, joining a row of others also waiting, with varying degrees of patience. One woman, who'd come to lodge a complaint against a neighbour for persistently ignoring blackout regulations – 'and that useless ARP warden never takes a blind bit of notice' – sat muttering imprecations against all and sundry to the woman next to her, 'People just don't care these days, that's the trouble. No public spirit . . .'

It seemed to Rowlands that the war – while bringing out the best in some – had also given encouragement to what Jane Austen had called 'voluntary spies', of which this woman was an example. Half an hour wore on. A man came to report that his car had been stolen. 'It's an Austin 7. Four years old. I only left it for a minute, when I nipped into the newsagent's to pay my paper bill . . .' A woman whose cat had disappeared said she was convinced it had been lured away by German agents. The desk sergeant said they would look into it. 'That's the third time she's been in this week,' he murmured to no one in particular. Somebody rang to report a break-in at their shop premises. 'Nothing stolen, you say? All right, I'll ask the constable on that beat to keep an eye out for any suspicious activity.'

'Frederick Rowlands? Inspector Dimmock will see you now.'

'Wonder what *he's* done,' muttered the woman who'd complained about the blackout, as Rowlands followed the young policeman out. 'Black marketeer, from the look of 'im, wouldn't you say, Elsie?'

Ushered into the inspector's office, Rowlands was subjected to another five minutes' delay, while the former shuffled through the papers on his desk. 'Smoke if you like,' he grunted, then, as the other lit up, 'How well did you know William Dobbs?'

'Not well,' said Rowlands, noting that Dimmock had used the past tense. 'Why? What's happened?'

'Only *he* seems to have been on familiar terms with *you*,' the inspector went on, ignoring the question. 'To hear him talk, anyone would have thought you two were thick as thieves.' He gave a satirical emphasis to the last word that Rowlands didn't like.

'Inspector,' he said, 'I don't know what you're implying, but I hardly knew Mr Dobbs, except in his professional capacity. He looked after Sir Ian's dog for me while I was staying at Brasenose two weeks ago. And as you know, it was he who alerted me to the fact of Dr Quine's death . . .'

'Indeed,' said the inspector. 'Indeed.' He made it sound as if he'd scored a point. Rowlands had had enough of this. 'I wish you'd tell me what this is all about,' he said. 'Has something happened to Mr Dobbs?' All Dimmock had told him on the telephone was that it was a 'matter of extreme urgency' that he should return to Oxford.

Now the policeman dropped his bantering tone. 'William Dobbs was found hanged late Tuesday night,' he said brusquely, then, in a milder tone, 'I can see that the news has come as a shock to you, Mr Rowlands.'

'Of course it's a shock! Who found him?'

'One of the army lot, coming back to the college after a heavy night. Gave him no end of a nasty turn,' added the policeman, with grim satisfaction.

Rowlands felt a jolt of sympathy for the unfortunate Junior Staff Officer. 'I'm sure it did. Did Dobbs leave a note?'

'You and your notes!' chuckled the inspector. 'No, there wasn't a note.'

'Then I don't see . . .'

'. . . where you come into it?' the other finished for him. 'I'll tell you. The night before he did away with himself, Dobbs went out drinking. It was his night off. Not that he was a great one for the drink, but this time he made an exception, according to others that were there – one of them being Ron Harkness, landlord at The Bear, where Dobbs fetched up. He'd had quite a skinful by then, Harkness said. He was buying drinks for all and sundry, too. Acting as if he'd come into money. That's when your name came up.'

'Mine?'

'Didn't I just say so? Oh yes,' went on the inspector with some relish. 'Way Bill Dobbs was telling it, you and him was best mates. "I've done him a favour, I have," he said to anyone who'd listen. "He'll see me right, will Mr Frederick Rowlands." I suppose none of this means anything to you?' said Dimmock slyly.

'You suppose correctly.'

'So there was nothing in his talk about a "green file"?'

Rowlands's heart sank. 'He mentioned that, did he?'

'He did indeed. Knew where it was to be found, too, he said. He'd just have to hand it over, and then you'd "see him right" . . . Is that how it was, Mr Rowlands? He'd found something you wanted to get your hands on, and you said you'd make it worth his while?'

Rowlands almost groaned aloud. That poor fool, Dobbs! What had he unleashed? 'I suppose I'd better tell you what I know,' he said. He'd never found it so hard to keep his expression impassive.

'I suppose you had,' said the inspector. 'And not before time.'

Having already decided to say nothing of his visit to the Air Ministry, and his meeting with VR Smith, nor of what the latter had told him about the plans for Operation B, Rowlands kept his account of the events leading up to the discovery of the green file – if one could call it a 'discovery' when the object in question hadn't actually been physically present – and why he'd kept the information to himself. 'I knew that the late Professor Challoner worked for MI5,' he said. 'So when he told me about the file as he was dying, I guessed it must have a bearing on his murder.'

'Yet you didn't think to mention this to the police?' The inspector's tone was one of barely controlled anger.

'No. That is, I . . .' *Trust no one*. 'I only realised how important it was after Dr Quine's death,' said Rowlands. 'It seemed obvious to me that the file had recently been in Quine's possession, and so . . .'

'Ah, yes. It was the smell of the thing that gave it away,

you said.' Dimmock's tone was sarcastic.

'Precisely. I decided that, as it was clear to me that possession of the file had led directly to two suspicious deaths, I ought to inform MI5 of my findings. It seemed the most direct approach,' added Rowlands, when the inspector said nothing.

When the latter replied at last, it was with a grudging respect hitherto absent from their exchanges. 'So you marched right into the lion's den?' He chuckled. 'Rather you than me, Mr Rowlands! I'm just a simple policeman, trying to do my duty. I steer clear of that crowd up at the palace as much as I can.'

Rowlands smiled.

'But you see my problem?' the other went on. 'I've another death on my hands – a death that, until now, I'd every reason to suppose was a suicide. Quite unconnected – so I thought – to MI5, or any of that "most secret" caper. Although,' he went on, in a ruminative tone, 'I won't say that there weren't a few suspicious circumstances surrounding Dobbs's death that I might've been about to look into. For instance, how did a man with only one arm manage to string himself up so effectively? He was found hanging from one of the coat-hooks in the lobby off the porter's lodge. Used his own belt. Choked hisself,' added the inspector with casual brutality. 'Anyhow, be that as it may, it seemed as if he'd died by his own hand, after having a few beers too many. Now you're telling me that there's a connection between William Dobbs's suicide (call it that) and the deaths of two members of the same college – the connection being this green file of yours . . .'

'Yes.'

'I'm not saying that if you'd spoken up a bit quicker about what you knew, Dobbs's death might have been prevented, but you do see how it looks to an outsider? Because apart from this blessed file – which nobody appears to have actually seen – the only other link between those three deaths is yourself, Mr Rowlands.'

It had been a *mauvais quart d'heure* all right, thought Rowlands, as he retraced his steps along St Aldate's. Of course he blamed himself for not warning Dobbs to keep quiet about what he knew – but how was he to know the poor fool would go blabbing to all and sundry about the wretched green file, and where it was to be found? It was always easy to be wise after the event.

The interview with the inspector had ended on a cautionary note. Having told Rowlands that he should remain in Oxford, in case they needed to call him for the inquest, Dimmock had added, 'You'd better watch yerself, Mr Rowlands. This man has already killed three people, as far as we know. I wouldn't want to see him make it a fourth.'

'I'll do my best to stay out of trouble,' said Rowlands.

'Do that,' was the reply. 'Because if Dobbs was at a disadvantage – having only one arm – when it came to defending himself, you're at a worse one, if you'll permit me to say so.'

Dimmock's words were ringing in Rowlands's ears as he reached the High, and entered the hotel once more. It had occurred to him that the inspector's warning applied to someone other than himself – someone who remained unaware of how dangerous it was for anyone asking questions about the whereabouts of the green file . . . The question posed itself: how to deliver that warning in the shortest possible time?

His first thought was to find Peter Bawden – although he hadn't much hope that the army officer would still be in situ, since it was now well past closing time, and the bar of the Mitre was deserted. The landlord, busily polishing brasswork, was applied to, but could offer no useful suggestions as to where Rowlands could find the young man. 'He's one o' them Brasenose lot, is all I know. Comes in here quite frequent, he does, with them other lads. Might be out at Port Meadow by now. That's where the army's carrying out manoeuvres, so I'm told.'

When Rowlands asked if his room might be available for another night or two, the landlord said that it was – 'seeing as we're not exackly swamped with visitors'. Rowlands thanked him, and decided to make Brasenose his next port of call, even though the chances of finding Bawden there were slim. But he could at least leave a message . . . When he reached his destination a few minutes later, it was to find his way barred by a uniformed policeman. 'Sorry, sir, but you can't go in there,' said the constable, planting his solid, serge-clad form between Rowlands and the gate. 'Police investigation in progress.'

Rowlands said that he understood this, but that he had an urgent message to deliver. 'I know it might sound ridiculous. But it really is a matter of life and death.'

'I'm sure it is, sir,' said the officer in a soothing tone. 'But it'd be more'n my life's worth to let you pass. You're not a member of the college staff – and you don't look like an undergrad, neither,' he added, guffawing at his own joke.

185

'If I could just leave a note at the porter's lodge . . .' began Rowlands.

'Porter's dead,' was the trenchant reply. 'Done 'isself in, poor bugger. So there's no one to leave a note with, sir. Maybe you could post a letter?'

'A letter might be too late.' Exasperated, Rowlands was starting to walk away, when a voice he recognised hailed him.

'Hello there! You! I've forgotten your name, but you're the man who can perfectly describe a room that he can't actually see. Most of us with eyes couldn't do half as good a job.'

'Dr Ponsonby-Smythe,' said Rowlands. 'How very nice to see you again.'

Chapter Fifteen

'Well, come in, if you're coming in,' said the vice-principal. 'I take it you have business in college?'

'Yes. That is . . .'

'Splendid. This gentleman is with me,' said Ponsonby-Smythe to the dumbfounded constable, as he sailed past (the word was peculiarly apposite, thought Rowlands, for a man wearing a doctor's gown). 'We'll have tea in my rooms,' he called back over his shoulder, as Rowlands hurried to catch up with him. 'I suppose,' he went on, as they crossed the quadrangle, 'that you'll have heard about our latest embarrassment?'

Rowlands guessed that he was referring to the porter's death. 'I've just come from the police station,' he said. 'Inspector Dimmock told me what had happened.'

'Ah yes. The admirable Dimmock.' The vice-principal lingered on the last word as if it were the name of some rare species of bird. 'I imagine,' he added, as they passed under an archway, 'that you must spend a good deal of your time fraternising with the likes of dear old Dimmock.'

Rowlands admitted that this was so.

'We go up here,' said Ponsonby-Smythe as they reached the foot of a staircase. 'First floor. I insisted on these rooms as a condition of accepting my present post. They're rather more spacious than the average set – so useful for entertaining people to tea – and I do like to spread myself a bit . . . I'm something of a collector, you know. Oh, not in a big way – these are just a few little *objets* I've found over the years, on my trips to Italy . . . Sadly,' he went on, 'there won't be any more of those, at least not while the present emergency persists. Do sit down. There's a comfortable chair two paces to your left.'

Rowlands took it.

'Yes,' continued his host. 'I'm very fond of my collection of bibelots. This charming little head, for example . . . I like to think it's School of Donatello. And this icon of the Black Madonna . . . picked up for a song in some disreputable emporium on the Rialto . . . Oh, yes, I've got some pretty pieces.'

'I wish I could see them,' said Rowlands politely. 'But your description gives me at least an idea of what the room looks like. I've been told its colour scheme is one of its most striking features. Blue and orange, isn't it?'

'Azure and amber,' Ponsonby-Smythe corrected him. 'But the overall effect is the same. Mediterranean. A glimpse of blue skies and terracotta walls . . . So necessary in this cold, grey climate, and surrounded as I am by all this cold, grey stone.' The speaker must have rung, for a moment later, a servant appeared. 'Tea for two, if you'd be so good, Thomas.' Then, to his guest, 'Do you prefer

Indian or China? Now tell me,' he went on, when the order had been given and the man had gone, 'what exactly brings you to Brasenose?'

Rowlands had already decided that he would make as little of this as possible. 'I wanted to leave a message for one of the officers billeted here. A Lieutenant Bawden.'

'Ah, yes,' said Ponsonby-Smythe vaguely. 'I believe I many have seen him about.'

'He and I know one another slightly,' Rowlands went on. 'And as I was passing, I thought . . . But it's really not important.'

'So it was pure coincidence, was it, that you happened to return to Oxford just as the unfortunate Dobbs decided to end it all?' enquired Ponsonby-Smythe slyly. 'One feels sorry for the fellow, of course – but he really couldn't have chosen a worse time, with college so short-staffed, and such a very large military element in residence . . .' They were interrupted this moment by the arrival of the tea. 'Ah, good. Thomas has brought us plenty of hot buttered toast. I hope you like hot buttered toast?'

Rowlands said that he did, very much.

'I myself think it far superior to muffins and teacakes and all the rest. I prefer mine with Gentleman's Relish – although it is also delectable on its own.'

Rowlands agreed, and the next few minutes were occupied with the business of eating and drinking, interspersed with Ponsonby-Smythe's remarks about what he saw as the deterioration of educational standards at the university, and the difficulty of preserving tradition in the face of what he called the 'creeping philistinism of progress'.

In the middle of one of these rants, he suddenly broke off, with a self-deprecating laugh. 'You will think me a dreadful old reactionary! But of course I realise that institutions such as this one cannot remain unchanged forever. Look at all the women's colleges we now have in Oxford! There was a great deal of resistance to them when they were first set up, as there was to their sister colleges in another place – something my esteemed cousin, Beryl Phillips, knows only too well.'

Rowlands said that he was afraid that this was so.

'Indeed. I must tell you that Berry – that is the name I have known her by since we were children – is rather an admirer of yours, Mr Rowlands. You see I do remember your name, after all! She – my cousin – was very struck by what she called your "moral certainty" during the time you . . . ah . . . were instrumental in solving that terrible case.'

'It's kind of Miss Phillips to remember me – although I can't claim to have "solved" the case. The police did that. I happened to be on the scene at the crucial time, that's all.'

'Oh, I think it was rather more than that! But let's not quibble.' He took a bite of toast. 'So who is it you fancy – if I might employ racing parlance – for the role of First Murderer in our own murder mystery?' Ponsonby-Smythe's languid tones did not disguise his keen interest in the answer to this question. 'I imagine you must by now have compiled a list of suspects?'

Rowlands must have looked startled, for the vice-principal laughed. 'Come, come, Mr Rowlands! No need to hold back. I'm well aware that the suspects for Professor Challoner's murder must be members of this college.'

'Well . . .'

'Unless you are of the opinion that Challoner was murdered by Dr Quine – as indeed the police were until quite recently, I understand?'

'I'm not privy to the details of the police investigation,' said Rowlands, playing for time. How much did Ponsonby-Smythe know?

The question was answered for him in the next instant, when the other said, 'Dr Summerby and I have of course been kept abreast of developments in the case over the past month – the most recent of which have indicated a shift, shall we say, in the way the evidence against Dr Quine has been construed.'

'I see,' said Rowlands.

'I believe you do. The fact is, Mr Rowlands, that certain discrepancies have become apparent, as regards Dr Quine's death . . . discrepancies of which the principal and I have become aware only through renewed questioning by the police, which has left us both with a strong impression that there is more to this case than meets the eye.'

'Yes,' said Rowlands. 'I imagine you would think that.'

'The police – as represented by that stalwart man of the people, Dimmock – have taken a peculiar interest in the question of whether or not the late Dr Quine was left-handed,' the vice-principal went on. 'A matter that would seem to have a bearing on the manner of his death. Cutting one's throat involving – it goes without saying – a degree of manual dexterity.'

'So I gather.'

'Distasteful subject, is it not? But the very fact of its having been raised shows that the police no longer regard this as a case of suicide. Which suggests that whoever killed Professor Challoner must also have killed Dr Quine, since he was physically incapable of cutting his throat with his right hand – as seems to have been done . . . But I see that none of this is news to you, Mr Rowlands – the fact that we have a double murderer on the premises.'

'No,' said Rowlands.

'Which brings me back,' said Ponsonby-Smythe, 'to my original question: whom do you suspect?'

Now it was Rowlands's turn to laugh. 'Even if I had a list of suspects, as you say, it would hardly be politic of me to advertise the fact, Dr Ponsonby-Smythe. You surely don't expect me to name names?'

'Perhaps not. But there's nothing to stop me from doing just that.'

'Do you mean you suspect somebody?'

'Oh, I suspect everybody,' he chuckled. 'One might say it was a part of my job – keeping an eye on the doings of my colleagues . . . In fact, I might be able to help you there, Mr Rowlands – since for obvious reasons you will have formed only a partial idea of the Brasenose fellowship. Might it interest you to hear my impressions of those who were present on the two nights in question – that is, the night of Professor Challoner's murder, and the night . . . it was Christmas night . . . when Dr Quine was last seen alive? I can assure you that my character sketches, although not always wholly impartial, will be as accurate as I can make them.'

'I should be interested to hear them.'

'Good. We will begin, as is only proper, with myself. Oh, yes. I realise that I must be a suspect, since I was present on both the occasions I have referred to, and might be said to have had as much – or as little – of a motive for doing away with my esteemed colleagues as, well, the rest of them. Having said that, I had nothing against Challoner, who seemed to me a pleasant enough fellow, if a little dry, the way these Secret Service types tend to be . . . No, it was the late Dr Quine with whom I had my differences. He was rather an irascible sort, as you'll have gathered. Took particular exception to some of the little soirées I organised in my rooms for the Pater Society . . . A few like-minded souls gathered together for the sake of art and beauty, and to enjoy a light collation and a few glasses of a decent vintage . . .' He sighed. 'Dr Quine complained of the noise – "carousing", as he called it – going on until the small hours. He threatened to get one of my party – a charming youth, with a penchant for reciting the poetry of Ernest Dowson – sent down for breaking bounds. Ridiculous. Yes, we did not agree on many things, Dr Quine and I. But I did not kill him.'

'No,' said Rowlands, with a smile.

'Then there is dear Dr Summerby himself—'

'I wonder,' interrupted Rowlands, 'if you would mind adding a brief physical description of each of the fellows? Only it would enable me to picture events more clearly.'

'Of course. I'm fifty-two. Tall, thin, rather stooping – too much time spent in libraries, I fear . . . I have grey hair – still plentiful, I am glad to say – and I wear pince-nez. However, I wasn't always such a specimen of what the academic life can do to a man. As a youth at this college I took to rowing – got my "blue", too – until distaste for the antics of the "hearties" made me give it up. There are only so many times one can endure a "debagging" with equanimity . . . Does that give you a picture?'

'It does. Do go on about Dr Summerby.'

'Dear old Summers! It's he who holds this college together, by sheer force of character – although you might not think it, of such a mild-mannered fellow. But where the interests of college are at stake, he has a will of iron. He had a fierce reputation as a barrister, too, before he was appointed to his present post. Oh, I have great admiration for the principal, even if he is over-fond of sport.' Ponsonby-Smythe gave a disdainful shudder. 'Quite a good cricketer, in his time . . . before his sight began to fail. Now, I fear, he is blind as a bat . . . Forgive me. One so easily slips into these crude colloquialisms.'

Rowlands inclined his head. 'One does.'

'In person: tall – a shade under six foot; tending to stoutness in his late middle-age. He wears spectacles, naturally; and he is fond – some might say, over-fond – of a glass or two . . . but you'll have gathered that. I don't believe him to be our murderer.'

'No, because he didn't leave the SCR until after Major Fraser and I had left,' said Rowlands. 'I heard him talking to Commandant Hastings as we went out.'

'Ah, so you were paying attention!' cried Ponsonby-Smythe. 'I expect you can tell me exactly who was, and who was not, in the room at any given time.'

'Only those whose voices I could hear,' was the reply.

'To be sure. Next on the list – in order of precedence, you know – is our senior tutor, Dr O'Halloran.'

'Yes,' said Rowlands. 'He was first to arrive at Professor Challoner's rooms after Major Fraser and myself. I don't think he was at dinner . . .'

'He was not. Dr O'Halloran suffers from poor digestion – he is nearly seventy, you know. He often has his meals in his room, instead of attending hall.'

Which would account for his being first at the scene, on the night of the murder, thought Rowlands. 'Go on,' he said. 'This is proving very helpful.'

'I'm so glad. Well, then there's our bursar, Dr Owen. He was out that night, I seem to recall. Welshman. Very good at his job. Efficiency the keyword. Plays the harmonium.' Ponsonby-Smith pronounced the word with a Welsh lilt. 'There is not much more to be said for him. The chaplain, Allbright, was also dining elsewhere that night, I believe. He spends more time at Christ Church than he does here.'

'I've met the Reverend Allbright.'

'Definitely a Christian of the "muscular" variety,' sniffed the vice-principal. 'Rugger player – and doesn't let one forget it! Then there's Dr Rawlinson, our tutor in philosophy. Pale, thin, sandy-haired. Aged about forty, I'd say. He was there that night, and at dinner on Christmas night, too . . . as was our lecturer in chemistry, Dr Aitken. Funny little chap. Under-sized, like a wizened child – although he must be fifty. Asthmatic. Not much to say for himself – all these scientists are the same. Dr Armstrong – our lecturer in physics – is as bad. No conversation, these people, unless it's about their precious molecules . . . What does he look like? Rather nondescript. Medium height, neither fat nor thin, with one of those faces one instantly forgets. Thirty-five or thereabouts. Last but not least is Dr Hobson. Historian. Bit of a card. Likes the sound of his own voice, but no harm in him.'

'What does he look like?' asked Rowlands, who had formed his own impression, and wanted to have it corroborated.

'Hobson? He's shortish . . . or perhaps you'd say medium height. Five foot eight or nine. Burly. Limps a bit.'

'A war wound?'

'Think he fell out of a window as an undergraduate, during some silly rag. These hearties are like overgrown children . . . But as I said, not a bad fellow, at heart. Oh! I almost forgot the venerable Dr Crawley, our professor of philosophy. Eighty, if he's a day. White-haired. Sharptongued. I don't think he'd have had the strength to kill anyone – unless it was with cutting remarks . . .'

'Thank you. I think I've got the picture.' Rowlands touched his Braille watch. It was past five o'clock. If he wanted to get to Keble in time for the return of the Blenheim bus, he ought to be making tracks. He stood up. 'Thank you for the tea, Vice-Principal.'

'I've enjoyed our talk. It's refreshing to step outside the academic circle, from time to time. Keeps one in touch with the real world.'

'Oh, one other thing: you didn't mention your subject.'

'French and Italian,' was the reply. 'But I do very little teaching these days. As for getting across to the Continent . . . well, that's no longer a possibility. Such a pity! I had some wonderful trips to Italy before the war, as I've said . . . as well as numerous visits to France, with my reading groups. There was a charming little chateau in the Loire valley one could rent for a month or two . . . Who knows if it's still there? This war has done terrible things, Mr Rowlands. Destroyed much that was precious and lovely.' Ponsonby-Smythe gave an uneasy laugh. 'I wonder if life will ever be the same?'

Exiting the college by the main gate, Rowlands pondered on what he had learnt during the past hour. Some of it was irrelevant, of course – the waspish musings of a frustrated aesthete. For Ponsonby-Smythe was certainly a fish out of water in this college of 'hearties', as he called them. Belonging to that class of Oxford men who had been young before the Great War – a time that seemed a 'land of lost content' to those privileged enough to have enjoyed its pleasures. The champagne suppers and the picnics on Boars Hill. The punting parties on the Cherwell, with young men in white flannels and striped blazers reciting poetry to the visiting sisters of their friends – or perhaps to the friends themselves – as they glided between the flowery banks . . .

Rowlands smiled to himself as he recalled what the vice-principal had said about the youth who'd liked Ernest Dowson:

I cried for madder music and for stronger wine,
But when the feast is finished and the lamps expire,
Then falls thy shadow, Cynara . . .

Yes, the feast was finished, all right, thought Rowlands, as an army lorry, full of soldiers, roared along Beaumont Street and turned, with a squealing of brakes, up St Giles'. And yet for someone like Ponsonby-Smythe, who had been a member of that fortunate set – the jeunesse dorée – the loss must have left a bitter taste.

He wondered how far he could trust the man. Not

that he suspected Ponsonby-Smythe of being a murderer – notwithstanding the latter's arch admission that there had been no love lost between himself and the late Maurice Quine. No, it was a feeling he had that the vice-principal, for all his apparent candour, had been throwing sand in his eyes. Throughout their colloquy, he'd had the distinct impression that the other had been holding something back. And why had he been so insistent on inviting Rowlands back to tea – and then quizzing him about the case? It all seemed a bit suspicious.

But that was the way things were, these days, he thought, with everyone suspecting everyone else. He was reminded of the woman in the police station who'd reported her neighbour for neglecting to put up the blackout. Had they really come to this, as a society? Shaking his head to dispel the unwelcome thought, Rowlands crossed the Broad and turned along St Giles', taking care to stay close to the wall on his right, to avoid collisions with passers-by. Even as he did so, a crowd of undergraduates came dashing out of St John's, released from their studies for the day, and no doubt heading for the Bird and Baby, or another of the local pubs.

Their voices, whether high and fluting ('I say, you fellows, hang on, won't you?') or deep and manly ('Lend us a quid, old man! I'm stony broke') seemed to him painfully young. As they shouldered their way past him, paying not the slightest attention to the old chap creeping along by the wall, he felt a rush of sadness, for the youth and strength that had once been his, and for these eager young men – children, they seemed to him – who appeared to have little awareness of how much they had to lose.

Reaching the gates of Keble, he discovered the Blenheim bus had been and gone, disgorging its cargo of female operatives, who must by now have disappeared into the Victorian red-brick reaches of the college. But when he asked at the porter's lodge, the man didn't seem to know what he was talking about. 'Blenheim Girls? I don't know nothing about any *girls*, sir! This is a college for young gentlemen, far as I'm aware . . .'

'Yes, yes, I know all that. But this is really important. I need to speak to Miss Angela Thompson – urgently, do you hear?' Then, when the other remained intransigent, 'Can I at least leave her a note?'

'You can do that, sir, for all the good it'll do,' said the porter stonily.

Of course he'd have had it dinned into him that security was of the essence, thought Rowlands, trying to control his exasperation. 'Look, if you could just see if she's in . . .' he began, when someone who had come into the porter's lodge behind him, said, 'Can I be of help?' It was a young woman's voice. 'You see, I know Angie Thompson. In fact she's my roommate.' Then, when Rowlands turned towards her, 'Are you a relative of Angie's?'

'Well . . .'

'Her uncle, perhaps?'

'That's right,' said Rowlands hastily.

'Then I don't see what harm there can possibly be in my taking you to her. It's all right, Mr Briggs,' she added to the – no doubt scandalised – porter. 'This gentleman's Miss Thompson's uncle. I expect he's got some news of her people. Come along, Mr, er . . .'

'Rowlands. This is most awfully good of you, Miss . . .'

'Cartwright. Jean. We go this way.' As they exited the porter's lodge, she took Rowlands's arm, with a confidence that showed she'd had experience of dealing with people in his situation – a fact she at once confirmed. 'My father's blind. A proud St Dunstaner. I noticed your badge . . .' This was the silver emblem, in the shape of a flaming torch, Rowlands wore on his lapel.

'Oh?' The name didn't ring a bell. And yet the man must be of his own generation.

'Yes. The Cape Town branch, not the London one. He was at the Somme. 1st South African Brigade. The Battle of Delville Wood.'

'Oh yes. They fought very bravely there.'

They were now crossing what Rowlands guessed was a wide quadrangle. Voices – one male, one female – floated towards them through the early evening air. 'Well, I say we go and see what's on at the flicks and then get a bite to eat.'

'Yes, but they always run out of any decent grub so early. I'm fed up with dining on stale rock cakes and stewed tea.'

'So tell me,' said Jean Cartwright, once the couple – still arguing – were out of earshot. 'What do you want with Angie? Or shouldn't I ask?'

Rowlands took a moment to reply, unsure how much he should divulge. And yet this young woman had helped him, without a moment's hesitation. 'It's connected with Miss Thompson's work at Blenheim,' he said. 'I'm afraid she may be in some danger.'

She took this calmly. 'It's not unknown for our people to fall foul of enemy agents,' she said. 'We're dealing with highly confidential material. Although the security at

Blenheim is pretty tight. I'd like to see any German agent getting past the MPs without a fight.'

Rowlands could attest to that. 'It isn't Blenheim I'm worried about.'

'You mean Angie could be at risk here?' Now she did sound alarmed. 'But nobody knows . . . I mean . . .'

'I'm afraid it's a pretty open secret in Oxford that the women billeted at Keble work at Blenheim,' said Rowlands. 'Whether it's widely known that they work for the Secret Service, I couldn't say. One thing's certain, though – at least one person does know – and could be intent on harming Miss Thompson.'

'You're scaring me, Mr Rowlands. But I'm glad you've told me. If Angie's friends are on the look-out for this person, we can stop him getting anywhere near her. Forewarned is forearmed.'

This was true enough, but being prepared only took you so far where a really determined killer was concerned, thought Rowlands. But he'd frightened this poor young woman quite enough.

Chapter Sixteen

They had reached a doorway that led to a staircase – a layout, he had come to see, that applied to all Oxford colleges, from the oldest to the newer variety, such as this one. The stairs brought them to a door on the second floor. It was evidently on the latch, for Miss Cartwright went in without knocking. 'No, I'm not coming out tonight,' said a voice Rowlands recognised as Angela Thompson's. 'I've a nice quiet evening planned, washing my hair and darning my stockings, so . . . Oh!' she exclaimed, catching sight of Rowlands over Jean Cartwright's shoulder.

'Good evening, Miss Thompson. I'm sorry to intrude on your quiet evening, but I've something I have to tell you. It's about the green file.' Because having taken Miss Cartwright into his confidence about the risk to her friend, he saw no reason not to spell out exactly what might trigger that risk – Angela Thompson's investigations into the whereabouts of the said file.

The latter seemed unconcerned by this. 'You can talk

freely in front of Jean. She and I worked together at the registry. The German section. Other sections deal with enemy networks elsewhere.' Such as Russia, thought Rowlands, recalling his brief visit to Section F in the Long Library. 'I believe the missing file is one of ours.'

'Yes,' said Rowlands. 'There would appear to be a German connection.'

He was careful not to say from whom he had learnt this – although she must have put two and two together, for she said, 'So that was why she brought you to the registry!'

'What's this?' said Jean Cartwright. 'I seemed to have skipped a page or two in this whodunnit . . .'

'Mr Rowlands here is a friend of Iris Barnes.'

'Not a friend, exactly. We've worked together on several occasions, that's all.'

'Yes, and she speaks very highly of you. It's thanks to you that I've been given the job of tracking down this precious green file – for which I'm very grateful. Anything to get away from all that boring clerical work . . .'

The more she said, the worse Rowlands felt about having got her into this. 'I don't know what Miss Barnes has told you about the chequered history of this file, but I think you ought to know that anyone in possession of it – or who shows too keen an interest in locating it – stands a very real chance of being killed.'

'There are always risks attached to intelligence work,' said Angela Thompson.

'That's what I said, too,' put in her friend. 'We're warned about consorting with dubious types, who might turn out to be enemy agents . . .'

'It's more than that. Two people have been murdered. A third has been found dead in suspicious circumstances. Did Miss Barnes tell you that?'

There was a shocked silence. When Miss Thompson spoke again, it was in a subdued tone. 'She did say there might be risks . . .'

'She' being the woman who had selected her for the task. Rowlands had always known Iris Barnes to be ruthless, but this seemed a step too far – exposing an inexperienced young woman to the machinations of a killer.

'Tell me what happened,' she said.

'All right.' He knew he'd already said too much to hold back now. 'You'll recall when we first met . . . in Oxford, I mean?'

'The day I nearly ran you down with my bicycle?'

'Yes. Well, as it happens, there was a reason for my being in Oxford just then.'

'Before you go on, I think I should make us all a cup of tea,' said Miss Cartwright. 'You've gone as white as a sheet, Angie.'

'I've used up my tea ration,' said the latter, with a brave attempt at a laugh. 'It'll have to be cocoa.'

Rowlands said he'd rather smoke, if they wouldn't mind.

'I'll join you,' said Angela Thompson. 'Go on with what you were saying, Mr Rowlands.' They lit cigarettes, then, as briefly as he could, he described the reasons for his initial visit to Oxford, and what had taken place subsequently. Miss Thompson listened in silence, only interrupting once, 'So this Professor Challoner was one of ours?'

'That's right.'

'I think I must have seen him at Blenheim. He was tall, rather gaunt, with white hair – distinguished looking. A typical Oxford don.'

'I wouldn't be able to say for certain – never having seen him. But I'd say you were probably right.'

'How beastly that anybody could have murdered him!' she said fiercely. 'And you're saying it was on account of this green file?'

'Yes. Professor Challoner was still alive when we . . . I . . . found him. His last words to me were to find the file.'

'Why didn't he tell you the name of the person who'd attacked him?' said Miss Thompson.

It was something that had also puzzled Rowlands. 'It may be that he didn't actually see the man,' he said. 'The attack came from behind, you see . . .'

Again she was silent, digesting this.

Jean Cartwright turned from the gasring where she'd been making cocoa. She poured some into a mug. 'Go on, drink this,' she said to her friend. 'It'll do you good. I put the last of my sugar ration in.'

'You're too kind,' and she took a sip of the sweet, comforting brew. 'You said there were two murders,' she said to Rowlands. 'You'd better tell me about the other one.'

'Very well. I believe I mentioned that it was the smell of the file that alerted me to the fact of its having been in Professor Challoner's room . . .'

'Ugh, that horrible smell!' put in Miss Cartwright. 'All the files we rescued from Wormwood Scrubs simply stank of smoke.'

'Indeed. Well, there was the same smell in the room

where the body of Dr Maurice Quine – another fellow of Brasenose – was found.'

'Was it he who'd killed the other one – the professor?'

'The police thought so at first. But the fact of the missing file suggests that whoever took it must have been responsible for both deaths.'

'Why do you think he – this Dr Quine – took the file in the first place?'

'Blackmail,' said Jean Cartwright, with satisfaction. 'It's obvious. This gets more and more like a whodunnit every minute.'

'Don't, Jean! It's horrible. How did Dr Quine die?'

Rowlands told her. 'The police thought it must have been suicide. But then certain . . . discrepancies . . . were found,' he added quickly, hoping that she wouldn't ask what those 'discrepancies' were.

Luckily, she seemed more interested in the question of who had taken the file from Quine's room. 'You're saying it wasn't there when you found the body – even though the burnt paper smell suggested it had been?'

'That's right. I asked Mr Dobbs – the porter at Brasenose, who was with me – to search the room, but he found nothing. Unfortunately, he – Dobbs – appears to have taken it upon himself to discover where the file was, and to boast about having found it – with fatal results.'

'What do you mean?'

'Mr Dobbs was found dead, in the porter's lodge, on Tuesday night – apparently by his own hand.'

'Crikey!' Jean Cartwright was no longer laughing. 'It looks as if anyone who gets their hands on this thing is likely to end up dead.'

'I'm afraid that's so,' said Rowlands. 'Now, perhaps, you can see why I was so anxious to warn you, Miss Thompson?'

'It was kind of you,' she said. 'Only it doesn't change things. In fact, it makes it all the more urgent to find this file, and expose the man who stole it, and who's behind these murders.'

'Well, yes,' he began. 'But surely . . .'

'You don't think anything you've said could dissuade me from carrying on with the job I've been assigned, do you? I mean, I'm grateful to you for the warning – but it's not going to stop me . . . if anything, it's made my task easier. Because it's obvious to me now that Brasenose is the centre of all this enemy activity. The missing green file must contain names – one of those will be that of the man we want. It's essential that I get into Brasenose, and find him.'

'And just how are you going to do that, you poor infant?' said Jean Cartwright. 'It may have escaped your notice, but Brasenose is a men's college. Unlike this one, it hasn't made any special provision for females like ourselves.'

'They have women working in the kitchens, don't they?' replied her friend. 'Bedmakers, too. In case it's escaped your notice, there's a war on – and a shortage of college staff.'

'No wonder,' said Miss Cartwright. 'Women can make better money working in the factories at Cowley than as domestic slaves for Oxford colleges.'

'Exactly. It's a perfect opportunity. All I have to do is present myself, and ask for a job.'

'No,' said Rowlands. 'What you're proposing is much

too dangerous. Didn't you hear what I said just now? The man we're after is a ruthless killer – and he'll be on his guard against anyone that strikes him as taking too much of an interest in college affairs.'

'That might be so if I were a visiting professor, or someone equally conspicuous. But who'll take any notice of a mere kitchen maid – or of a woman who makes the beds? In fact, I think that's the job I'll apply for. It'll give me the perfect excuse to go ferreting around in people's rooms.'

Rowlands shook his head. 'I don't like it. A woman on your own . . .' Yet even as he said it, he had to admire the cleverness of the plan. People didn't notice servants – except when they wanted something fetched or carried, or a meal served . . . Poor Dobbs had doubtless taken advantage of this invisibility when he'd gone sniffing around in the private papers of Brasenose fellows. His mistake had been to broadcast his findings. 'I don't suppose I can stop you,' he said wearily. 'But do take care. I've no idea how you people operate, but surely if you're going to do this, you ought to keep someone else informed of your movements? Miss Cartwright, for instance?' Suddenly he had a better idea. 'Isn't Lieutenant Bawden billeted at Brasenose? Maybe you should take him into your confidence?'

'Oh, Peter'll only try to dissuade me from getting involved. I'm better on my own. But I will let Jean know when I'm inside the college.'

'You'd jolly well better,' said her friend.

'Then if anything goes wrong, you can alert the authorities,' went on Miss Thompson calmly. 'I begin to like this plan more and more. Just imagine, being able to go into all those rooms, and poke about in all those masculine secrets . . .' She made it sound as if it were no more than a lark, and not the deadly game Rowlands knew it to be. She must have seen his grave expression, for she added, 'Don't worry. I'm not a complete fool. I'll be on my guard. I've also had a certain amount of training in self-defence. And I won't take any unnecessary risks. The minute I come across anything untoward, I'll be straight on the blower to Blenheim.'

With which Rowlands had to be content. But as he made his way back to the Mitre, and the prospect of a solitary supper, he couldn't shake off a feeling of foreboding.

The bar of the Mitre Hotel was as busy as it had been at lunchtime – this time with the RAF, rather than the army. As Rowlands settled down with his pint, he could hear voices rising above the general hubbub, 'I mean to say, you chaps, I nearly went for a Burton that time . . . Flew so low I clipped the tops of the ruddy trees.'

'All right, all right. We all know you're a blinking daredevil.'

'But I mean to say . . .' The owner of the voice sounded young, excited, and just a little bit drunk. Pilot Officer Holifield. That was the name, wasn't it? Rowlands had helped to carry his trunk up the stairs. He was obviously making a night of it. 'Give a chap some credit! It's not every man who could pull off a stunt like that.'

'Surprised you weren't put on a charge for hedge-hopping,' said another voice Rowlands recognised. Holifield's roommate, Flight Sergeant Andrews, if he wasn't mistaken. 'Risking the Spit like that.'

'To say nothing of risking your neck,' put in another, more sympathetic, colleague. 'I tell you, they positively *encourage* it at Benson—' began Holifield, then checked himself, as one of his companions – the dour Andrews, perhaps – elbowed him in the ribs.

'Pipe down, old man. People are listening.' A warning, Rowlands guessed, that must have included him, since he was sitting at the next table.

But this injunction to silence only drew the loquacious pilot officer's attention to the older man. 'I say! Isn't that the chappie who helped us move in? I owe you a drink, old boy . . .'

This last was to Rowlands himself, who made a deprecating gesture. 'Thanks, but there's really no need.' It seemed he was fated to be bought drinks by grateful service personnel, however, for – ignoring his muted protest – the young RAF officer got to his feet, and stumbled across to the bar.

'Another round of the same, if you'd be so kind, landlord . . . and same again for the gentleman on the right.' His attempt at a man-of-the-world tone made him sound very young, thought Rowlands. For all their tales of derring-do, these were mere children. He supposed the 'hedge-hopper' must be all of nineteen.

The drink arrived. Rowlands thanked his benefactor gravely. Young and foolish the lad might be, but he was still one of those risking his life for his country. 'Have you settled in all right?' he asked, to move the conversation on to a less contentious topic. The surly Andrews had been right to shut his friend up. Spies might be found in the most innocuous places – an Oxford pub not being the most unlikely.

'Rather!' was the reply. 'Wizard digs, I'd say. Makes me quite sorry I didn't try for Oxford myself – but the RAF looked like more fun . . . Still, I've ended up here anyway. College life isn't so bad, from what I can tell. Grub's pretty good, too.'

'I'm glad to hear it.'

'Yes, we're enjoying life at jolly old Brasenose College, aren't we, Andrews, old man?' A grunt from the taciturn flight sergeant was the only reply to this. 'Bit of a facer the other day, though,' went on the garrulous Holifield. 'One of our chaps – not I, thank the Lord – came back to find the porter'd done himself in . . .'

'Belt up, Holifield.'

'No, but I mean to say. Not the sort of thing you want to walk in on, after a night on the tiles.'

'No indeed,' said Rowlands. 'It must have been a dreadful shock.'

'You've heard about it, then?' said Andrews suspiciously. Rowlands said that he had. He saw no reason to offer an explanation to this truculent youth, whose sojourn in Oxford evidently hadn't improved his temper.

Holifield was still musing on the unpleasantness of his fellow officer's discovery, 'Poor old Daintry! Rotten luck to come upon that. Not surprised he was brassed off.'

'War does terrible things to people,' said Rowlands – a remark that might have been taken to refer equally to the unfortunate Dobbs, and the man who'd found his body. He suppressed the thought that this probably wouldn't be the last time Daintry, or his comrades, experienced violent death.

Somebody else at another table, who either hadn't

heard Andrews's sharp reminder of the need for discretion where military matters were concerned, or who'd heard it, but didn't care, piped up, 'Yes, I've been told they rather go in for "dicing" at Benson. Chap I know who's based there flies a Mossie. Never saw such stunts. Glad I'm stuck with the old Flying Cigar. Couldn't clip a hedge with that if you tried.' There was laughter at this; then the talk moved on to other things.

Having finished his drink, Rowlands went to ask if the landlord couldn't rustle him up something to eat. He'd handed in his ration book on arrival, to cover breakfasts, but guessed the coupons might be made to stretch to supper. 'Certainly, sir. Got a nice bit of pork, left over from luncheon. Pork sandwiches do you?' Rowlands accepted the offer gratefully. After his long journey, and the grilling he'd had from the Oxford police, he was ready to turn in.

But sleep, when he eventually closed his eyes, proved hard to come by. Fragments of his conversation with Angela Thompson kept going around in his head. *Just imagine, being able to go into all those rooms, and poke about in all those masculine secrets . . .* No he wasn't happy about her plan at all. Doughty and resourceful she might be, but she was still no match for a determined killer.

Over breakfast (porridge and a boiled egg, paid for with another of his ration coupons), Rowlands tried to decide what to do. A night's sleep had failed to calm his fears for Angela Thompson's safety, and – since she'd been deaf to his pleas to give up her plan of infiltrating Brasenose College – he considered what measures he could take to protect her. The obvious answer was to make another attempt to contact Peter Bawden. He guessed Miss Thompson wouldn't thank him for doing so – but after all, what harm could it do, to ask the young man to look out for her? He'd have to be careful what he said, though, since he suspected that if Bawden knew the whole of it – that the young woman who'd engaged his affections was planning to go undercover in order to hunt down a Nazi agent – he might decide to intervene, with disastrous consequences.

Although the man would find out soon enough what she was up to, if only because he was bound to meet her around the college, carrying out her tasks as a bedmaker. Rowlands shook his head at the absurdity of it. Cloak-and-dagger stuff. So many young women these days – he thought of his eldest daughter, Margaret – were becoming involved in the secret world, in one way or another. It was all part of the struggle of good against evil that was being played out across the world.

He thought of what Ian Fraser had said about the 'war to end all wars' that he, and the rest of their generation, had believed they were fighting. And yet the war was still going on, against an enemy that seemed merely to have gone underground during the twenty-odd years that had passed. Now it had re-emerged, stronger and far more dangerous, because its sinister ideology had captured people's minds . . . He shivered, then shook himself out of his black mood. It did no good to give in to such pessimistic thoughts. Time to beard young Bawden in his den – assuming he hadn't yet left to join his unit. It was still early – not yet eight o'clock. With luck, he'd find the young man still at breakfast.

Having collected his coat and stick, Rowlands set off

along Turl Street. It was no more than a minute's walk to the gates of Brasenose, and having walked it a number of times since his latest arrival in Oxford, he strode along with a confidence he did not always feel in a city that remained largely unfamiliar. What a difference it had made, having a dog to guide him! He decided that, as soon as he was back in Brighton, he'd follow up his application to have a dog of his own.

It was just about here he had to cross, wasn't it? He slowed his steps, as there came the sound of a car approaching, at some speed. In the same instant, he felt a sharp push between his shoulder-blades, which caused him to stagger, lose his balance and fall, right into the path of the vehicle. The last thing he knew was a shattering impact that jarred his whole body from the base of his spine to the crown of his head. He tasted blood. Then he knew nothing more.

Chapter Seventeen

They were taking the wounded to the dressing station. He knew that was where they were going, because he could hear the cries and groans of his injured comrades . . . many cried for their mothers; some cursed and raved; others were merely silent as if the horror of what had happened to them – the stripping away, in a brutal instant, of life and strength – was too much to take in. He himself had been silent, for much of that journey. Being jolted about in the back of the ambulance as it lurched over the ruts and potholes had taken all his reserves of courage to endure. Someone had tied a rudimentary bandage around his eyes. Later, the RAMC officer had removed this, in order to assess the damage. He remembered thinking, *This isn't real*, as the man gently lifted first one eyelid, then the other. Now he wondered if in fact he'd died that day, and everything since had been a fevered dream . . .

When he woke at last – it might have been hours, or even days, later; they'd taken away his watch – it was to a medicinal smell, and the touch of smooth sheets against his skin. He was in hospital, then. Somebody said, 'He's awake. Better tell Sister,' confirming this.

Then – incredibly and wonderfully – he heard his wife's voice, 'Fred? Can you hear me? It's Edith.'

He tried to open his eyes, but a heaviness, as of approaching sleep, possessed him. He reached, instead, for her hand. 'Where am I?'

'St Hugh's Military Hospital. It's where they treat head injuries. They've got the top man from the Radcliffe Infirmary . . .'

'How long have I been here?'

'Three days. Oh, Fred . . .'

'What happened?'

'You were knocked down by a car. The driver saw you, but couldn't stop in time. You must have stepped out . . .'

'I was pushed,' he said. 'Didn't the driver see the man who did it?'

'No. All he said was, you weren't looking where you were going. Oh, Fred, you might have been killed.'

'No more talking now,' said a stern voice. The sister's, he supposed. 'You can come back at visiting time.' This was to Edith, who at once got up.

'I'll see you later,' she said, bending to kiss him. 'Try and get some rest.'

Over the next couple of days, he had several more visitors. Angela Thompson came, bringing him a tin of toffees, and the news that she'd started her job as bedmaker at Brasenose College. 'I've found nothing useful yet,' she confided in an undertone, since the ward was full of visitors for the other patients – young servicemen, most of them, recovering from head wounds. 'But I'm confident I'll turn up something very soon.'

'What does Lieutenant Bawden think of your . . . initiative?' He'd been on the point of saying 'escapade', but restrained himself.

'Oh, he's furious with me, of course,' she said cheerfully. 'But I told him I didn't suspect him of being a German spy.'

Bawden himself came another day, bringing Rowlands a pack of cigarettes, which the nurse confiscated. 'Angela's told me of her damn-fool plan. Said you'd tried to stop her, but it did no good. That girl's stubborn as a mule,' he added angrily. 'If she doesn't look out, she'll find herself at the wrong end of a German Luger . . . The worst of it is, I can't be around to protect her as much as I'd like. Some of us are being sent to Manchester for special training next week, so I won't be at Brasenose for a while.'

'I'll keep an eye on her while you're away,' put in the amiable Ginger Jarvis, who'd accompanied his friend to St Hugh's (the hospital was housed in what had been a women's college, requisitioned for the duration).

'That's what I was afraid of,' grunted the other.

Inspector Dimmock came, bringing a box of candied fruits. 'The wife got given 'em for Christmas, but neither of us like 'em,' he confessed. 'I must say, Mr Rowlands, you have got yerself into a pretty pickle,' he added lugubriously. 'What did I tell you about not putting yerself in harm's way?' Because Rowlands had told him that the 'accident' had been nothing of the kind. 'You were lucky that the driver of that Morris wasn't going any faster. As it was, you went clean over the bonnet of the vehicle, instead of under the wheels. You were lucky, like I said.'

'I don't feel very lucky,' said Rowlands ruefully. In the past few days, his injuries – two broken ribs and extensive bruising – had started to make themselves felt. 'But I'm hoping to get out of here soon. What was the verdict at the inquest on William Dobbs? I'm sorry I wasn't able to give evidence.'

'I doubt you'd have been called. Verdict was "suicide while of unsound mind". It's what I'd hoped for. No sense in alerting the chap that we're onto him.'

'You mean the murderer?'

'I do,' said the inspector. 'He'll think he's got away with it – and that might make him careless.'

Of those whom he might have expected to visit him in hospital, only Iris Barnes failed to appear. But then, thought Rowlands, it was like her to make herself scarce just when he'd wanted to have things out with her – not least about the way she'd made Angela Thompson a cat's paw in the dangerous game she was playing.

Ten days had passed since the accident that had nearly cost Rowlands his life, and from which he was still feeling the effects. The concussion that had made him of interest to the distinguished neurosurgeons of the Radcliffe Infirmary had all but passed off, leaving him only with a vestigial headache, and a persistent feeling of tiredness. His broken ribs were another matter; he'd be feeling the pain from those for weeks yet, the junior doctor who discharged him said cheerfully. 'Try to get as much rest as possible.' *Chance would be a fine thing*, thought Rowlands, but he thanked the young man for his advice.

He said his farewells to the nurses who'd looked after

him, and the men in his ward with whom he'd become friendly. 'Hope you make it back to your unit soon,' he said to Ralph Partridge, an RAF navigator, who was keen to get back in the fray, and 'Good luck,' to naval rating Bernie Fisher, whose ship had been sunk by a torpedo in the North Sea and whose chances of getting back to any semblance of normal life looked slim.

Rowlands made his way outside. The lawn where the brick huts that housed the wards and occupational therapy rooms were located had once, in happier times, been the setting for tea parties and games of croquet, when St Hugh's was still a women's college. Now, shadowy forms in pyjamas and dressing gowns – 'Sorry, old man! Didn't see you there' – tottered back and forth, guided by uniformed nurses.

Exiting onto St Margaret's Street, he listened out for the ticking sound that would herald the approach of the taxi he'd ordered, hoping that by standing in front of the college's ornamental iron gates, he'd make himself conspicuous to the cab driver. All he wanted now was to collect his suitcase from the Mitre, where it had been stored at his request for the past ten days, and get himself to the station to catch the London train. He felt as if a hundred years had passed, not just a few weeks, since he'd first set foot in Oxford. The place had that effect on one – casting a spell (not always a benign one, Rowlands thought) that made it difficult to leave.

Where had the man got to? He'd made a point of asking the young woman at the taxi firm who'd taken his call to make sure his driver would be on time – 'I'm blind, you see – so he'll have to look out for me' – to no avail, apparently. Ah, what was this? For a car had pulled up a few paces from where he stood. 'There you are!' he cried, hastening towards it. 'At last!'

'Why, were you expecting me?' said a voice. It was one he'd heard only a couple of weeks before. VR Smith's. 'Now I'm convinced you must have extraordinary powers of perception!'

Abashed, Rowlands came to a halt. 'I'm sorry,' he began. 'A misunderstanding. You see . . .'

'On the contrary, I call this a piece of luck,' said Smith, opening the nearside door. 'Well, get in, do. Where do you want to go?'

Rowlands hesitated only a moment before getting into the car – an MG sports car, with a fold-down roof (thankfully not folded down at that moment). 'This is really awfully good of you,' he said, as, having ascertained where it was they were heading, the car sped off towards the centre of Oxford.

'Yes, it was a good thing I happened to be passing,' was the reply. 'I've just popped in to see Lindemann, my old supervisor at the Clarendon Laboratory, you know . . . It's just up the road from St Hugh's. Were you visiting someone there or . . . ?'

'I've just been discharged. I was hit by a car ten days ago.'

'Bad luck. Must be the kind of thing that happens to you more often than not.'

'Well, no, actually,' said Rowlands, piqued that this forthright young man should suppose him to be more accident-prone than most. 'I take great care when crossing roads, as a rule. Only on this occasion, I was put in harm's way.'

'Like that, was it? I must say, you do lead an interesting life!'

Within a short space of time, they arrived in front of the Mitre Hotel. 'Thanks for the lift,' said Rowlands, opening the car door.

'Hang on, hang on!' said Smith. 'Are you planning to stop in Oxford?'

'No. I'm collecting my bag, then catching the train to London.'

'Oh, if that's the case, I can save you the trouble,' was the reply. 'I'm going back to London myself. Don't mind if we call in somewhere along the way, do you?' Rowlands said that he did not. 'Good. Then fetch your bag and we'll get going.'

As he settled back in the passenger seat of the MG, Rowlands felt he now understood how it was that this young man had managed to convince no less a personage than the Prime Minister of his exceptional abilities. It was sheer force of personality – a quality in which Churchill himself was not deficient. Of course the fact that he – Smith – was no doubt highly accomplished in the field of science in which he specialised must also have counted for a lot. But without the forcefulness with which VR had evidently delivered his 'pitch', he wouldn't have captured his distinguished audience so quickly.

There was also his quick-wittedness. 'I've told you why I was in Oxford – what was it that brought you there?' Smith said, as they left the city behind and headed into the Oxfordshire countryside. As briefly as he could, Rowlands told him. 'Hm,' said Smith at last, when the recital was over. 'It seems to me, from what you've said, that your suspicion that somebody tried to do for you, by pushing you under a car, was entirely reasonable. I suppose this chap Dobbs was murdered, too?'

'I'm sure of it.'

'Nasty business,' said the scientist. 'At least you're well out of it now. I don't suppose,' he went on, 'that before your brush with death you came across anything in the line I suggested to you when we last met? No mention of Freya, or radio beams, or the French coast?'

'I'm afraid not.'

'Pity. But then again, it's rather good news for our side. Things being at a crucial stage,' he added mysteriously. He began to whistle under his breath – Cherubino's aria from *The Marriage of Figaro* – and conversation ceased for the moment.

They had been travelling for a little over an hour when he said, 'Fancy a spot of lunch? I know a little pub on the Henley Road where we can get a pint and some fodder.'

Rowlands eagerly agreed to this proposal, and after a short while, they pulled up in front of the said hostelry. 'The Dog and Badger,' said Smith. 'Friend of mine recommended it. Serves a decent pint of Brakspear's.'

They entered what Rowlands judged – from the oak beams supporting its low ceiling (on one of which he nearly bumped his head) and its worn flagstone floor – to be a building of ancient lineage. A good fire was burning in the inglenook, and oaken benches were set against the rough-plastered walls. Smith, who was first to the bar, offered to buy a round, but Rowlands said, 'Let me get them. You've saved me a tiresome journey.'

It was still fairly early – just after midday – and they

were among the only customers – apart from a couple of old men in the chimney corner, whose gnomic remarks concerned the state of the weather, as far as Rowlands could make out. He gave his order to the landlady, who seemed to know Smith, for she greeted him with some cordiality. 'Come to see us again, have you, sir?' And to Rowlands, 'That'll be one and ninepence, sir, if you please.'

Carrying their pints, the two men sat down at a table, next to the fire. For a few moments, a contented silence reigned. Then Smith said, 'I'll get Judy to cut us off a bit off that ham, shall I? They kill their own pigs here, so it'll be worth eating.'

On returning from this errand, he brought someone else with him. 'Talk of the devil,' he said. 'Dickie, I want you to meet a friend of mine – Fred Rowlands.' Then, to Rowlands, 'This is Dickie Walsh. One of the glamour boys we're all so indebted to. He's based not far from here.'

Rowlands offered his hand, and felt it warmly grasped.

'As you'll have noticed, Rowlands here is a veteran of the previous war,' said Smith. 'Doesn't stop him getting himself into scrapes, now and then, does it, old man?'

Rowlands smiled, but said nothing.

'Not that old Dickie hasn't had a few escapades in his time,' went on VR Smith, with what sounded to Rowlands suspiciously like envy. 'He's flown that Spitfire of his over some very dangerous spots. Talk about dicing with death . . .'

'All in a day's work,' said Dickie Walsh, raising his glass. 'Well, here's luck.'

By contrast with his ebullient friend, Squadron Leader Walsh was a taciturn individual, confining his remarks to a few cryptic observations about the weather – 'Cloud looks as if it'll clear later. Might be all right by the time I take her up' – and technical jargon to do with photography, of which Rowlands could make little. 'Trouble is, I'm just too bally slow,' he complained, after one such discussion of shutter speeds and stereoscopic images – conducted in an undertone, for the pub was now filling up with its lunchtime clientele. That these were mainly, if not exclusively, local men, Rowlands could tell from the Oxfordshire accent – but it didn't do to assume that anybody was 'safe' in these uneasy times . . .

Perhaps the same thought had struck the squadron leader, for he abruptly changed the subject. 'Enough of this chit-chat, VR. We're boring Mr Rowlands. Remind me what it is you do,' he added, addressing the latter, who had not, in fact, said what he did for a living.

'I'm with St Dunstan's – the institute for the war-blinded,' he accordingly replied. 'I run the Brighton end of things.' He smiled. 'Routine stuff, compared with what you do, but it suits me.'

Walsh made some polite response; then Smith – who could never leave well alone, it seemed – piped up, 'Mr Rowlands is being far too modest. He's a detective. Cracked a good few cases, too.' There was never an answer to this, and so Rowlands merely smiled and shook his head.

Fortunately, Dickie Walsh was of a more discreet tendency than his friend. 'You don't say?' he merely replied, then, addressing Smith, 'How's Violet?'

'Top-hole, thanks. Seeing her tonight, as it happens.'

'Lucky man. Some of us,' added the RAF officer wryly, 'don't have time for a social life . . . Speaking of time, I ought to be pushing along. Got to get back to Benson for a briefing at two.'

Rowlands was reminded of the 'hedge-hopping' Pilot Officer Holifield, last encountered in the bar at the Mitre – hadn't he been based at RAF Benson too? Evidently, they favoured the dare-devil type there.

'We're dropping in at Danesfield House,' said Smith. 'Want a word with Wavell about this new piece of kit.'

'I get the picture, old man.' Walsh sounded distinctly uncomfortable at what Rowlands guessed must have been another indiscreet remark on the part of his friend. 'Good to meet you, Mr Rowlands. See you around, VR.'

'I can give you a lift back if you can hang on a bit longer,' said the man thus addressed.

'No, thanks,' said Walsh. 'Got the BMW with me. I'll be back in two shakes.' Then he was gone. A moment later, there came the sound of a motorbike's engine revving up, then accelerating away with a roar. 'Good chap, old Dickie,' said Smith, as he finished his beer. 'Wonderful flier, too. Why, I could tell you some of the things he's got up to in that plane of his that'd make your hair curl . . .'

'I think,' said Rowlands quietly, 'you'd better tell me about them in the car. It's getting a bit crowded in here.'

Another few miles brought them to the place Smith had mentioned as their next port of call. 'Welcome to Danesfield House – otherwise known as RAF Medmenham HQ. It's rather a monstrosity,' he said cheerfully, as the MG pulled into the drive. 'Looks like a wedding cake – all white stucco and fake battlements. Typical Edwardian country gentleman's retreat. Lot of interesting work going on here, though. You recall what I was telling you just now about old Dickie's exploits in the Spit? Low-level flying and so on?'

'Yes.'

'Well, the idea is that the plane can get close enough to the target – say, a German radar station – to take accurate photographs.'

'I gathered as much from what you and Squadron Leader Walsh were saying in the pub.'

'Did you? That's more than most people would have done.'

Unless they were enemy agents, thought Rowlands. 'Go on,' he said. But the MG had now come to a halt, in front of what he guessed must be the main entrance.

'Come on,' said VR Smith. 'I'll show you the kind of thing I've been talking about.'

Chapter Eighteen

They entered a large entrance hall – the ground floor of one of the towers that flanked the central portion of the house, Smith said. 'The architects of these places were partial to towers . . .' Rowlands recalled last year's visit to the sprawling Victorian Gothic pile of Bletchley Park – another country house that sported its share of turrets, domes, crenellations and other architectural frivolities, and had also been requisitioned by the government. *There must be a wealth of such over-sized dwellings scattered across the British Isles*, he thought – *many of them now dedicated to furthering the aims of the secret war*. 'In here,' said VR Smith, opening a door.

It was a large room that might once have been a ballroom: high-ceilinged and illuminated by several tall windows. At intervals across the floor, from which the carpet had been removed, large tables had been set out, at which industrious rows of young women were engaged in poring over maps. Rowlands gleaned this much by a combination of observation (the murmured conversations of the women, as they discussed points of interest; the scratching of their pencils on paper; the scraping of chairs against the parquet floor as they got up and moved about the room); and what his companion was in the process of telling him.

'This is the map room – it gets the most light, with those big windows. These girls – they're WAAFs, of course – spend all day piecing together the images retrieved by the photographic reconnaissance pilots. The photographic labs are in the Nissen huts behind the main house, so fresh images are being developed all the time . . . On the wall over there, they're pinning up the latest pictures that have been sent over from the labs during the last few hours. With every new image, we get more and more detail.'

With a touch on the arm, he drew Rowlands across the room, to where a group of uniformed men – whom Smith introduced by their respective ranks – were contemplating a series of photographs, taken that morning. 'Group Captain Hoskins, Flight Lieutenant Ormerod, Flying Officer Brown . . . This is Mr Rowlands, who's come to see what we're about – and keep us up to the mark, eh, Rowlands?'

'Hardly,' said Rowlands, wondering anew at VR's audacity. He seemed to say whatever came into his head – and get away with it. The RAF officers thus mentioned clearly knew him of old, and seemed unperturbed by his brashness.

'Got a few things to show you that might be of interest,' said one – the group captain, Rowlands guessed. 'Nice, crisp detail in this one. You don't even need a magnifying glass to see it.'

Smith was silent a moment, studying the photographs. 'These are really extremely good,' he said at last. 'Better than the last lot.'

'Dickie Walsh took them.'

'Thought I detected his hand in this! Must've been flying very low indeed to capture this kind of detail.'

'Mad bugger,' said one of the airmen, with a mixture of envy and awe.

'What's this shadow . . . here . . . do you think?' said Smith, ignoring this. 'Could it be the apparatus we're looking for?'

The others gathered round. Opinions were offered.

'Certainly looks like a possibility.'

'Could just be a smudge on the camera lens.'

'Trouble is, we'd need to get even closer to make absolutely sure, and that's not humanly possible.'

'Where's Wavell?' demanded Smith suddenly. 'Said he'd be here today.'

'Oh, he's about somewhere,' said one of the RAF men. 'You know old Wavers . . . always beavering away in the lab.'

'Well, I need to see him,' said Smith. 'Hey, you! Blondie!' This was to one of the WAAFs, seated at a nearby table. 'Be a good girl and go and find Squadron Leader Wavell for me, will you? Tell him it's urgent.'

'Yes, sir.' The WAAF scurried off to do VR's bidding.

'He's promised me all sorts of marvels,' went on Smith, to the men gathered around the table. 'Some new device for gauging the height of an object from aerial photographs – what does he call it, again?'

'The Altazimeter,' said a voice from the doorway. 'You

needn't have sent for me, VR – I was on my way.'

'Yes, yes, so I see,' said Smith impatiently. 'Well, now that you're here, perhaps you can take a look at these photographs and tell me how you're going to get the information we need from them?'

'It's quite simple,' said Wavell. An older man, to judge from his voice, thought Rowlands – or perhaps it was merely the calm authority with which he spoke that made it seem so, in contrast with the excited tones of the volatile Smith. 'One can determine an object's height from a flat image by multiplying shadow length by the tangent of the sun's altitude. Here, for example . . .' His fingernail tapped the glossy surface of the print. 'An interpreter needs only to know the latitude of a location, the scale and orientation of the photograph taken, and the date.'

'You make it sound like a piece of cake,' said the group captain drily.

'Oh, but it is,' was the reply. 'Take this photograph in front of us. That indistinct shape in the bottom right-hand corner might be nothing but a smudge, or a depression in the ground – or it might, using my method, that is to say, spherical trigonometry, prove to be a . . . what is it you call it, Smith?'

'A Würzburg,' said Smith. 'Otherwise known as a radar dish.'

'I say, old boy!' protested the group captain sharply. 'That information's confidential. You ought to be more careful about who might be listening.'

Rowlands supposed he was alluding to the presence of a stranger – himself – in their midst, and felt annoyed with Smith for putting him on the spot. He hadn't asked to be brought to Danesfield House, to be made to feel like an interloper. But then Smith said, 'Mr Rowlands here has been busy these past two months, trying to track down an enemy agent – at considerable risk to his own life, I might add. It's thanks to him, and others like him, that our splendid enterprise hasn't already become known to the Germans. So I think we can trust him with the "gen", don't you, Hoskins old boy?'

The group captain muttered something that might have been an apology. Rowlands gave an embarrassed shrug. He rather saw the group captain's point. But when a maverick like VR Smith started throwing his weight around, one had little choice but to grin and bear it. Further conversation of a desultory nature followed. Rowlands felt his attention drift. The winter sun, streaming in through the room's enormous windows, was warm on his upturned face. That, and the lunchtime beers he'd had, was making him feel sleepy.

He was jolted back to the here and now by Smith's saying, 'All right. Keep me posted about any developments, won't you, Wavers?'

The older man said that he would.

'I'd like to be informed as soon as you get anything definite on the location in question . . . All right, all right. I wasn't going to say where it is! Time's of the essence with an operation like this one. The weather's got to be right, and the terrain perfect, before we can achieve what we're hoping to achieve . . . Anyway, that's that, for the present. Come along, Rowlands old man. Let's get you back to London. Good to see you, Wavers. So long, gentlemen.'

There was a valedictory murmur from the RAF group.

'Wonderful chap, Claude Wavell,' said Smith, as they exited the building. 'The CIU – that's the Central Interpretation Unit – is lucky to have him. He spent years in Brazil, surveying the country. That's where he developed his photographic techniques. Now he's doing invaluable work for us. That precious Altazimeter of his will give us the edge we need to win this war.'

With little traffic on the road, apart from the occasional farm cart or army lorry, they were in London within two hours – Smith bound for his office in St James's (and later, a meeting with his fiancée at a nearby pub) and Rowlands for Victoria station and the Brighton train. On this second leg of the journey, which had taken them from rural Buckinghamshire to the heart of Westminster, via the Great West Road, Smith had regaled his companion with tales of his undergraduate days at Oxford, ten years before. There'd been a spectacularly ill-conceived prank, cooked up with a fellow chemistry student, that had – quite literally – reduced the population of Oxford to tears, after vials of a chemical ('a rudimentary tear gas') had been smashed on the city streets. The 'rag' had turned out to be all too effective, chuckled Smith, with ambulance crews dispersing the weeping crowds with cries of 'Mustard gas! Clear out!' – no doubt recalling for many the horrors of the war that had ended a few years before. 'In retrospect, it wasn't all that funny,' said Smith.

'No,' agreed Rowlands. 'It doesn't sound funny at all.'

But, such youthful misdemeanours aside, it seemed that VR's heart was in the right place. When, a year or so after the tear gas incident, the Oxford Union held its infamous debate on the motion 'This House would not in any circumstances fight for King and Country', Smith was one of those who fiercely opposed it. 'I even wrote a letter to my mother, apologising for the behaviour of the university,' he laughed. 'I told her not to judge Oxford by the antics of a few Union politicians. I've never taken the "conchie" line.'

'Quite right,' said Rowlands, although he had known a few pacifists in his soldiering days. Quakers, mostly. Some of them had been stretcher-bearers, or had driven ambulances, ferrying the wounded back from the front line. He'd always thought they were as brave as everyone else, in their own way.

'Yes, my father was at Neuve-Chapelle,' said Smith, expanding on his remark. 'British Expeditionary Force. Got his arm smashed up, so that it was useless afterwards . . . I suppose you must have been in the war, too.'

'If you mean the last war – yes, I was. Although, like it or not, we're all in this one, together.'

'We are.' He was silent a moment. 'You know, sometimes,' he went on, with the wistful note in his voice Rowlands had noticed earlier, 'I wish I were one of those doing the fighting – like old Dickie – instead of being a back-room boy.'

'You're making it possible for the ones doing the fighting to do so more effectively,' said Rowlands. 'And probably saving some of them from ending up like your father – or myself.'

'Would that be so bad? To know one had done one's bit . . .'

A lot of people had thought like that, in 1914, thought

Rowlands – himself included. It was only when you'd seen what war was like that you found yourself questioning the myth of heroic sacrifice. But he said nothing. It was Smith who spoke, 'I'm sorry. That was an utterly crass thing to say. It's just that I sometimes feel that I'm having an easier time of it than my peers.'

'Don't think that,' said Rowlands. 'Just remember that your work – and that of your fellow scientists – is helping to shorten the war. That's all that matters.'

Rowlands thought of this conversation later that night, as he sat beside the fire in his own home, with his wife and mother-in-law seated nearby, and only the gentle ticking of the mantlepiece clock, and the soft click of the women's knitting needles, disturbing the quiet. 'You look tired, Fred,' said Edith, after a while. 'I'm not at all sure that the hospital should have let you go so soon.'

'I'm fine,' he said. 'It's doing me more good being at home than any amount of time spent in that hospital.'

'Fred's right,' said Helen Edwards. 'One recuperates far more quickly at home.'

'Especially with a trained nurse to look after me,' added Rowlands with a smile. Edith had been a VAD. 'Although I will turn in early. It's been a long day.'

As January moved into February, life resumed its familiar pattern for Rowlands; it was as if the events of the past few weeks had never happened – or had been part of some fantastic dream. Starting back at the office, after an enforced absence, had meant putting in extra hours to cope with the backlog of tasks that had accumulated, and with which his secretary had been unable to deal on her own.

There were also household jobs requiring his attention – a tap that needed a new washer; a cracked pane in the bathroom window; a patch of damp that had appeared on the bedroom wall. It was humdrum stuff, but he was glad of it – if only because it distracted him from thinking about the still-unsolved Oxford murders.

A visit from their middle daughter, Anne, who had been granted a forty-eight-hour pass from the RAF base where she was stationed, had raised concerns of a different kind for both her parents. Relations between Anne and her mother had never been of the easiest, it was true – but of late it seemed as if they couldn't spend an hour in one another's company without falling out. Anne's refusal of a second helping of potatoes at lunch had elicited the remark from Edith that she was getting too thin (his wife never could restrain herself from making such remarks). 'We're all thin, Mother, in case you hadn't noticed,' had been the tart reply. 'There's a war on.' Nor had Anne's fondness for turning up the radio when a favourite song came on escaped her mother's condemnation. 'I happen to like Duke Ellington, Mother. I'm sorry if he's not to your taste.' Worst of all, his daughter had refused to accompany her mother and grandmother to church. 'I get enough of all that at Church Parade.'

No, it had not been a happy few days.

'I do wish she'd find herself a nice young man,' complained Edith to her husband as they were getting ready for bed on the last night. Perhaps she had, thought Rowlands, and that was the reason for her bad temper. The course of true love and so forth . . .

'Are you all right, old thing?' he'd ventured to ask, as

he was walking Anne to the station to catch her train. He half-expected a dusty answer; but his daughter merely sighed.

'I've known things to be better. But it's nothing for you to worry about. It's just this war . . .'

It was what everybody said when setbacks arose, whether great or small. When they'd run out of bread by the time one got to the front of the queue; when one's train was cancelled, resulting in a two-hour wait; or when one got back to find one's house was no longer standing . . . 'It's this war,' people said, with a shrug. 'It's this wretched war.'

Even so, Rowlands couldn't help feeling that there was something more behind his beloved daughter's melancholy mood than just the conditions under which they were all living. 'You know you can always talk to me about anything that's troubling you,' he said.

'I know, Daddy. And there's really nothing. I'm sorry I was cross.' Then the London train was announced, and the waiting crowd surged towards the barrier. She kissed him, and went to join a group of her fellow WAAFs who were travelling by the same route. Waiting until she and her friends had boarded the train – 'Don't wait, Daddy. We won't leave for another ten minutes yet' – he felt his heart ache. What had become of his lively, cheerful girl? The war had changed her – as it had so much else.

It being a Sunday, he had no particular reason to hurry back. Edith and her mother would still be at evensong, and they'd none of them want more than a sandwich after Sunday lunch. Not that the meal had been up to much, Edith had lamented. Woolton pie was no substitute for the

Sunday roast. But it couldn't be helped – it was the war. And so Rowlands made his leisurely way down Queen's Road, passing the Royal Standard and the Queen's Head – both of them open for business, to judge from the hum of voices from within, and the smells of rough tobacco and freshly poured pints. He was tempted to stop for a quick one. But then he reproached himself. Poor Edie would be feeling blue now that Anne had gone. Even though they quarrelled like cat and dog, he knew there was real affection there. It was the war – always the war – he thought. It put people out of sorts.

The icy winds of January had given way to a damp, cool February. Moisture clung to his hair and to the woollen pile of his coat. He'd be glad to get back inside and warm up by the fire, he thought. Turning along Church Street, he quickened his pace, using his stick to keep a safe distance from the edge of the kerb. Since his 'accident', he'd become more cautious about crossing roads. Reaching Dorset Gardens, he hesitated, listening out for the sound of any approaching vehicle. And there was a car pulling up, across the road – just in front of his house. Now, who could this be at this time on a Sunday evening?

His unspoken question was answered in the next instant. 'Is that you, Mr Rowlands?' – the absence of street lighting making this uncertain for a moment.

'Good evening, Miss Barnes.' Then, because she obviously hadn't arrived there for no reason, 'Won't you come in? My wife and mother-in-law should be back fairly soon. May I offer you a cup of tea in the interim?'

'I'd like that very much.'

He unlocked the door, and stood back to let her precede him into the hall, conscious of how narrow and poky it must seem to her after the spaciousness of Blenheim Palace. 'The sitting room's to your right.'

'Thank you. May I put on the light?'

'I'll just do the blackout.' When the bay window was safely shrouded, he switched on the standard lamp. Fortunately the fire was still in. He stirred up the coals with the poker. 'Do sit down,' he said. 'There's another lamp on the table next to you. My wife likes to have plenty of light for her sewing.'

She switched on the lamp. 'What a charming room! So cosy and welcoming. I do like that painting over the fireplace. Is it one of Percy Loveless's?'

'Yes. It was exhibited at the Royal Academy show, some years ago.'

'It's a good likeness. He's really caught your expression,' she said.

He smiled. 'I wouldn't know about that. I'll make some tea.'

'Don't go yet. There are some things I need to tell you. I've been away – in France, as it happens. I only got back late yesterday night. The fact is, things are reaching a critical point as far as the enterprise of which I've told you is concerned. I gather Victor Smith has filled you in on the purpose of the mission . . .'

'In the vaguest terms,' said Rowlands. 'I don't have any real information about what's involved.' *Nor do I want it*, he thought. Such information was likely to endanger whoever possessed it.

'Be that as it may,' said Iris Barnes, 'something's arisen

that you ought to know about . . . Is it all right if I smoke, by the way?'

'Go ahead.' Although Edith disliked people smoking in her sitting room, saying that the smell of cigarettes lingered unpleasantly. He pushed the box on the low table between them towards her. 'Won't you have one of these?'

'Thanks, but I've become addicted to the French brands. Horribly strong-smelling, I know, but . . .' She lit one, inhaled, and blew out a cloud of pungent smoke. 'Oh, I'm sorry. Would you like one?'

He declined.

'Anyway,' she went on. 'You'll have gathered from what I've said – and from what Victor may have told you – that the mission . . . operation . . . whatever one calls it . . . is to take place in France. That's why I was there – talking to our networks. They've given us the information we need to put the plan into operation.'

'I see. But what has this got to do with me? It's been two weeks since Mr Smith took me to Danesfield House, on the way back from Oxford. It was kind of him to give me a lift, in the circumstances, but . . .'

'Yes, I was sorry to hear about your accident,' she said. 'I hope you've recovered from your injuries?'

'I have, thanks. But you haven't answered my question.'

'I was coming to that.' She hesitated. 'When did you last see Angela Thompson?' For the first time she sounded embarrassed.

'She came to see me in hospital, the day after I was knocked down. Why? Has something happened to her?'

'Nothing untoward,' said Miss Barnes quickly. 'At least, not as far as I'm aware . . . The fact is, she's disappeared.'

'What?'

'Oh, don't get excited! I'm sure she's perfectly fine. She's probably with that young man of hers . . . Lieutenant Barton . . .'

'Bawden,' said Rowlands. 'Is he missing too?'

'Not exactly. That is, he's been away on a training course. It's all rather connected to what we've been talking about.'

'I don't follow.'

'You've been to Danesfield House. You heard about the photographic intelligence the RAF have been retrieving . . .'

'But Bawden isn't RAF; he's with the army.'

'He's got a part to play in this, nonetheless. An important one.'

'Where does Miss Thompson fit into all this?'

'I was hoping you could tell me that,' she said. She opened the bag she was carrying and took something out. A letter. 'This was left for you at the Brasenose porter's lodge.'

'You'd better read it, then.' Although he was sure she already had.

'Very well.' She unfolded the single sheet of paper and read aloud: '"I think I've found what we were looking for. But there's nobody I can trust, except you. Come to the porter's lodge on 10th February, at midday . . ."'

'That's tomorrow.'

'Yes. Now do you see why meeting you tonight was so urgent?' said Iris Barnes. 'It sounds as if she's got the information we want. We mustn't lose any time.'

'Does she say anything else?' he said, because it seemed to him that Angela Thompson's message had broken off

240

rather abruptly. 'Just this,' she replied. '"If I can't come myself, I'll send someone who'll bring you here . . ." I wonder where that is?' mused Miss Barnes. 'It isn't Keble, because we've already checked. That friend she shares rooms with hadn't seen her for days . . . or if she had, she wasn't saying.'

'She wouldn't,' said Rowlands, recalling Jean Cartwright's no-nonsense manner. 'It sounds to me as if Angela Thompson's in danger – and knows it.'

Chapter Nineteen

It seemed to him that there was a pattern to all this, if only he could make it out. It was as if the pieces of a jigsaw puzzle had been thrown up into the air, and had landed on the table any old how . . . It was his job to put all the bits together to form a clear picture. 'I suppose you want me to come back with you?' he said to his visitor, who now sat, apparently lost in thought, as she smoked her French cigarettes. 'I should warn you, though – I won't agree to anything that will expose Miss Thompson to more danger than she's in already. She's been thrown in at the deep end, and if anything happens to her, it'll be on my conscience . . .' *As it will be on yours*, he thought, but didn't say.

Iris Barnes took a deep drag on her Gauloises. 'Oh, we'll give her all the help she needs. If she's identified our traitor . . .' The sentence ended in a coughing fit. 'Damn these filthy things! Yes, we'll be keeping a look-out for her, you can be sure. And yes, I think it would be a good idea for you to come back to Oxford with me, Mr Rowlands.

As I said, things have reached a critical point . . . But this must be your wife coming in,' she added, as there came the sound of voices in the hall. A moment later, the door opened. 'Good evening, Mrs Rowlands. Your husband took pity on me and offered me a cup of tea.'

'That was decent of him,' said Edith drily. 'It's Miss Barnes, isn't it? We met around five years ago, in Cornwall.'

'Of course. Such a memorable holiday.'

It had certainly been that, thought Rowlands grimly, recalling the circumstances that had brought Iris Barnes and himself together.

'I don't believe you've met my mother, have you?' Edith went on. 'Mother, this is Iris Barnes, the writer.'

'Delighted,' said Helen Edwards. 'One doesn't often get the chance to meet a writer. Although I was introduced to Mr Galsworthy once, at a tea party before the last war.'

There was a small, awkward silence.

'Fred, I don't see any tea things,' said his wife. 'Surely you haven't already cleared them away?'

'No, no. I was just going to make the tea . . .'

'Well, don't let us stop you.'

He wasn't entirely happy about leaving the women alone together. One never knew what Edith would come out with. As for Miss Barnes, she was capable of saying anything, if it served her purpose.

'I'll come with you, Fred,' said Mrs Edwards, who didn't approve of men doing household tasks. 'I'll make the tea and you can carry the tray.'

It was frustrating, not knowing what the two of them might be saying to one another, he thought, as he waited for his mother-in-law to arrange things to her liking. 'Teapot.

Milk jug. Plates. Napkins. I hope there's enough of that seed cake left to go round . . . Sugar basin. We're rather low on sugar,' she murmured. 'But she's very slender, your Miss Barnes, so I don't suppose she takes it.'

On returning to the sitting room, he was in time to hear his wife quizzing their guest about her work. 'Do you still write those awfully exciting murder mysteries? I remember you were finishing one when there was all that dreadful business at the hotel.' The dreadful business in question had been the murder of one of the guests, of which Rowlands had – very nearly – been a witness.

Miss Barnes seemed unperturbed by the allusion. 'That's right,' she said. 'Ooh, seed cake – lovely! No, I've moved on from writing novels. Just lately, I've been involved with films.'

'What, acting, do you mean?'

'Heavens, no! I couldn't act to save my life. This is strictly on the production side. Government-sponsored films, you know. Nothing very artistic, I'm afraid. It's all about keeping up morale.'

'It sounds like a very good thing,' said Mrs Edwards. 'Staying cheerful is so important when there's a war on, don't you feel?'

It was a three-hour drive to Oxford. For Rowlands it passed in a kind of dream. To begin with, he and Iris Barnes made desultory conversation, but after they left Brighton behind – taking the coast road, and then turning inland towards Winchester – she was silent, unless it was to ask him to light her another of her infernal cigarettes, the smoke from which soon filled the car. What she'd said to Edith, to convince her of the necessity of this trip, he couldn't imagine, but his wife had put up no protest, disappearing to pack his overnight bag, while he and the woman who was about to carry him off stood awkwardly about in the hall.

Outside Newbury, Miss Barnes pulled over to the side of the road, and switched off the Jaguar's engine. She retrieved a flask from the back seat. 'Coffee,' she said, pouring out a cup for herself and one for Rowlands. 'It'll wake us up.' She lit another cigarette, and this time Rowlands did the same. 'It's funny,' she said. 'This reminds me of that long drive we did across France and Spain, in '37 – do you remember?' He said that he did. 'Dodging the Francoist bullets, as we drove through the mountains . . .' Iris Barnes laughed. 'Those were simpler days. One knew who one's enemies were. Now, it's less obvious.'

He wasn't so sure about that – recalling the vicious in-fighting between factions supposedly on the same side, which had characterised the Spanish Civil War – but he allowed her her moment of nostalgia.

They were in Oxford by eleven. Miss Barnes dropped her passenger off at Brasenose, assuring him that it was all arranged with the principal. 'I'll be staying at the Randolph Hotel,' she said, as he got out at the porter's lodge. 'I'd like to know as soon as you've heard from our Miss Thompson. She'd no business to disappear without warning – although I grant you, she might have had good reason.'

The porter who'd replaced poor Dobbs was a retired policeman by the name of Higgins. An Irishman. 'Dr Summerby said as you was to look in, sir, if you was agreeable,' he said, having taken charge of Rowlands's bag. 'Often sits up late, does the principal.' He chuckled. 'Says he and I are the only night owls in college, he does . . .'

And so, a few minutes later, having ascertained from Higgins that he was in the guest room in Old Quad that he'd occupied before, Rowlands found himself once more in the principal's comfortable quarters, being offered a whisky (which he gratefully accepted) and a cigar (which he declined).

'Well, well,' said Dr Summerby, as the two of them settled themselves in front of the blazing fire. 'Here we are again, Mr Rowlands. I trust that you have now recovered from your very nasty experience?'

Rowlands guessed he meant the accident. 'I have,' he said.

'I'm glad to hear it. Do you know, I couldn't help feeling responsible, since it happened just outside the college gates. I realise that it must of course have been a coincidence . . .' Rowlands was sure that it was not. '. . . but I felt a good deal of chagrin, all the same.' The principal ventured a small joke. 'We blind men have to take extra care when crossing roads, you know!'

Rowlands said that he did know.

'But tell me,' said Dr Summerby eagerly. 'Are you any nearer to solving the mystery of these murders?' He dropped his voice as he pronounced the last word, although there was no one to hear. 'Oh, I don't expect you to tell me the name of the culprit, but I would be grateful for a hint. Only some rather strange things have been happening in College lately . . . Yes, what is it, Travers? I thought I said . . . Oh, it's you, Vice-Principal! My eyes are getting worse and worse . . . Come in, my dear fellow, come in.'

'I don't want to disturb,' said Ponsonby-Smythe. 'But I heard voices and thought . . . Good evening, Mr Rowlands! So you've come back to us, have you?'

'For a little while.' Rowlands smiled.

'We were just having a nightcap,' said Summerby. 'Care to join us, Vice-Principal?'

'Well . . . maybe just a teeny one. Whisky keeps me awake, you know . . .'

'You were saying, Dr Summerby, about strange goings-on at Brasenose,' prompted Rowlands.

But Summerby affected to have forgotten what he had been going to say. 'Do you know, it's gone clean out of my head! It's not just my eyes that are failing . . .'

'I can tell you one strange thing that's happened,' said Ponsonby-Smythe. 'The theft of my lecture notes on Dante's *Inferno*. I swear I left them on my desk . . . but when I looked for them, they were nowhere to be found. Whoever took them made a complete mess of my study. Books put back in the wrong places, and papers strewn around . . .' He shuddered. 'When I think what else might have been stolen . . . My Donatello head for instance . . . it makes my blood run cold.'

'I'm sure the notes will turn up,' said the principal in a soothing tone. 'You've probably just mislaid them. More whisky, Mr Rowlands?'

But the latter was now ready for his bed. Still puzzling over the 'strange things' of which Summerby had spoken, he said goodnight to the two academics, and made his way to his now-familiar staircase.

* * *

It was after nine by the time Rowlands had had his bath and dressed – unusually later for him, but then, yesterday had been an unusual day. As he'd woken at last, he'd become aware, in his drowsy state, of the life of the college going on around him: the clanking of cisterns as people ran baths and flushed lavatories; the banging of doors and clattering of footsteps as they hurried downstairs; the shouts from below the window as they began the business of the day. That this would consist, for some of them, of lectures and tutorials, and for others, of marching, saluting and other activities that were part of the military agendum, was apparent from the snatches of talk that penetrated his consciousness.

'Hurry up! Old Stodders'll have a blue fit if we're late for his chinwag on Chaucer.'

'Jumbo! Get a move, on will you? We'll miss rollcall at this rate. And for Pete's sake do up your buttons! Do you want to be put on jankers?'

This last reminded Rowlands that he wanted a word with Peter Bawden. Perhaps he'd be back from his training course by now? But when he descended the stairs to breakfast, it was to find Old Hall deserted, except for a few of the senior fellows. On the surface, all was as it had been when he'd first entered these walls on that afternoon in late December that had proved so fateful. Here were to be heard the same voices – affable, civilised voices that spoke of a world of ease and privilege, a world that seemed secure even as the tides of war swirled around it. Here was Dr Aitken, grumbling about the coffee, and Dr Armstrong, wondering aloud whether they'd fixed that leak in the ceiling of the squash courts, because he for one could do with a game . . . Here, too, was jovial Dr Hobson, 'Back again, are you?' he said to Rowlands.

'Yes. They can't keep me away.'

'Jolly good,' laughed Hobson. 'Glad to see you looking so well. You had us all quite worried after that accident of yours, didn't he, Professor Crawley?'

'Oh, indeed. Quite worried,' said the old man. 'That's a dangerous crossing in front of college. And the way these young fools drive, it's no wonder more of us haven't been killed.'

'I'll take better care next time,' said Rowlands, finishing his coffee. There was still a couple of hours to kill before he had to meet Miss Thompson – or her emissary. He decided to settle for a smoke in the SCR.

'Hello? Anybody there?' he called, as he entered the room – hoping that if the answer was in the affirmative, whoever replied would be somebody he knew. Even though he had become something of a fixture around Brasenose College during the past two months, he knew he was only here under sufferance. There was no reply, however, and so he went in, intending to park himself by the fire, which – thankfully – had already been lit. But something – a memory of that first visit with Fraser – made him hesitate. The room, with its massive stone fireplace occupying most of one wall, was large – he recalled that it had held over a hundred people, without any sensation of overcrowding. Might it not be large enough to allow somebody to seclude himself from the general throng?

Rowlands decided to investigate. He accordingly began to circumnavigate the room, turning first to his right, and moving along the adjacent wall, whose two large windows, set in deep embrasures, had a view over the Fellows' Garden. There were certainly possibilities for concealment here. Turning left, he came to the wall in which the fireplace was set, around which chairs were placed in a rough semi-circle. At the end of this was a wall in which there was another door, which led to the dining hall.

But there was still another part of the room, as yet unexplored – a large alcove, closed off by folding doors, which could be opened to extend the space. The doors were open now. He went inside. Yes, here were some more chairs, and a grand piano, presumably used for concerts. It was here, he realised, that somebody had sat concealed, while he and Fraser were talking, on that first afternoon . . .

The door to the SCR opened. Two people came in. 'I shouldn't worry about it, my dear fellow,' one of them was saying. Rowlands recognised Ponsonby-Smythe's voice. 'I'm sure we can settle this to everyone's satisfaction.'

The other man – Rowlands realised it was Hobson – seemed unconvinced by these emollient words. 'I hope you're right, Vice-Principal. It's just that some people . . . naming no names . . . become absurdly defensive when their own little fiefdom is under threat.'

'Yes, well . . . Tempers do get frayed,' said the other. 'But I'll see what I can do. Leave it with me, dear boy . . . Oh! Mr Rowlands! You quite startled me.'

Because Rowlands had decided it was time to emerge from his hiding-place. 'I . . . I was just hunting for some matches,' he said. 'I seem to have left mine in my other jacket. Have either of you gentlemen got a light?'

It was the best he could come up with. Hobson, at

least, seemed to accept this, for he said, 'Here you are. Have mine,' handing over a box of Swan Vestas, then, when Rowlands attempted to return them, having lit his cigarette, 'Keep them. There are only a couple left in the box.'

Rowlands thanked him, not without a feeling of awkwardness that was perhaps no more than having been discovered in the not-entirely honourable position of overhearing what had obviously been a private conversation. Although it hadn't been his intention to eavesdrop . . . He was relieved when, a few minutes later, the door opened once more and several other fellows came in – among them Dr Aitken, Dr O'Halloran and the Reverend Allbright. Conversation became general. As soon as he'd finished his smoke, Rowlands got up and made his way out. He'd be early for his meeting with Miss Thompson – but it was preferable to feeling de trop.

There was nobody about as he crossed Old Quad; evidently the RAF and army contingents were carrying out their duties elsewhere. After what he had learnt on his visit to Medmenham, he supposed that the young airmen he'd encountered in the bar at the Mitre Hotel would be putting the dangerous skills they'd been learning into practice, in readiness for the mission that lay ahead. It sounded as if the army, in the person of Lieutenant Bawden, would be also be involved, according to what Iris Barnes had let slip . . . Not that she would have done so by accident, he thought. He knew that there was calculation behind all her utterances.

From the porter's lodge came the plaintive notes of 'The Minstrel Boy', being whistled by Higgins, the porter.

The minstrel boy to the war is gone,
In the ranks of death you'll find him . . .

The words of the beautiful Irish melody seemed all too apposite, thought Rowlands, as he paused on the threshold, unwilling to break the spell. Then Higgins spotted him, 'Mr Rowlands, sir! What can I do for ye, now?'

'I'm just waiting for someone.'

'Well, come in out o' the cold, do! It's a nasty, raw day, so it is.'

Rowlands gratefully accepted. 'I suppose,' he said, warming his hands at the lodge's iron stove, 'you must see all the comings and goings in college, Mr Higgins?'

'I do, sir. And I can tell ye, it takes a bit of doing, learning all the young gentlemen's names . . . not that I haven't had a bit of practice. After I retired from the police service, I was porter at St Hugh's for six years – only that was young ladies. Now they've turned the college into a hospital, so when poor Bill Dobbs came to such a sad end . . . that was the man before me, ye know . . .'

'Yes, I knew Mr Dobbs,' said Rowlands.

'Terrible thing, sir. Terrible . . . Anyway, that's when I came here.'

'Well, I'm sure you've got your work cut out, what with all the army officers and airmen billeted here, as well as the undergraduates to look after.'

'To be sure, we've a full house now,' chuckled Higgins.

'I don't suppose you know Peter Bawden – that's Lieutenant Bawden?' enquired Rowlands. 'He's with the Junior Staff Officers' School.'

'Certainly I know the lieutenant,' was the reply. 'In

fact I saw him not half an hour ago, roaring away on that motor-bicycle of his, the young devil . . .' The porter broke off. 'Begging your pardon, sir, if I was speaking out of turn.'

'Oh, I don't think Lieutenant Bawden would object to that description.' Rowlands smiled. 'Tell him I was looking for him, will you, when you next see him?'

'I will, sir. Now, who can this be, making such a commotion?' For a car had pulled up outside, with a grinding of gears and alarming banging sounds emanating from its engine. 'That's an old model, and no mistake.'

A moment later, the owner of the vehicle put his head around the door. 'I'm looking for a Mr Frederick Rowlands,' he said, in a pleasant, unassuming tone. Rowlands put the speaker's age at about forty. He declared himself, and held out his hand. The other shook it. 'Andrew Carlton-Bray,' he said. 'Angela said you'd be expecting me. Shall we make tracks?'

Chapter Twenty

The car – an old Morris Cowley – was indeed a bit of a rattletrap. Rowlands guessed it must be twenty years old. 'She's a bit wheezy, this morning,' confessed the driver. 'Took me a while to get her started. She doesn't like damp weather. But once I've got her going, she's as right as a trivet . . . So tell me, Mr Rowlands,' he went on, raising his voice above the roar of the engine. 'How is it you know our Angie?'

'I met her when she was an undergraduate at St Gertrude's College,' replied Rowlands. 'My wife and I were attending the end-of-term festivities at the college.'

'Good old Gertie!' cried Carlton-Bray, as, with something of an effort, the car ascended the Woodstock Road. 'I was at Cambridge myself, a number of years before Angela. King's,' he added. 'I do a bit of teaching there now, as a matter of fact – when the War Office allows me to.' He didn't enlarge upon this, and Rowlands guessed that his lecturing duties must be combined with another sort of desk job, perhaps of a military kind. 'Of course it can be a bit of a nuisance getting to Cambridge these days,' he said. 'We're rather out in the sticks here, as you'll see, and I don't qualify for extra petrol, so it's the Varsity Line for me – and a very tedious journey it is, too.'

With another of the sudden changes of subject that characterised his conversational style, Carlton-Bray said, 'I must say, you're not my idea of a police detective! But then, my idea of a detective probably bears little relation to reality.'

Rowlands smiled. 'You're not the first to notice that I'm hardly Bulldog Drummond material,' he said. 'And I'm not a policeman.'

'All the better for it,' replied Carlton-Bray. 'Angie tells me you solved that murder case at Gertie's . . .'

'I was on the spot,' said Rowlands. 'That meant I had access to certain evidence, which was useful to the police, that's all.'

'All right, I know when I've been warned off!' laughed Andrew Carlton-Bray. 'One thing, though. I'd be obliged if – detective or no – you'd use your skills to look out for Angie. She's a very dear girl, and my wife and I think the world of her . . .'

Rowlands said that it was certainly his intention to look out for Miss Thompson. He didn't ask why it was she had taken French leave from her job – surely a serious offence? – nor why he himself was being brought here, to the wilds of Oxfordshire. Let her tell him herself. Then conversation lapsed, as Carlton-Bray focused his attention on navigating a series of steep hills, up which the Morris climbed with a great deal of complaining – and murmured encouragement from her owner ('Come on, old girl! You can do it!'). From the almost total absence of traffic sounds – nothing but a labouring tractor and, before that, a passing motorbike, disturbed the quiet – Rowlands guessed they had entered a very rural area. It wouldn't do to break down here . . .

After twenty minutes or so, the car turned off the main road into a narrower thoroughfare. They drove on for another ten minutes, bumping over the ruts of what was apparently no more than a cart track. Then Carlton-Bray said, 'Here we are! Welcome to Chastleton House. Sorry about the bumps . . .' Because the car had now pulled off the road and entered a weed-infested gravel drive that seemed as full of potholes as the lane outside. 'Like the rest of the jolly old place, it's sadly in need of repair.'

They got out of the car. 'I'll take it round to the stables in a while,' said Carlton-Bray offhandedly. 'I say, do you need to take my arm?' he added, echoing the enquiry the Duke had made at a similar moment.

'Thank you. I'll manage,' said Rowlands, as he'd done on the previous occasion. 'But do let me know if there are steps.' Because he guessed they were now approaching the entrance to the house, which from the sound of it, must be of a substantial size.

'Six of 'em,' was the reply. 'All a bit uneven. Watch your step.'

Rowlands negotiated these successfully, with the aid of his stick. 'I gather it's an old house,' he said, knowing that most owners of such properties liked talking about them – as indeed was the case here.

'Jacobean,' said his host. 'We think about 1608. With

bits tacked on in the eighteenth century . . . and not much done to it since,' he added, with a laugh. 'Do come in. This is the Great Hall. We do sit in here, when it's a large party, but there's no fire lit at present.'

The Great Hall certainly lived up to its name, thought Rowlands – being of vast size, with a ceiling rising to a considerable height above their heads, to judge from the echo, and a stone floor covered with rather worn and threadbare carpets. It was also extremely draughty. So he was relieved when Carlton-Bray added, 'We'll sit in the White Parlour. It's directly ahead of you. My wife prefers it. Much cosier, she always says . . .'

'What do I always say?' said a voice from inside this room. A rather drawling, cultivated voice. Rowlands put its owner in her mid-thirties.

'Hello, darling. We're just back, as you see,' replied her husband, as they went in. Rowlands was relieved to find that this room, at least, was warm. 'Might there be a cup of coffee?'

'There might. Why don't you introduce our guest, Andy, before we get on to beverages?'

'Oh, yes. This is Frederick Rowlands. Rowlands, my wife, Beatrice.'

They shook hands. 'You're older than I expected.' Mrs Carlton-Bray evidently believed in speaking her mind. 'From the way Angie's been singing your praises, I was picturing a cross between D'Artagnan and Sexton Blake.'

'Beatie – really!' said a voice from across the room. It was Angela Thompson. 'You're being frightfully rude to poor Mr Rowlands.'

'I'm sure I didn't mean to be rude,' said Beatrice

Carlton-Bray in an injured tone. 'I was just going on to say . . . when I was interrupted . . . how relieved I am to find that Mr Rowlands is flesh and blood, and not a fictional character.'

'Coffee,' said her husband. 'I'll make it. You must excuse my wife, Mr Rowlands. She was brought up in rather bohemian circles. Such people tend to say the first thing that comes into their heads.'

'Do sit down, Mr Rowlands,' said his hostess, as Carlton-Bray set about brewing the coffee on a small Primus stove in the corner of the room. 'You see I do have some manners! Oh, just chuck all that on the floor,' she added, as Rowlands, attempting to follow this injunction, found the chair he had selected piled high with books and magazines.

'Give those to me,' said Miss Thompson, taking these from him. 'Really, Beatie! You might have tidied up a little . . .'

'You know I can't be bothered with all that,' said the other woman carelessly. 'Mr Rowlands must take us as he finds us. I hardly think a bit of mess will bother him, as he can't see it.'

'Beatie!'

'It's perfectly true,' said Rowlands, now seated in the rather lumpy armchair, with his cup of coffee perched on the rickety occasional table at his elbow. Although in truth, he was acutely aware of mess and clutter – especially when, as now, it constituted a potential hazard. He took a sip of the coffee, which was surprisingly good. 'So, Miss Thompson . . .'

'Do call me Angela.'

'Angela, then. Are you going to tell me what this is all about? I gather that your . . . er . . . employers don't know of your whereabouts . . .'

'Oh, Andy and Beatie know I've been working for Five,' she interjected. 'They've both signed the Official Secrets Act. You can speak freely in front of them.'

'Very well. Then I'd better tell you that Miss Barnes wants to know where you are. You're to get in touch with her – she's at the Randolph Hotel – as soon as possible.'

'I can't do that.' For the first time, Angela Thompson's air of self-confidence faltered. 'You don't understand. I'm not safe in Oxford . . . or at Blenheim. Someone's trying to kill me.'

'Now, Angela, you don't know that for certain,' said Carlton-Bray. 'It might have been an accident . . . well, that first time anyway,' he added, when she gave an exasperated sigh. 'You said yourself that you weren't sure what happened.'

'I was taken by surprise, that's all. One minute I was cycling merrily along the High, the next I was flat on my face in the middle of the road.'

'You might have hit a pothole.'

'No. I was pushed. Someone hit me quite hard between the shoulder blades and knocked me off balance. I only avoided being hit by a passing baker's van by a miracle.'

'I still think you might have been imagining things,' said Carlton-Bray. 'The shock of the fall, you know, and then . . .'

'I wasn't imagining things,' said Miss Thompson fiercely. 'And even if I was, how do you explain the other time?'

'That is more of a puzzle,' said Carlton-Bray.

'Go on,' said Rowlands. From what he'd heard about Miss Thompson's accident, he needed no further convincing that she was in danger; but he wanted to know how serious the threat to her life might be. Being pushed into the stream of traffic might just – like his own 'accident' – have been a warning.

'This was two days ago,' she replied. 'I was in my room at Brasenose . . . you remember that I've been working as a bedmaker there? Well, I've a room in one of the attics – over the kitchen. Of course I've left most of my things at Keble, with Jean, but I thought that, for verisimilitude . . . I think that's the word . . . I ought to spend a few nights at Brasenose. I was afraid that if I was spotted cycling back to Keble every night at the end of my shift, somebody might get suspicious . . .'

'Yes, how did you convince the college authorities that you were a humble bedmaker, and not Miss Angela Thompson MA, late of St Gertrude's College, Cambridge, and an employee of MI5?' said Beatrice Carlton-Bray sardonically.

'I managed,' was the reply. 'I'm not such a bad actress as all that . . . Anyway, I'd gone to bed, two nights ago, as I said. I was dead tired. Cleaning forty rooms a day takes it out of you. I'd left the gas fire on, because it was a miserable night, but I'd taken the precaution of setting up my usual alarm, so that I wouldn't forget to turn it off.'

'And what's that?' said Rowlands.

Angela Thompson gave an embarrassed laugh. 'A string tied around my big toe, and fastened to the bedpost,' she replied. 'An ingenious method of my own devising. When

I'd turn over, thus pulling on the string, it'd jerk me awake. Never failed. And it didn't on this occasion – for which I'm heartily thankful.' She was silent a moment. 'It must have been around half an hour later. I'd fallen into a light sleep, and was on the point of becoming more deeply unconscious, when—'

'You turned over,' supplied Mrs Carlton-Bray.

'Don't interrupt, Beatie! Yes, I turned over, and was jerked instantly awake by the string tied to my toe. I sat up, to untie myself, and then to switch off the fire, when I smelt gas. The room was full of it. It had given me the most shocking headache. For a moment, I thought I must have made a mistake, and forgotten to light the gas after I'd turned on the tap. But then I saw that the spent match with which I'd lit the fire earlier was lying on the tiles in front of the fire, where I must have dropped it. The tap was still turned on full. But the gas was out.'

'Perhaps the wind blew it out?' But Rowlands didn't really believe this.

'The window was closed. I've told you, it was a miserable night. And someone had plugged up the gap under the door with newspaper.'

Her three listeners were silent, contemplating the implications of this.

'Of course,' went on Angela Thompson, in a voice that trembled a little, 'whoever did it no doubt planned to remove the paper next day, once they knew I was dead – so that it would look just as you said it would look – like an accident.' She gave a tremulous little laugh. 'So I wasted no time ringing up Andy and Beatie. And here I am.'

'You'll be safe with us,' said Beatrice Carlton-Bray. 'Let

anyone try and get in here, and we'll drop them in one of Chastleton's deepest dungeons . . . or spike their head on the battlements . . .'

'If you've quite finished with these bloodcurdling reflections, I'll go and put Jemima away,' said her husband – referring to the car, Rowlands guessed. His host accordingly left the room, his footsteps rapidly retreating across the flagstones of the Great Hall.

'There's something else,' said Angela Thompson. 'Something that's convinced me it wasn't an accident, when I fell off my bike, and that I didn't forget to light the gas . . . Wait here, Mr Rowlands. I'll go and get it.' Then she, too, hurried out.

'She's been badly frightened,' said Beatrice Carlton-Bray. 'Whoever it was who tried to kill her – or at the very least to frighten her off – must have something they very much want to conceal.'

'I think so, too,' said Rowlands.

'As you will have gathered from Angela's remarks, my husband and I are both working in different ways for the government. Andrew works in a voluntary capacity, for the Royal Air Force Reserve, and I'm involved in operational research for RAF Bomber Command. We analyse photographic evidence, to assess the effectiveness or otherwise of British air raids on German cities. So you see, Mr Rowlands, we take a keen interest in the work Angela has been doing for MI5 . . . But she'll tell you more about that herself.' The door to the sitting room opened. 'That was quick,' said Mrs Carlton-Bray. 'You must have run all the way to get to the Sheldon Room and back in such a short time.'

But it wasn't Angela Thompson who appeared.

'Look who I found skulking about in the shrubbery,' said Andrew Carlton-Bray to his wife and Rowlands, as he ushered in another person – none too gently, it seemed, for the latter gave an indignant cry.

'Ow! No need to jab a man in the back. And stop waving that gun around! You're making me nervous . . .'

'Don't think I wouldn't use it,' snapped Carlton-Bray. It was hard to believe this was the same mild-mannered individual who'd welcomed Rowlands to his domain not long before. 'I've had weapons training, so I'm quite capable of blowing off your treacherous head, Mr Whoeveryouare . . .'

It was Rowlands who supplied the name, 'Lieutenant Bawden,' he said. 'What are you doing here?'

'Mr Rowlands!' The relief in the young man's voice was obvious. 'Please ask your friend here to stop poking me in the back with his Webley, and I'll explain.'

'I think you might put down the gun,' said Rowlands to his host. 'This is Lieutenant Peter Bawden. He's with the Junior Staff Officers' School at Brasenose. I'm sure he's got a reasonable excuse for turning up here.' He hoped, as he said it, that it was true. Bawden struck him as a bit of a hot-head.

But Carlton-Bray seemed convinced, for he lowered the gun. 'I don't much like intruders,' he said, by way of apology. 'But if Rowlands here will vouch for you, then I'll give you the benefit of the doubt. So you're with the army, are you?'

'As you can see,' was the curt reply. Bawden wasn't doing himself any favours by adopting this truculent manner, thought Rowlands.

'Just because a man's wearing a uniform doesn't mean he's necessarily all he says he is,' retorted Carlton-Bray. 'You've heard of fifth columnists, I suppose?'

'Yes. I . . .' But whatever the young lieutenant had been going to say died on his lips as the door opened once more. 'Hello, Angela,' he said. 'I . . . I was hoping I might see you.'

'Peter! How on earth did you get here?' She sounded anything but pleased to see him.

'Just on the old motorbike, you know,' was the feeble reply. 'It was easy, once I got on the trail of your friend's car, at the traffic lights in St Giles' . . .'

'You mean you followed us all the way from Oxford?' demanded Carlton-Bray. 'But how did you know which way to go? You weren't at the college when I called for Rowlands here. I'd have seen you.'

'It was the porter who put me on to you. He said you were looking for me, Mr Rowlands, and that if I were quick, I might just catch you. He said you were going to see Angela. The car was an old Morris, he said – you couldn't miss it.'

'He seems to have said quite a lot,' remarked Rowlands, thinking he ought have a stern word with the garrulous Higgins.

'I caught up with the car in the Woodstock Road,' went on Bawden. 'Wasn't difficult with an old banger like that. You could hear it groaning away five miles ahead . . . So it led me here,' he finished awkwardly.

'You should never have come,' said Angela Thompson furiously. 'You've no idea of the damage you've done.'

'Oh, but I have,' said Peter Bawden sheepishly. 'That's why I had to come. To apologise . . . and make things right.'

'What are you talking about, you chump?' she said softly. She had wandered over to the fireplace, and now stood idly swinging her foot against the brass fender. Bawden followed her. It was as if, for these two, nobody else in the world existed.

Beatrice Carlton-Bray evidently felt she had had enough of this casual disregard for the formalities. 'I don't want to sound like a stuffy old maiden aunt,' she said acidly. 'But I don't seem to have been introduced to this gentleman.'

'Sorry,' said Angela, not sounding at all sorry. 'Beatie, this is Peter Bawden. Peter, this is a dear family friend, Beatrice Carlton-Bray. The chap waving the gun around is her other half, Andrew. You still haven't said why it is you followed me here,' she went on, returning her attention to her suitor.

'No.' Bawden said nothing for a moment. 'I think I may have put you in danger,' he said at last.

There was a silence. Then Carlton-Bray said, in an affable tone, 'Why don't we all sit down? I'll make some more coffee. Unless . . . Beatie, is there any of that sherry left? It must be time for a glass of something before lunch.'

'What lunch?' muttered his wife. 'You've still to kill that chicken . . . Sherry's in the tantalus,' she added. 'Make mine a large one. I feel I need it.'

The drinks had been distributed. Peter Bawden took a sip of his, perhaps to give him courage. 'You'll remember that I was at Brasenose, Mr Rowlands?'

'Of course. That's where we met.'

'Oh, I didn't mean as part of the officers' school – I mean before. I did two years of a modern languages degree – French and Italian – from '39 to the end of the Michaelmas term, last year. I was hoping to do research, once I graduated—'

'What has all this to do with Angela?' interrupted Carlton-Bray.

'I was coming to that,' was the reply. 'My specialist subject was the Italian Renaissance, and the formation of the nation state. I had very good hopes of being offered a bursary – and perhaps the chance of an exchange visit to one of the Italian universities.'

'Well, that won't happen now,' said Carlton-Bray.

'No. And of course I had to drop my studies as soon as I joined up.'

'You're far from being the only one.'

'True.' Bawden was silent a moment. 'But when the war ends, there might be a chance of resuming my research,' he said. 'Or so I was led to believe.'

Chapter Twenty-One

'It was strange to be back at the old place – Brasenose, I mean,' the young man went on. 'Stranger still not to be a part of it, but just there under sufferance, as it were.'

'You were serving your country,' Carlton-Bray reminded him sternly.

'Oh, I know all that! But I missed it . . . missed the chance I'd had of making a contribution to scholarship . . . I wouldn't expect you to understand.'

'Of course he understands. He's a university lecturer,' interjected Beatrice Carlton-Bray. 'Never stops pining for the dear dead days beyond recall, do you, my sweet?'

'Shut up, Beatie,' said Angela Thompson. 'Go on, Peter.'

Despite this encouragement from his inamorata, Bawden hesitated before continuing. 'Soldiering keeps one pretty busy, of course. But there were times in between – times when I wasn't occupied with shouting orders at a bunch of useless conscripts, who had to be knocked into shape in readiness for the battlefield – that I revisited my old haunts in college. The library was one of these. I was looking at a book on the war machines of Leonardo da Vinci – did you know he invented the machine-gun, and a rudimentary form of tank? – when I ran into my old tutor.' He named him. 'He invited me back to his room for a glass of this stuff . . .' He took another sip of sherry. 'We had a good talk about old times. He told me that I'd always been one of his most interesting students . . . and that he'd predicted great things for me.'

Bawden gave an embarrassed laugh. 'I was flattered, of course – especially when he said that there might be a chance for me to resume my studies after the war. He'd see to it, in fact, that the two years I'd already done would be taken into account, so that I could start at a higher level – perhaps as a junior research fellow . . . which was music to my ears. This was over several conversations, you understand? I'd got into the habit of slipping round to his rooms, after dinner, for a chat and a smoke. It made a change,' he added softly, 'from the endless talk about the war.'

'I still don't see how Angela comes into this,' said Mrs Carlton-Bray impatiently.

'Shut up, Beatie.'

'I never meant to bring her into it,' said Bawden. 'It happened like this. I'd had a pig of a day. Old Harold . . . sorry, I meant Commander Hastings . . . had been more than usually cantankerous. Tore me off a strip for neglecting my duties, whereas the fact of the matter was, I'd been given special leave because of . . . well, no need to say.'

'No indeed,' said Carlton-Bray sharply. 'You can keep anything of that nature to yourself.'

'I'd dropped round to . . . to my tutor's rooms that

evening. I'd not long been back from . . . well, the special leave I'd been given, so hadn't been to see him for a couple of weeks. I'd been looking forward to resuming our conversations about Italy. He'd spent a lot of time there before the war. Knows a lot about Italian art. Politics, too. Only that night he wasn't in the mood for intellectual conversation. In fact, he seemed quite agitated. Someone had been going through his possessions, he said. He'd noticed that things had been disturbed, and put back in the wrong place. He was afraid that one of the college servants might have been responsible . . .'

Bawden paused, as if nerving himself to continue. 'He asked me if I'd noticed anyone of that sort acting suspiciously. For instance, there was a fair-haired girl, who was new. He'd noticed her going in and out of rooms where she'd no business to be. He'd poured me a drink, by this time – it was whisky, not sherry. College still has reserves of this stuff. I'm afraid I rather indulged myself that evening . . . Anyway, when he said that – about the fair-haired girl – I couldn't help laughing. It was so exactly the way I'd pictured Angela, carrying out her snooping, so I said, "I think I know who you mean, sir. And you needn't worry about her. She's on our side."'

'You said that, did you?' said Rowlands.

'Yes. And then he said, "So she's not what she seems to be? I rather suspected as much."'

'Then what?' said Angela Thompson.

'Then nothing. We talked of other things. We had some more whisky and after a while, I staggered off to bed. It was only when I woke up next morning – with a terrible head, I might add – that I realised that I'd given you away, Angela. Then when I heard you'd disappeared from Oxford . . . well, I feared the worst.'

'With reason,' said Carlton-Bray grimly. 'Two attempts have been made on Angela's life since you made your incautious remark.'

'Then that means . . . But that's impossible! I can't believe the man would be capable of . . .'

'Murder? Treason?' said Rowlands. 'As he himself said, people are not always what they seem to be. I think, Lieutenant Bawden, we'll have to pay your former tutor a visit.'

'Not before lunch,' said Mrs Carlton-Bray. 'I've got the range nice and hot, so if you'll just deal with that chicken, Andy, I'll get on with cooking it.'

Muttering something about being a domestic drudge, her husband followed her out of the room, leaving their three guests together in a rather awkward silence. Peter Bawden was the first to break this. 'Is it true?' he said, in an agitated tone. 'That he tried to kill you, I mean.'

'Well, somebody pushed me into the traffic on the High . . . and turned on the gas in my room,' said Angela Thompson. 'But I suppose it could have been unrelated to your cosy little chats about Italian art.'

'Angela, please! I never meant . . .'

'I know you didn't,' she said. 'But you've caused a lot of upset, nonetheless.'

'I'm a fool,' said the young man humbly.

'Oh, you are. A complete fool.'

Rowlands had the feeling that they were now gazing into one another's eyes. Probably holding hands, too. He cleared his throat officiously. 'There was something you were going to show me, Miss Thompson . . . Angela, I mean. You'd just gone to fetch it when Lieutenant Bawden arrived.'

'Oh yes.' She picked up the parcel from the floor where she'd deposited it, and unwrapped it. At once, a disagreeably acrid smell filled the room. 'I found this in one of the fellows' rooms at Brasenose,' she said. 'It was shoved under a heap of other files. It's the one we've been looking for – the smell of the thing gives it away. Unfortunately, there's nothing in it.'

She handed the thing to Rowlands, and he weighed it in his hands for a moment. The famous green file, which had caused so much mayhem. Whatever secrets it had once held had been destroyed, or hidden elsewhere . . . He handed it back. 'Whose room did you find it in?' he asked. She told him. It wasn't one of the names he'd had on his list of potential traitors, but as he'd just remarked, appearances could be deceptive. 'We'd better pay him a visit, too.' The ugly thought that there might have been a conspiracy behind the theft of the file, and the killings that had ensued, flitted across his mind.

'Faugh! What an infernal stink!' exclaimed Peter Bawden in disgust. 'Wrap the thing up again, won't you?'

'I'll thank you to speak more respectfully about this piece of vital evidence,' said Angela. 'While you were swanning about in . . . wherever it was . . .'

'Manchester.'

'I didn't hear that. While you were playing at being a hero, as I said, I was uncovering evidence of treachery. I'll now return it to its hiding place, until such time as it needs to be produced.'

'An empty file – what's the use of that?' scoffed Bawden as she got up to leave the room.

'Quite a lot of use, as it happens,' said Rowlands. 'In that it's marked a trail . . . from one murder to the next . . . that will lead eventually to our traitor.'

'I know, I know. I was only ragging,' said the young man. He lit a cigarette, then offered the pack to Rowlands.

'Thanks, I'll smoke my own. I find those too rough on the throat.'

The two men smoked for a moment or two in silence. Then Bawden said, 'If anything happens to her because of my stupid blunder, I'll never forgive myself.'

They were in Oxford by five o'clock. Lunch – which Rowlands suspected had been further advanced that Beatrice Carlton-Bray had suggested – had been consumed with much enjoyment on the part of all those present. The roast chicken was perfectly cooked, as were the potatoes and Brussels sprouts – 'from our own little plot', said Mrs Carlton-Bray modestly. When lunch was over, 'Jemima' had been retrieved from her berth in the stable block and started up (a process that involved a good deal of effort on the part of her owner, accompanied by encouraging cries of 'Come on, old girl!') and they were ready to go.

In spite of Peter Bawden's efforts to dissuade her, Angela had insisted on being one of the party. 'How many more attempts on your life will it take to keep you away from Oxford?' he'd demanded, in exasperated tones, to which she replied that a) she wasn't going to be scared off by some Nazi stooge and b) if he thought she was going to miss out on the fun, he had another thing coming. At which superb piece of bravado, Bawden snorted, 'On your own head be it, darling,' climbed onto his machine, and having kickstarted the engine, roared away along the drive.

'Oaf!' muttered his lady-love crossly. When she was seated in the back of the Morris, however, she admitted that her only reason for wanting to return to Oxford was to 'face the music' at the Randolph Hotel. Here, her superior officer would doubtless be waiting to hear her explanation for having deserted her post. With her, she had brought the errant green file (or what there was of it) as evidence that she hadn't entirely wasted her time as an undercover agent. That she felt uncertain how this encounter would turn out was evident from her nervous chatter – 'I do feel a bit of a beast, leaving Beatie to do the washing-up' – and the more sombre note struck by her question, 'Might they put me in prison for going AWOL, Andy?'

'Bound to,' was the latter's not-entirely serious reply. 'Bread and water for thirty days, I should think.'

Having dropped her off in front of the hotel, Carlton-Bray drove the by-now complaining Morris along the narrow streets that led to the college. 'Want me to come in with you?' he asked, as Rowlands got out of the car.

'Thanks – but I think I'd like to see the man in question by myself, in the first instance,' replied Rowlands. 'But I'd be grateful if you'd wait here. Young Bawden should be along any minute with the police – that is, if he's managed to convince Inspector Dimmock of the urgency of the situation.'

'All right,' said Carlton-Bray. 'I'll give you a quarter of an hour before I send in reinforcements. This fellow sounds like a dangerous customer. Want my gun?' he added, by way of afterthought.

'No thanks,' said Rowlands. 'I'd probably end up shooting my own foot off. But I appreciate the offer.'

He had hoped to slip past the porter's lodge without attracting Higgins's notice, but the man must have spotted him. He darted out. 'Mr Rowlands! Mr Rowlands, sir! Did the young gentleman find ye?'

'He did.'

'I told him if he was quick, he'd just catch ye,' said the porter. 'I made sure that motorcycle of his was more than a match for the other gentleman's motor car.'

'It was. Now, I really must—'

'He – our young gentleman – was delighted to have news of the young lady,' Higgins went on, obviously fishing for further information on this interesting topic.

Rowlands thought about telling him that he had been exceeding his duties in bringing Miss Thompson into it. But there was no time for this. 'I can't stop to chat, Mr Higgins.'

'To be sure. Is it the principal ye're wanting, sir?'

'It's the vice-principal. And there's no need to telephone. He'll be expecting me.' Which wasn't true, but there was no time for explanations.

'Very well, sir. As Dr Ponsonby-Smythe is expecting ye . . .'

But Rowlands had already walked off along the path that led across Old Quad, and the vice-principal's quarters.

At the foot of the staircase, he took a moment to collect himself. In the hours since Bawden had told him of that late-night conversation with Ponsonby-Smythe, in which he – Bawden – had been so indiscreet, Rowlands had been trying to decide how to approach the subject with the vice-principal. The idea of waltzing in and accusing him of treason – and murder – seemed ludicrous. What, after all, was the evidence against him? Only the account of a single conversation related by a young man who, by his own admission, had been half-cut at the time. No, it wasn't a moment for wild accusations. He'd have to proceed carefully.

Reaching the door of the vice-principal's room, he knocked, and, at a summons from within, entered. Ponsonby-Smythe was at his desk, evidently writing – for there was the soft scratching of a pen moving rapidly across paper. He continued writing for a moment, then looked up. 'Ah,' he said, in a tone nicely poised between surprise and pleasure. 'Mr Rowlands. How nice to see that you have not yet left Oxford. I gather, then, that the . . . ah . . . research you have been undertaking has still to be completed?'

'I think,' said Rowlands carefully, 'that I am close to completing it.'

'That is excellent news! But do sit down, my dear fellow. There is a chair just in front of you . . . unless you would prefer a softer couch? The sofa next to the fire?'

'This is fine.' Rowlands seated himself on the upright chair facing the desk where the vice-principal was sitting.

A moment's silence followed, during which he was uncomfortably aware that he was being scrutinised – an impression confirmed when Ponsonby-Smythe said, 'You know, you interest me, Mr Rowlands. You are not – forgive my bluntness – what one would describe as an "Oxford man" . . . which is not to say that you lack refinement.' He gave an affected little laugh. 'I fear there are all too many people at this university of whom that cannot be said . . . Whereas you, a man of, shall we say, rather more humble origins than most of us here, can take your place at, say, high table, without embarrassment. You are a chameleon, Mr Rowlands. A man who is at home everywhere – and nowhere.'

'Dr Ponsonby-Smythe . . .'

'A moment more, I pray. You must allow me to continue my little character sketch. You are a chameleon, as I say. You have made yourself quite at home at Brasenose – and elsewhere in our beautiful city, I have no doubt. You listen a great deal, but you do not say what is in your mind.' Again, the vice-principal laughed. 'I confess I am a little afraid of you, Mr Rowlands.'

If Rowlands had expected anything of this interview, it was not that he'd be interrogated himself. He decided he'd had enough of this fencing. 'Vice-Principal,' he said. 'I'd like to ask you a few questions. It shouldn't take long.'

'Ah,' he replied drily. 'I see that I am hoist with my own petard! I complain that you do not speak your mind – and now you have spoken it. Ask your questions. I will do my best to answer them.'

'Thank you,' said Rowlands. 'When we met in the principal's room yesterday evening, you said that your possessions – papers and the like – had been disturbed by someone searching your study. Some lecture notes had been taken . . . on Dante's *Inferno*, I think you said . . .'

'What a memory you have!' laughed Ponsonby-Smythe. 'As it happens, the notes on *Inferno* turned up this morning. They were in my attaché case all along.'

'But you do think that the study had been searched?'

'It was just untidy . . . untidier than usual,' said the vice-principal, adding with a yawn, 'Is there some point to this? I am, of course, happy to chat with you for as long as you wish, Mr Rowlands, but I am a busy man . . .'

'Can you recall exactly when you discovered that someone had been in your study, and had searched through your papers?' persisted Rowlands. 'Was it two days ago? Three?'

Ponsonby-Smythe emitted a gusty sigh. 'Is it really important?'

'It is.'

'Let me see.' He consulted a mental calendar. 'My lecture on Dante was supposed to be given last Thursday. So four days ago. But I fail to see . . .'

'You had a conversation that same evening, I believe, in which you complained that someone – possibly a college servant – had been into your rooms and had disturbed your papers.'

'A conversation?' echoed Ponsonby-Smythe. 'I don't recall . . .' He broke off, evidently remembering both the conversation with Peter Bawden and what had been said. 'Oh,' he remarked drily. 'Someone has been very indiscreet.'

'It was last night – Sunday – that you mentioned the matter of the missing lecture notes to the principal and me,' said Rowlands. 'Had you mentioned it to anyone else?' Because the longer he sat there, listening to this petulant and self-important man, the harder it was to believe Ponsonby-Smythe a murderer. While he'd certainly been present on all the occasions when murder had been committed – the dinner at Brasenose that first night; the Christmas feast; and, conceivably, when Dobbs had been carrying out his ill-advised search for the green file – he had betrayed no obvious motive for the killings. Of course, if he were a spy, then his motive would be to conceal the fact from any interested party – if necessary, by eliminating the latter.

Now, in answer to Rowlands's question, he replied ill-temperedly, 'I might have done. Why? Does it matter?'

'Only that, in doing so, you might have endangered another person's life,' replied Rowlands gravely. 'But I have another question for you, Dr Ponsonby-Smythe. What do you know about a green file?'

'I . . .' Ponsonby-Smythe gave a nervous giggle. 'Curiouser and curiouser,' he said. 'A green file. That sounds like something out of a mystery story by Edgar Wallace.'

Rowlands waited, certain now that the man knew something.

'Now you mention it,' he went on, 'perhaps I have seen something of the kind somewhere . . . I suppose you aren't going to tell me why it's important?' When Rowlands said nothing, Ponsonby-Smythe went on, in a ruminative tone. 'Hmm. Let me see. A green file. Yes, I believe I have seen it . . .'

In the same moment, there came the creak of footsteps on the stairs outside. The door opened. Rowlands felt a surge of exasperation. For Carlton-Bray to have sent in reinforcements now, just when he was getting somewhere . . . But then the vice-principal said, 'Hello, dear boy! Talk of the devil! Mr

Rowlands here was just asking me about that green file of yours, and I said—'

There came the deafening sound of a shot. With a groan, Ponsonby-Smythe slumped forwards over the desk. In the same moment, someone else came pounding up the stairs and burst into the room. 'Drop that!' cried a voice. It was Carlton-Bray's. There followed the sound of a scuffle. But while this timely intervention had certainly saved Rowlands's life, it wasn't enough to prevent the intruder from escaping. Having knocked Carlton-Bray to the floor, the man was gone, his footsteps thumping unevenly down the stairs.

Unevenly. Suddenly, Rowlands knew beyond a shadow of a doubt who it was. 'Get help!' he cried to Carlton-Bray, who was stumbling to his feet. 'I'm going after him.' Descending the stairs at a run, he hurtled out of the archway onto Old Quad, startling a couple of undergraduates coming the other way, and ran towards the porter's lodge. Perhaps struck by the unusual sight of someone running in those hallowed precincts, Higgins stuck his head out. 'Did you see where he went?' panted Rowlands. He named the man he was after.

'Indeed I did, sir. Saw him not two minutes ago, walking towards the Radcliffe Camera. Is it a message you want me to give him, sir?'

Ignoring the question, Rowlands sprinted across the road that lay between the college and the famous Oxford landmark, and cut along the path that led to the main door. Here, he hesitated only a moment before starting to climb the broad spiral staircase – 'like the inside of a giant sea-shell', as his brother-in-law had once described it to him – to the first-floor reading room. He judged that the ground floor of the library might be busier than the rest of the place, and was therefore best avoided – guessing that his quarry would have made the same calculation.

Chapter Twenty-Two

Sure enough, in that moment of deliberation, he heard the faint echo of a halting step, as the miscreant laboured up the stairs ahead of him. Then came the hollow reverberation of a door slamming shut, as the latter entered the Upper Camera. Reaching this floor in his turn, Rowlands pushed open the heavy oak door and went inside. Here was an atmosphere of hushed concentration, with only the sound of pens scratching and the occasional creaking of a chair, as its occupant shifted position, to disturb the quiet.

Again, Rowlands paused, unsure where to go next. The last thing he wanted was to attract attention – especially if the librarian had chosen that moment to pay a visit to the upper floor. But then he heard something else: the sound of footsteps from somewhere above his head. He remembered, from his long-ago visit, that a gallery ran around the Upper Camera; it was reached by another spiral staircase – this one made of iron. He located this by circumnavigating the outer edge of the room until he found it, then climbed the stairs, holding on to the polished wooden banister, until he reached the top, where he stood wondering which direction to take. The question was answered for him. 'Over here to your right, Mr Rowlands,' said a voice softly. 'Ten paces should do it.'

He followed these instructions, which brought him level with one of the oak tables that were set at intervals around the circular space. 'Sit down,' said the man he had been chasing, still in the same quiet tone. 'And keep your hands where I can see them. I've a pistol pointed at your heart, so don't try anything stupid.'

Rowlands sat down.

'Well, well,' said the other. 'So you've caught up with me at last! I must say, I admire your determination, if nothing else.'

Rowlands forced a smile, although he didn't feel much like smiling. He was all too aware that sitting across from him in the tranquil surroundings of the reading room was a man who had killed three people – perhaps a fourth. 'Why did you do it?' he said, keeping his voice low. 'I mean, I know Challoner was onto you . . . and Quine was blackmailing you . . . but what had poor Dobbs ever done to you? As for Dr Ponsonby-Smythe, I thought you and he were friends.'

'I'm afraid you're rather to blame for the last,' said the other indifferently. 'If you hadn't been so obsessed with finding that file – which, by the way, is no more – my revered colleague would still be alive. But I didn't kill Dobbs – what makes you think I did?' Then, perhaps seeing the startled look on the other's face, 'No need to look so alarmed at my plain speaking, Mr Rowlands! We are quite safe here, for the present. This, you know – or rather, you do not know – is the history department, and I, being a respected doctor of history, command certain privileges. One of these is that, when I am in situ – this is my preferred desk, you understand – the librarian on the floor beneath us has instructions not to let any of the undergraduates onto this mezzanine. So we can talk without fear of being overheard.'

'Not always the case in the senior common room.'

'Ha ha! No, indeed. It was fortunate for me that I heard you come in, with your friend – the good Major Fraser – as I was secluded in my little nook. Your conversation proved most illuminating. Then when that Challoner man joined you, with all his talk of spies, I saw that I had to act – and act fast – if I were not to be exposed.'

'You killed him,' said Rowlands.

'I did. The foolish man had left the instrument of his own destruction to hand, on the desk in front of him . . . a weapon stolen from a better man.'

'The German officer's dagger.'

'Precisely. It was to avenge his honour – the dead officer's – that I chose that method.'

'Stabbing a defenceless man in the back.' Rowlands did not attempt to conceal the contempt he felt. 'Hardly an honourable killing.'

'He insulted the Fatherland!' snapped the other. 'And he would have betrayed me to the secret police.'

'We don't have those here.'

'That's what you think. What was Challoner, if not a member of that clandestine fraternity? But let us not quibble, Mr Rowlands. You and Major Fraser stumbled upon the body, not moments after I had quitted Challoner's rooms.'

'It was you who passed me on the stairs,' said Rowlands. 'I recognised your step.'

'But not soon enough to identify me. And I had retrieved what I wanted . . .'

'The green file.'

'Exactly. I was only just in time – because you turned up.'

'Yes.'

'With Challoner dead, and the file in my possession, I had nothing more to fear. If only you had not insisted on pursuing the matter, Mr Rowlands, nothing more would have come of it. The police were happy to let MI5 take care of things, as he was one of their own, and—'

'What about Dr Quine? He pursued the matter, too – if you're referring to the green file.'

'Yes, Quine was foolish – and greedy. He saw me slip away from the SCR that night, and return with the file under my arm. He guessed that it contained something important, since by the time you and your friend had raised the alarm, I had placed the file in my study for safe-keeping. It was there Quine found it – a cursory read told him he had ammunition to blackmail me. He was always jealous of my success. A petty little man.'

'So you killed him, too – and with the utmost brutality.'

'It was quick and merciful. One moment we were chatting pleasantly, the next . . .' He broke off. 'But I do not have time to argue with you over semantics. The fact is, I needed to retrieve the file, and do so before it could fall into anyone else's hands.'

'What was in it that was so important?' asked Rowlands, although he thought he already knew some of this.

The other shifted impatiently in his seat. 'How you do like asking questions, Mr Rowlands! It can surely mean nothing to you, since you are not a secret policeman. But I will gratify your curiosity, since you will not be able to enjoy your knowledge for very much longer. The green file contained my history – the history of a historian, that is rather good, is it not? My past. My . . . I suppose you would say "political affiliations" . . . I prefer to call them my "credo". As well as the visits I have made to Germany. The friends I made there. The documents I may or may not have brought back with me . . . It was all in the file, you see – the one they were so busy reconstructing, after the original was lost with the others. All bombed to smithereens by our Luftwaffe.'

He chuckled. 'That was a piece of divine luck if ever there was one . . .'

Or infernal luck, thought Rowlands.

Something of the distaste he was feeling for the glee with which the other had spoken must have shown on his face – usually so impassive – for the man said, with a burst of venom, 'Yes, I imagine you think very differently, Mr Rowlands! But it was luck, no doubt about it, when almost all the files containing years of research conducted by British Intelligence into the lives of "subversives" like myself were destroyed in one night. Lucky for the subversives, that is.'

Again, he chuckled. 'Although even you must admit, Mr Rowlands, that it was foolhardy, to say the least, that those files, containing all that hard-won information, were stored in so insecure a place . . . Ach, you will say, will you not, that there could not have been a more secure place than a prison – Wormwood Scrubs, no less – in which to store such documents? By the by, I have always found that a peculiarly apposite name for such a place – "wormwood" representing the bitterness experienced by the prisoner; "scrubs" alluding to the menial work imposed on the incarcerated – or perhaps to the shapeless prison garments . . .'

It struck Rowlands that he was enjoying his moment of triumph – of revealing to a captive audience how clever he was, and how far above the common herd. It was a delusion Rowlands had encountered before, in his dealings with murderers of a certain type.

'Where was I? Ah, yes. The prison. A very secure place, you might suppose, to house not only the worker bees of MI5 but its most sensitive case files. What carelessness, then, to place the said files in so insecure a building – the glass-roofed prison workshop – where they might be destroyed by the action of a single bomb, shattering the glass and everything beneath it . . . an illustration, if ever there was one, of the old adage that people in glass houses shouldn't throw stones.'

He chuckled at his own bon mot. 'But to return to the matter under consideration . . . The files. Or rather, the file – green in colour – that concerned myself. I mean my real self, not the confected nonsense . . . Ah, I see you understand what I mean by this! Yes, the persona (such a useful Greek word) that I presented to the world. A jovial "buffer", I think you might say? A pettifogging man of letters. Harmless. Foolish. A bit of a bore . . .' He laughed delightedly. 'It was a convincing piece of theatre, was it not, Mr Rowlands? It certainly took you in.'

'Not entirely.'

'So you say – and yet . . . here you are,' replied the other coldly. 'If it is true that you had your doubts about me, you have left it rather late in the day to act upon this. Not that it matters,' he added. 'By the time you are found – dead, I am afraid to say – I will be out of the country. Home and dry, as the saying goes. The man I was will be dead, too – as far as the world knows – and I will have assumed my true identity.'

'That of a traitor,' said Rowlands.

'If you choose to put it like that. I myself would have used the word "patriot". But each to his own.' He was silent a moment. 'Come, Mr Rowlands, we will now take a little walk. I feel the need for some fresh air. Get up,' he went on, dropping his jovial tone for a colder one. 'And don't make any sudden moves. You and I are going to admire the view – a splendid view it is, too, comprising the whole of the Oxford skyline. Such a pity you cannot see it.'

Rowlands did as he was told, feeling the gun nudging his spine, as the two of them walked towards a door that was set into the curved wall, and which led out onto a balustraded parapet. 'It is a fine day – if a little misty,' said the other as they stepped onto the slatted leads. 'We will finish our conversation here, in sight of the architectural beauties of this city. Eastward stand the twin towers of All Souls, with New College visible behind, and Queen's, with its green copper dome. Look southward, and there is Magdalen, the Schools and University College. Merton is to the north, with the spire of St Mary's behind. Westward, there is Christ Church, with its looming Tom Tower – bringing us full circle to our own dear Brasenose, with St Aldate's and Carfax beyond . . . As I say, a beautiful city. I feel quite sentimental about it, now I am so soon to be leaving.'

'Yet you have betrayed it, and all it stands for,' said Rowlands.

'Ah, there you go again!' said the other. 'Mistaking patriotism for its opposite. As a matter of fact, it was his patriotism that first attracted me to Heinz Albrecht. He was the man who first showed me what it means to love one's country. Not that I understood the import of what he was saying at first.' He gave a self-deprecatory laugh. 'I'm afraid I found it all rather absurd – his talk of the Fatherland, and the necessity of sacrificing oneself for the "cause". '

'The Nazi cause, I suppose,' said Rowlands. He was determined to keep the other talking for as long as possible. Surely help would arrive before too long? Carlton-Bray must have informed the authorities of the vice-principal's murder by now – and young Bawden would doubtless have returned with the police . . .

'Heinz didn't have to name it,' was the reply. 'But I knew that was what he meant. This was in '33, of course. Heinz and the other German Rhodes Scholar had joined us in the Michaelmas term of that year. I was in the second year of my research studies. Goethe and the Romantic Revolution: from Werther to Faust,' he added. 'Not that it matters . . . although naturally I have always had the highest regard for German culture. But it was Heinz who showed me that there was more to it than that. We were a month apart in age. Twenty-two. The best age to be, in my opinion. A young god,' he breathed. 'Heinz, that is. Oh, I was good-looking enough in those days, but nothing to compare with him. Such hair . . . like spun gold. Such eyes . . . Ice-blue. And what a physique!' He was silent a moment, as if recalling that vision of long-lost beauty.

'You became friends,' said Rowlands. Would the others never come?

'Oh yes,' was the reply. 'Although I was only one of many acolytes. You cannot imagine how popular Heinz was – with those looks, and his sporting prowess . . . Rowing. Riding. Archery. Shooting. He excelled at everything. Then, of course, there was his skill at languages. He spoke English so beautifully, with hardly a trace of an accent. French and Italian, too. Oh, he had all the talents . . . But it wasn't until we went to Germany together, in the summer of '34, that we became fast friends.'

Another silence, which Rowlands was loath to interrupt this time, sensing that, as long as the other remained in his nostalgic dream, he would be less inclined to act. 'Yes, that was when I saw the truth of the matter,' he said once more. 'Oh, Heinz had been very patient with me. "I was sure you would come over to us at last," he told me. "Once you had seen for yourself the miracle that Our Leader has wrought in Germany . . ." And I was convinced by what I saw. Overnight, the country had been transformed – given a new pride in itself. The spirit of the people was different. More optimistic. Forward-looking. "We will bring about a great revolution, you will see," said Heinz. "It will be the triumph of the will. The overthrow of the old, corrupt order . . ."'

Rowlands must have looked sceptical, for the other said, 'Ah, I see you do not agree, Mr Rowlands! That is because you, too, belong to the old order. The way of decadence and decline.'

'Your "new order" depends rather a lot on killing anyone who disagrees with you,' said Rowlands.

The other man laughed. 'I suppose you are referring to the late Professor Challoner?' he said. 'He deserved to die. As did the blackmailer Quine. Anyway, enough of this idle talk, Mr Rowlands. It can do no good, since neither of us is about to convince the other. The time has come for you, too, to join the great majority. Do not be afraid. It will be quick. You are about to fall from this balcony onto the pavement below. An unfortunate accident. You must have leant too far over, and lost your balance. I was unable to prevent you going outside, although I warned you that the leads might be slippery. Alas, I was too late to save you . . .'

He must have drawn closer as he was speaking, for his prospective victim could hear the rapid sound of his breathing, and smell the sour tang of his breath. Determined not to surrender without a fight, Rowlands lashed out with his knee, hoping to bring the other down – or at least inflict an injury to the groin he would not forget.

'Ach, you would, would you?' jeered the other. Then came a stunning blow to the back of the blind man's head. He tasted metal, as if the gun's barrel had been jammed between his teeth, rather than its butt being used as a club. Then he knew nothing more.

When he returned to his senses, it was to the sound of a scuffle. Blows being traded; grunts and thuds; then the sound of a gun being dropped, and skittering away across the leads. He tried to sit up, but the effort made his head swim, and he could only lie there, helpless, as the wordless struggle went on. It didn't last much longer. There came the ugly sounds of someone choking – or being choked – followed by a strangled cry. Then came a silence – disturbed only by the wind, blowing around the spires and domes of Oxford, and by the mournful crying of rooks.

How long he lay there, drifting in and out of consciousness, he could not afterwards have said. But that he was alone for a time on that rooftop parapet, he was certain. Whatever fate had overtaken his assailant – and he had a dreadful suspicion that he knew what this was – the man was no longer there. He remembered there'd been a struggle . . . but who else had participated in this, he couldn't have said for certain. He head ached damnably. He abandoned the effort of trying to work it out, and let himself slide into unconsciousness once more.

The next thing of which he was aware was the sound of voices. One of these was familiar. 'Easy now,' said Inspector Dimmock. 'You get hold of this arm, Alcock, and Hedges, you take hold of t'other. No need to jostle him about . . .'

At this – albeit careful – manhandling, Rowlands let out a groan. 'Back in the land of the living, are you?' said the inspector cheerfully. 'Thought you was a goner, for a while.'

'What happened to the other two men?'

But the policeman seemed not to have heard the question. 'Take it slowly, now, sir. Take it slowly. Let's see about getting you down those stairs.'

Rowlands's head was still ringing, and waves of sickness threatened to overwhelm him, as the little party, with Dimmock in the lead, made its halting progress down the spiral staircase, and out onto the lawn in front of the building. At once, all was bustle and confusion. There seemed to be a lot of people milling about. That some of these were police officers was apparent from the orders now being shouted by the inspector, 'Come along there, you men – look lively! Sergeant! I want these onlookers dispersed at once – they're blocking the path of the ambulance . . .'

A moment later, the vehicle, its bell clanging, drove up, coming to a halt just outside the iron railings that surrounded the Radcliffe Camera. Doors opened and people – these would be doctors, thought Rowlands – clambered out. More orders were shouted. 'It's this way! Bring a stretcher!'

Having detached himself from his two police escorts, who were instantly dispatched on other errands by their superior officer, Rowlands had seated himself on the kerb in front of the railings. Now somebody – one of the doctors – peered at him. 'Is this one in need of medical attention? He doesn't look too good.'

'You should see the other fellow,' was the laconic reply. 'You'd better take a look at him, first. Not that there's much left to look at.'

It was strange, thought Rowlands drowsily, being in the middle of all this commotion, and yet not knowing the first thing that was going on . . . like switching on the wireless halfway through a play – one of the modern, 'experimental' kind – and trying to work out who the characters were and what they were doing.

'Mr Rowlands? Frederick? Are you all right?'

'Hello, Miss Barnes.' Here, at least, was a familiar character. 'Yes, I'm fine. I'd just like to know what's going on.'

'Don't you remember?' Her voice was gentle. 'You've been hurt. There was a struggle – at the top of the Radcliffe Camera. The other man got the worst of it.'

'You mean . . .' He named him.

'Yes. He's dead. Fell from the parapet.'

'And I'm supposed to have pushed him?'

'So it would seem. But don't worry about it now. Whatever happened, it must have been self-defence. He had a gun. Come on.' She took his hands, and helped him to his feet. 'Let's get you to hospital. I don't like the look of that cut.'

Chapter Twenty-Three

It was Miss Barnes who drove Rowlands to the hospital – the ambulance crew having been preoccupied, unsurprisingly, with the removal of the pathetic remains of the man who'd fallen – nobody could explain how – from the top of the Radcliffe Camera, dashing himself to pieces on the pavement below. That this was Jeremy Arthur Hobson, doctor of history at Brasenose College, had been confirmed by the police – the body having been identified by the principal, Dr Summerby, lately summoned from the hospital bedside of his second-in-command. For the vice-principal had survived the attack that had been made upon him by his former friend and colleague, it transpired. All this Rowlands was to learn later. At that moment, cocooned in the swiftly moving Jaguar, he thought about the dead man, and the persona he had constructed for himself, and about all the lies he had told to maintain it.

That Hobson had been a German agent was not in doubt – the man had revelled in the fact, during their strange tête-à-tête on the parapet of the Radcliffe Camera. But when Rowlands tried to tell his companion what he had learnt from this conversation, she seemed curiously uninterested in the details. 'The main thing is that he's been stopped. He can't do any more damage. Yes, you may congratulate yourself, Mr Rowlands, on having disposed of a very nasty individual. A spy who might have endangered a vital operation . . . a triple murderer, too.'

'He said he didn't kill Dobbs,' said Rowlands.

She seemed not to hear this. 'Here's St Hugh's, at last,' she said. 'I remember when this was all tennis parties and reading groups on the lawn. Now it's just another wing of the Infirmary. What times we live in . . .'

The doctor who had examined Rowlands after he'd been hit by the car took a dim view of his return to the hospital a mere matter of weeks later. 'A head injury such as the one you sustained a month ago is a serious thing,' he said. 'You were lucky not to fracture your skull. This latest blow to the cranium might have finished what the other started. How's your vision? A bit blurred?'

Rowlands started to explain, but the young medical officer forestalled him. 'Oh, I see – it's all in your notes. "Blind in left eye. One-eighth vision in right. Shrapnel injury during military service, July 1917." That wouldn't have done your head any good, either! Well, we'll keep you in for a day or two for observation. Let me know if your symptoms get any worse. Headache. Sickness. Fainting spells. All that.'

Left alone in the ward, Rowlands could have groaned aloud. To be stuck in a hospital bed once more, when all he wanted was to go home, and think over all that he had learnt in the past twenty-four hours. But there was to be no escape from Oxford just yet, it seemed.

Oxford, as before, was prepared to come to him – his first visitor being the principal of Brasenose. He'd just come from visiting his colleague, Dr Ponsonby-Smythe, in the infirmary, said Dr Summerby. It was a convenient distance from there to St Hugh's Military Hospital. 'Poor Ponsonby-Smythe is very lucky to be alive,' he said, seating himself down beside Rowlands's bed with a little grunt of effort (Dr Summerby was of a rather corpulent build). 'The bullet merely "winged" him, as I believe is the expression. Had it been an inch or so to the left it would have pierced his heart. One must suppose,' the principal went on, 'that in his haste, the man was shooting wildly.'

Or that he had, consciously or unconsciously, shot wide of the mark, thought Rowlands. Ponsonby-Smythe had, after all, been his friend – whatever that meant to a man prepared to betray both friends and country.

'Such a terrible thing for college,' said Summerby, in his gentle, melancholy tone. 'To have harboured such an individual under its roof . . .' He had not, so far, named Hobson. 'We found a wireless set in his rooms,' he added mournfully. 'Tuned to a German frequency.' All those concerts Hobson had claimed to be enjoying on the radio, thought Rowlands. 'One wonders how much information he succeeded in sending the enemy's way.'

It was what Rowlands himself had wondered. Because how much information would the late history don have been able to collect on his own? Without at least one other collaborator, he would have been limited to retailing university gossip, and whatever he could pick up in the usual course of events about public morale. That he had been a Nazi sympathiser was obvious; whether he had been an active spy was less so. Surely the zeal with which he had done his best to cover up his connections to the current German regime pointed rather to the past than to the present? He had killed Challoner and Quine because both had threatened to expose him as a traitor – but of what, exactly, had that treachery consisted?

As he lay there in his hospital bed, Rowlands turned these questions over and over in his mind. There was the fact that Hobson had denied killing the porter, Dobbs. Why would he have lied about that, when he had boasted of carrying out the other killings? And there were, in addition, the attacks on Rowlands himself, and on Angela Thompson. No mention had been made of these, either. Unlike the murders of the two Brasenose fellows, these had taken place outside the college – or in the servants' quarters, where a fellow of the college like Hobson would have been unlikely to venture. It was true that, in letting slip to Hobson what Peter Bawden had said about the inquisitive bedmaker's being "one of ours", the vice-principal had unwittingly exposed Miss Thompson to danger. But was it Hobson who had made the two attempts on her life – or had it been somebody else?

Round and round went these questions in Rowlands's head, until it ached as if from another blow. Was there perhaps another enemy agent at work in Oxford? Someone who had passed on information to Hobson, so that he could pass it on in turn by means of his radio set . . . or who was working independently? If that were the case, then the contents of the green file – now destroyed – assumed a more sinister significance. Might it have contained not only Hobson's name, but that of another – his 'handler' within MI5?

Lying sleepless as, around him, his fellow patients snored and grunted in their sleep, Rowlands recalled the silent struggle on the parapet two days before, of which he had been an unwitting witness. He was as sure as he was of anything that Hobson had still been alive when he, Rowlands, had been knocked out – because it must have been the history don who had struck him. It had not been Rowlands who had tipped the man over the balustrade to his doom. Someone else had been there, moments after he himself had been disabled by a blow from the butt of Hobson's gun. It was that man who had thrown Hobson to his death, and who had strangled William Dobbs before him – the same man who had pushed Rowlands into the path of the car, and shoved Angela Thompson off her bicycle. He it was who had stolen into the rooms reserved for college servants, and had turned on the gas in the sleeping woman's room.

Whoever it was – and Rowlands had only the barest suspicion – this was a far more deadly opponent than the foolish and boastful Jeremy Hobson. It was he, and not the Brasenose don, who presented a greater threat to the British war effort.

From all he had gleaned over the past few months of his sojourn in Oxford, there was an important operation afoot – one that might, if he'd understood all that he'd been told – by Iris Barnes, and the mercurial VR Smith – change the course of the war. That it was due to take place very soon, he had also gathered. Chance remarks and scraps of information he'd overheard – not amounting to much in themselves – together formed a pattern. The 'hedge-hopping' ace Dickie Walsh, and his daredevil stunts over the French coast, to capture photographic intelligence in his plane . . . The men and women putting all this intelligence together at Danesfield House, in order to plot a mission . . . The special training being given to army officers, Peter Bawden being one . . . It all added up to something it was vital to keep secret.

He's still around, thought Rowlands, lying restless in the dark. Hobson was dead; but this was a greater adversary.

Another visitor was Angela Thompson – this time bringing somebody else with her. 'I found her wandering around in the grounds, looking a bit lost,' she said. 'So I said I'd show her the way.'

'Hello, Daddy.'

'Margaret! How did you get here?'

'Oh, the usual way – on the Varsity Line,' was his eldest daughter's reply. She kissed him. 'How are you feeling, Daddy?'

'All the better for seeing you.'

'Mummy's letter said you'd been in the wars again,' said Margaret. 'So I telephoned her to say I'd be the one to visit this time . . . Oh, Daddy, what have you been up to? I do wish,' she added in a low voice, 'you wouldn't get involved in this kind of thing' – his daughter knowing only too well, from her experiences of a few months before, what 'this kind of thing' entailed.

Rowlands smiled. There was no answer to this. 'I

assume you had permission to come to Oxford?' he asked.

'Yes. Don't worry, after what happened last time, I wouldn't dream of taking French leave.' This allusion to the occasion when she had done just that, and nearly paid a terrible price for it, seemed to renew her anxiety on his behalf, for she said, 'You'll be going home when you're fit enough to travel, won't you, Daddy?'

'Oh, I think so,' he said with a laugh. 'I've had my fill of university life.'

'Only Angela said you'd been caught up in that dreadful murder case at the college,' said his daughter, keeping her voice low – although there was nobody in the next bed, and the rest of his fellow patients were either having a smoke in the corridor, or taken up with their own conversations. 'There wasn't much about it in the paper, but . . .'

'No, I don't suppose there was.'

'Oh, Daddy, I do wish—'

But what she wished she never got to say, for at that moment the ward sister bustled in. 'No more than one visitor at a time,' she said sternly, seeing the two women beside Rowlands's bed.

'I'll wait outside,' said Margaret; but Angela Thompson forestalled her.

'No need. I can't stay long as it is. Just wanted to say goodbye, Mr Rowlands. I'm going away.'

'I see.' He knew he mustn't ask where. 'Will it be for long, do you think?'

'I couldn't say. But it'll make a nice change from my present employment,' she said drily. 'A bit of excitement after all that dull office work.'

'Well, good luck.' He held out his hand and she shook

it. 'Please send my good wishes to Mr and Mrs Carlton-Bray,' he said.

Carlton-Bray had been one of Rowlands's first visitors. 'Glad to see you're still alive, old man,' he'd said. 'I must say, I was rather worried about you for a time, after you set off in pursuit of that pistol-waving maniac. But all's well that ends well.'

It was not quite how Rowlands would have put it, but he appreciated the sentiment.

'Of course,' replied Angela Thompson. She started to walk away, then turned. 'Peter asked me to say goodbye. He's . . . he's going away, too. I mean . . .' She gave an embarrassed laugh. 'We'll be going to different places, of course, but . . .'

'Send him my best,' said Rowlands.

'I will. See you later, Margaret.'

'So, how's everything?' said Rowlands to his daughter, when they were alone once more. This vague query might have covered a multitude of things, from Margaret's general well-being, to the situation at her place of work, which was Bletchley Park.

Her reply was similarly vague. 'Oh, just the same as usual, you know.'

'Good. And how's everyone at home?' Because Edith's last letter had mentioned that their eldest daughter had had another weekend's leave.

'They're all well. At least . . . I didn't see Anne, but I gather she's getting on all right. Very busy, of course – but we all are, just now.'

'Yes.' Busy fighting a war – or trying to forget about fighting a war. Both took time and energy.

'Joan's captain of the school hockey team this term,' Margaret went on. 'That child's getting as tall as I am! She certainly eats enough,' she added fondly. 'Mother was complaining that there wasn't a biscuit left in the house after Joanie went back to Aunt Diana's.'

'How's Frank?'

'He's well, as far as I can gather. So much of his last letter was blacked out by the censor that it was almost impossible to read. Just "hope this finds you as it leaves me" and "thanks for the socks" had passed muster. He never says where he is, of course . . . but sometimes there's a clue – such as "I think my nose has got frostbite" and "please send warm clothing soonest".' She laughed. 'Unfortunately for Frank, I'm not much of a hand at knitting. I rely on Mother and Granny to keep the production line of socks and pullovers going.'

'Very wise.' From the far end of the ward came the rattle of the tea trolley. 'Would you like a cup?' he said. 'I'm afraid I can't offer you anything to eat, unless there's a biscuit going . . .'

'That's all right, Daddy. Angela's treating me to lunch in Oxford. She said that since I'd come all this way, I might as well take a look at the "Other Place" while I was about it. Did you know she was at St Gertrude's, a couple of years before me?'

'I did,' he said. 'It's then that she and I met.'

'She's awfully nice, isn't she?' said Margaret shyly. 'I do hope we'll be friends. I thought when she first introduced herself that she must be working for one of the Oxford colleges in some capacity, because she's not in uniform – but when I said that, she only laughed. "You wouldn't catch me working at the university!" she said. "Nothing but the palace will do for me." I suppose she must have been joking.'

'Almost certainly,' he said.

'Well,' said Beatrice Carlton-Bray as the ancient Morris drew up in front of the east wing of Blenheim Palace. 'Here we are at last. No bones broken, I hope?' Because the journey from Oxford in the rattling vehicle that her husband had christened Jemima had not been a smooth one. The car seemed to have developed several more faults since the last time Rowlands had been a passenger – a tendency to stall at traffic lights and intersections being one of them – although he wondered whether the discomfort of the journey owed as much to Mrs Carlton-Bray's erratic driving technique as to the deficiencies of the motor car. But he said politely that he was fine, and that he was grateful to his companion for giving up the time to bring him here.

'Don't mention it,' was the reply. 'Always glad of a chance to look up Mary . . . My hat!' she exclaimed, evidently taking in the extent of the façade in front of which they were now standing. 'It doesn't get any smaller, does it? How they manage in a place this size beats me . . .' Coming from the chatelaine of Chastleton House, itself of no inconsiderable size, this struck Rowlands as rather amusing. Although he conceded that Mrs Carlton-Bray's house would have fitted into this one several times over. It was all relative, he supposed.

'Steps here,' said his companion, breaking into these irreverent thoughts.

'Yes, I remember. Two of them, aren't there?'

'That's right. Oh, hello, Crawford. We're here to see Her Grace.'

'Of course, madam. She's in the small sitting room.'

It had only occurred to Rowlands on the spur of the moment, as Mrs Carlton-Bray was about to leave the ward at St Hugh's the previous day – having 'popped in' to see him (as she put it), on the off-chance that he hadn't already been discharged – that she might be the answer to the question of how he was going to get to Blenheim. Because get there he must – even if it meant taking the bus to Woodstock and walking from there. It hadn't been the thought of the bus journey, nor of the walk, he'd minded, as much as the thought of having once more to explain himself to a brace of no-doubt sceptical military policemen at the gatehouse. He couldn't count on the timely arrival of the Duke in his Bentley to release him from their clutches this time, either.

So when Mrs Carlton-Bray said, 'Of course I'll take you. We can go and visit Mary,' he'd seized the chance with alacrity. Formidable as the security arrangements at the MI5 headquarters were, they were no match for the claims of friendship. Although at first sight it seemed an unlikely friendship – the daughter of a viscount and the bohemian artist (for Beatrice Carlton-Bray 'painted a bit', she said). It seemed their worlds could not have been further apart. But Rowlands had reckoned without the invisible links that united one world and the other . . . the fact that the godfather of the artist had been a famous man of letters, and that her circle included many other celebrated artists and writers, was one such. The Duchess, in any case, was used to artists – her own portrait having been painted many times.

Another link was that the two families were neighbours. 'Oh, Chastleton's only half an hour's drive from here,' Beatrice Carlton-Bray had said as the car bumped over the ruts and potholes left by the military vehicles. 'Andy and I have been to quite a few of their parties . . . Their youngest girl's the same age as ours.' Another link. 'Then of course,' she added, with the vagueness people adopted when such matters were mentioned, 'there's her war work.' Meaning the Duchess's.

Whatever the reason for their friendship, the two women greeted one another with what seemed a genuine warmth. 'Hello, Beatie. I could hear that car of yours from a mile away.'

'Yes, she does make a frightful racket,' agreed the other cheerfully. 'Andy says it's the spark plugs, or something. Unless it's the carburettor.'

'Probably both,' laughed the Duchess. 'How nice to see you again, Mr Rowlands. Do sit down, both of you. There'll be some coffee, in a minute.' She must have rung, for in less than that time, a servant appeared, and the order was given. 'Well,' said the Duchess, when the parlourmaid had gone out. 'Tell me all the news.'

'Nothing much to tell,' said Mrs Carlton-Bray. 'With Andy spending half his time at King's, and the other half at the War Office, we hardly see one another, except at the weekends – and then we just want to loaf about, reading the papers.'

'Rather the same story here,' said the Duchess. 'How's Audrey?' This, Rowlands surmised, was the Carlton-Brays' daughter.

'Oh, she's thriving, thanks. Loves school – unnatural

child. Of course, they let her mess about with paints and charcoal, so she'll doubtless come to a bad end . . . How's your brood?'

'All well. We've just had Sunny back for the half-term holiday. He seems to have grown at least another foot since he was last home. The two elder girls are as madly busy as ever. Rosie's taking part in her first gymkhana. Terribly excited about it. Charles is getting to be quite a little man. I must take you up to the nursery to see him.'

The coffee arrived. Rowlands, taking sip of his, was wondering how he was ever going to interrupt this lively discussion of domestic affairs in order to make his request, when Beatrice Carlton-Bray said, 'I was forgetting. Mr Rowlands has something to ask you, Mary.'

'Yes.' It was an effort not to stammer. 'I . . . I wondered, Your Grace, if I might ask a favour . . .' He did so.

For a moment, the Duchess seemed to be considering what her answer should be. 'Well,' she began in a doubtful tone, 'there's a typewriter in my husband's study, but he's out at the moment, so . . .' She made a decision. 'I don't suppose he'll mind.'

'Thank you, Your Grace,' said Rowlands.

'I'll get someone to take you to the study,' said the Duchess, touching a bell. 'No. Wait,' she amended. 'I believe there's a typewriter in the Smoking Room. It's nearer.'

Chapter Twenty-Four

Leaving the two women to their conversation, Rowlands followed this functionary across a hall to what he'd have guessed, from the lingering aroma of cigars and pipe-smoke, to be a Smoking Room – even if he hadn't been told. Here was a desk, on which a typewriter had been set up. The footman waited while Rowlands sat down in front of this machine, selected a sheet of the headed notepaper from the pile he found in the left-hand desk drawer, and threaded it into the platen. He took a minute to familiarise himself with the keyboard and settings. A newish model Remington. He'd trained on one of these – although of course it had been an earlier type. He squared up the paper, then typed the date.

The footman watched all this with interest from the doorway. 'I think I can manage now,' said Rowlands, disliking the feeling – all too familiar to a blind man – of being looked at without being able to look back. When he heard the door close behind the man, he drew a breath and typed 'Dear Miss Barnes . . .'

It took him all of fifteen minutes to finish the letter. He had just signed it, with one of the pens that stood ready in the silver inkstand, folded it carefully, and was inserting it into an envelope he'd found in the right-hand drawer of the desk, when he heard the door open once more. Thinking it was the servant, returned to collect him, he said, 'I won't be a moment . . . although I could have found my own way back.'

'I'm sure you could,' said a voice with some amusement. It was a voice he knew.

Abashed, he stumbled to his feet. 'Your Grace. I must apologise. The Duchess said it would be all right . . .'

'If she said so, then it must be,' said the Duke, then, to someone else who had come in with him, 'Winston, this is Mr Rowlands.'

'Delighted,' said a voice that was also familiar to Rowlands – as it was to tens of thousands of others – if only from the radio broadcasts and newsreels from which its extraordinary cadences had issued over the past few years.

Rowlands stood dumbfounded for a moment, then recollected himself. 'It's an honour, sir.' He held out his hand, and felt it firmly grasped.

'Mr Rowlands is an old soldier, like ourselves,' said Marlborough.

'I can see that,' was the reply. Because Rowlands must unconsciously have stood to attention at the sound of the Prime Minister's voice. 'What brings you to Blenheim?' the latter asked. 'Not that one needs any particular excuse, of course. Mine is that I am insatiably curious about the goings-on of British Intelligence. Also I have a fondness for the place. It was here that I was born, and here that I proposed to my dear wife.'

'My own reason is this,' said Rowlands, realising that there was no point in beating about the bush where either of these men were concerned. He held out the letter, now in its envelope. 'I wonder if you would be kind enough to take charge of this, Your Grace, until Miss Barnes returns to Blenheim? I have no other way of getting in touch with her, and it is of vital importance that I do so.'

'Hmm. Yes, she's a rather wayward creature, is our Iris,' said the Duke, taking the letter from Rowlands and pocketing it. 'I'll see that she gets this. Iris Barnes is one of our MI5 people, Prime Minister,' he said to Churchill. 'And a dear friend of Mary's and mine.'

'I suppose you're not a secret policeman?' enquired the eminent statesman to Rowlands, with a rumble of laughter. The latter said that he was not.

'Oh, Mr Rowlands is something much more interesting than that,' said the Duke. 'He's a detective – works in an auxiliary capacity to the police. You remember the Castleford case?'

'Good Lord, yes. Poor old Neddie. That was you, was it?' said the elder statesman, with what sounded like a quickening of interest. Rowlands murmured that he was glad to have been of assistance to the police in clearing up the matter. 'Splendid.' For the second time that morning, Rowlands felt himself the object of scrutiny. This time he didn't mind a bit. Edith would never believe him, he thought, as he took his leave of the two men.

As he was closing the door of the smoking room

behind him, he heard the more famous of them say, in that characteristic growl, 'So where's that cigar you promised me, Bert? A man can't last all morning without a decent smoke . . .'

Returning to the Duchess's sitting room, Rowlands found the two ladies still immersed in conversation. Somebody's engagement was being discussed, he rather thought. 'I'm not sure she's really right for him,' the Duchess was saying. 'But, after all, what can one do? Men think they know their own minds . . .'

On Rowlands's arrival, this interesting discussion ceased abruptly. A few more general remarks were exchanged; then Mrs Carlton-Bray rose to take her leave. 'Do stay to luncheon, won't you?' said the Duchess; but her friend said she had to be off.

'No rest for the wicked, you know. It's back to the office for me – and I've got to drop Mr Rowlands at the station, first.'

The two women kissed, and then Rowlands thanked the Duchess for her kind hospitality. 'I hope you found what you were looking for?' she asked. He said that he had.

'Come along, Mr Rowlands. We'll go out this way,' said Beatrice Carlton-Bray. 'Goodbye, Mary.'

Exiting from the east wing by a door other than the one by which they'd entered, they found themselves in a vast courtyard. 'I'll go and see what they've done with the car,' said Mrs Carlton-Bray. 'Wait here. I'll pick you up in a couple of minutes.'

Glad that he hadn't had to find his way through the labyrinth of rooms and courtyards unaided, Rowlands tried to look as if he was there with a purpose, rather than merely loitering. It was a mild February day – almost springlike, he thought – and he was looking forward to getting back to Brighton, and his own, blessedly ordinary, life. Around him, all was still, with only the cries of the water birds on the lake, and the soft rustle of the wind in the bare branches of the beech trees, to disturb the quiet.

Just then, someone came down a flight of steps to one side of the east colonnade, and crossed the courtyard towards where Rowlands was standing. He knew before the other spoke who it must be. 'Mr Rowlands. We meet again.'

'It would seem so,' he replied.

'Strange how our paths keep crossing.'

'Yes.' He made a decision, turning to face the other squarely, as he said what he had to say. 'You were there, that day, on the parapet of the Radcliffe Camera. It was you who threw Hobson to his death.'

The other seemed unperturbed by this bald accusation. 'You were unconscious,' he replied. 'You couldn't possibly have known what happened. You were severely concussed.'

'It's true that I didn't actually see you do it,' said Rowlands. 'But it's the only thing that fits. I didn't push Hobson over the edge, so somebody else must have done it. You're the only one with both the motive and the expertise to carry out such a crime. You first applied sufficient pressure to Hobson's carotid artery to make him black out, before tipping him over the balustrade. It's the same method – partial strangulation – you used to disable William Dobbs, before stringing him up with his own belt.'

'I did that too, did I?' The man made no attempt to

conceal his amusement. 'That was very resourceful of me! You said I had a motive for these crimes. Might I hear what it is?'

'You're a German spy,' said Rowlands. 'You've been passing on secret information concerning British troop movements to the enemy. When Hobson threatened to expose you . . . or perhaps when his erratic behaviour looked as if it might draw attention to you, you killed him, as he killed Challoner and Quine. It was your name in the green file, which Dobbs boasted of having found – which was why you killed him, and why you tried to kill Miss Thompson and myself. I thought at first that Hobson was the enemy agent, but I now think that he was just a Nazi fellow-traveller. A useful idiot. You used him to distract attention from your own activities. He never got close to British Intelligence sources – whereas you, Captain Fawcett, work at the heart of MI5.'

'Mmm,' said Fawcett, in the clipped, dry tones that characterised his utterances. 'I do sound like a double-dyed villain! But of course . . .' He took a step closer to the blind man, so that the latter could hear the faint sibilance in his voice. A cold hissing. 'You have no proof of any of this.'

'None,' agreed Rowlands. 'I know it to be the truth, however. It was convenient for you when Hobson killed Professor Challoner, because the latter had come very close to identifying you. Your code name, in conjunction with other facts, would have led him to you eventually. Before that could happen, Challoner was killed, and the green file containing your name and Hobson's was stolen by the latter . . . only to be recognised for what it was by Dr Quine.'

'That foolish man,' said Fawcett contemptuously. 'He thought he could make terms with a murderer. In that he was mistaken.'

'Just as Jeremy Hobson was with you,' said Rowlands. 'It suited you to have him identified as an enemy agent – in which endeavour, I myself played an unwitting part. It was only when I came to reflect on those other murder attempts – one of which was successful, I am sorry to say – that I realised that I was dealing with two different sorts of crime. The first two were opportunistic murders, committed on the spur of the moment. The stabbing of Challoner with the German officer's dagger, found on his desk. The cutting of Quine's throat with his own razor. By contrast, the attempts to kill Miss Thompson and myself, the killing of Dobbs, the porter, and that of Dr Hobson, were cold-blooded crimes, planned and executed with the military precision typical of your comrades in the Gestapo.'

Fawcett was silent a moment, evidently digesting all this. When he spoke at last, his voice was not much above a whisper. 'You spin a pretty tale, Mr Rowlands – but you have, as you yourself have admitted, no proof of any of this. I should be very careful – very careful indeed – to whom you tell such tales. For a man in your . . . shall we say, vulnerable situation, it could prove dangerous . . .'

'Oh, I've already told someone,' said Rowlands. 'Someone in a position to do something about it, too. So if anything were to happen to me, there's a record of everything I've said. I don't think it'll take very much to convince this person that what I've alleged is true. After all, I was there when you murdered Hobson – even though I didn't actually see you do it. I suppose you must have hidden in the Upper Camera afterwards, until all the commotion died down?'

But Fawcett admitted nothing. 'You will regret this,' was all he said.

'I doubt it, Captain Fawcett. Ah, here's my lift . . .' Because at that moment, the unmistakable sounds of Jemima's approach could be heard. The car pulled up, with a great banging and creaking, and Mrs Carlton-Bray leant across and opened the passenger door.

'Hop in,' she said. 'Sorry I was so long – they'd taken the car round to the stable block, would you believe? I had to walk miles . . . I say, who was that chap in uniform you were talking to just now? He looked ill, I thought. Like death warmed up.'

Two weeks went by. Back in Brighton, Rowlands settled back into the routines of his daily life, as if he had never been away. It was a relief to have finished with his sleuthing activities, he admitted to Edith. He was getting too old for such things. Leave the daredevil stuff to the young. She agreed wholeheartedly.

Then, one morning – it was Sunday, the first of March – he'd just taken a sip of tea, and was about to attack his breakfast egg, when Edith gave an exclamation. Since she'd just unfolded one of the newspapers – they took the *Sunday Times* and the *Sunday Graphic* – he guessed that this was to do with what was in it.

His assumption was confirmed a moment later. 'Listen to this, Fred! "FULL STORY OF PARATROOP RAID. HEAVY CASUALTIES INFLICTED".'

So they'd done it, he thought. 'Go on.'

'"*With faces blacked even to the teeth*" . . . Oh, Fred, it's so exciting!'

'It sounds it. Read the rest, would you?'

'Of course. "*With faces blackened even to the teeth, the British paratroops who landed in France were dropped in moonlight through concentrated anti-aircraft fire. They not only smashed up the enemy radio-location station, which was their objective, but brought back prisoners*" . . .' As she read the description of the daring raid, whose vivid detail made Rowlands suspect that the author of the piece might well have used more than a bit of poetic licence, he reflected on the part he had played to ensure that the operation was a success, and that no word of it had leaked to the enemy. As seemed, to judge from these ecstatic reports, to have been the case.

Further confirmation of this came a few days later. Returning from work, Rowlands found his wife waiting for him in the hall, in a state of some agitation. 'I don't want you going away again, Fred,' she whispered. 'You've still not recovered from the last time.'

'What are you talking about?' he said, kissing her. 'I've no intention of going anywhere.' But when he entered the little sitting room, the smell of French cigarettes alerted him to the cause of her distress. 'Good evening, Miss Barnes,' he said. 'What brings you to Brighton?'

'Nothing bad,' she replied. 'I'm sorry if I alarmed you, Mrs Rowlands. I promise I won't stay long, but I thought you should know—'

'Edith, do you think we might have some tea?' he interrupted. 'Our visitor's got a long journey ahead of her, and might like some refreshment. All right,' he went on, when his wife had taken herself off to carry out this injunction. 'You'd better tell me what you've come to say.'

'I got your letter,' she replied. 'Oh, I'm sorry! Would you like a cigarette?'

'No thanks. So you got the letter?'

'I did – and it confirmed what I'd suspected about . . . our friend . . . we needn't name him.'

'No. So what I told you proved of use?'

'It did. Not least because it enabled us to take steps to conceal certain information concerning a particular operation from that individual . . . You'll have seen the papers, I expect?'

'Yes. But how . . .'

'Oh, we know he was continuing to supply information to the enemy all along, but you see . . .' She exhaled a mouthful of smoke. 'It was the wrong information. This not only served to confuse the Germans, and prevent their side learning about Operation B . . . but also to confirm that the traitor was, in fact, our man.'

Rowlands remembered with an involuntary shiver Fawcett's words to him outside Blenheim Palace. *I should be very careful to whom you tell such tales . . . It could prove dangerous.* All the way back to Brighton on the train, he had listened out for the unexpected footfall behind him . . . dreaded the shove in the back, the hands around the throat, that could have fulfilled the threat. 'So what's happened to him?'

'Nothing good, I'm glad to say. Oh, we haven't done anything to him . . . it's his own side who've dealt with him. They don't like being made fools of – and he had made fools of them, by passing on dud intelligence.'

Again, Rowlands shivered. What a dirty game it was.

'Ah, here's Mrs Rowlands with the tea, now!' said Iris Barnes. 'Just what I need to see me on my way.'

'Back to Oxford?' said Edith brightly, setting down the tray.

'Actually, I think I'll be going rather further than that,' said the spy.

Acknowledgements

With thanks to Antonia Keaney, archivist at Blenheim Palace, for her invaluable comments; also to Helen Sumping, archivist at Brasenose College; and Peter Monteith, archivist at Keble College, for allowing me to use the college archives.

CHRISTINA KONING has worked as a journalist, reviewing fiction for *The Times*, and has taught Creative Writing at the University of Oxford and Birkbeck, University of London. From 2013 to 2015, she was Royal Literary Fund Fellow at Newnham College, Cambridge. She won the Encore Prize in 1999 and was longlisted for the Orange Prize in the same year.

@christina.koning
christinakoning.com